Code Noir

"Just another day in a city where magic and high technology meet. . . . De Pierres continues to play fast and loose with post-cyberpunk sensibilities while fleshing out the slums and characters she set up in *Nylon Angel*."
—Jon Courtenay Grimwood, *The Guardian* (UK)

"Parrish Plessis remains an enjoyable creation. . . . [Marianne de Pierres] has a knack for spinning her tales at breakneck speed."
—*Vector*

"High-stakes intrigue and adrenaline hits."
—Warpcore SF

"[A] high-tech, fancy-free world. . . . The writing is vivacious."
—SF Crowsnest

Nylon Angel

"A compelling blend of *Mad Max* and *Dark Angel*."
—*The Age* (Melbourne, Australia)

"A fevered romp."
—*Vector*

"*Nylon Angel* has the body of an excellent crime noir hidden beneath its cyberpunk glad rags."
—*The Guardian*

"[A] good gangster . . . the ultimate postfeminist . . . An exciting, adrenaline-pumping read."
—*The Sydney Morning Herald*

continued . . .

Code Noir

THE SECOND PARRISH PLESSIS NOVEL

Marianne de Pierres

A ROC BOOK

ROC
Published by New American Library, a division of
Penguin Group (USA) Inc., 375 Hudson Street,
New York, New York 10014, USA
Penguin Group (Canada), 90 Eglinton Avenue East, Suite 700, Toronto,
Ontario M4P 2Y3, Canada (a division of Pearson Penguin Canada Inc.)
Penguin Books Ltd., 80 Strand, London WC2R 0RL, England
Penguin Ireland, 25 St. Stephen's Green, Dublin 2,
Ireland (a division of Penguin Books Ltd.)
Penguin Group (Australia), 250 Camberwell Road, Camberwell, Victoria 3124,
Australia (a division of Pearson Australia Group Pty. Ltd.)
Penguin Books India Pvt. Ltd., 11 Community Centre, Panchsheel Park,
New Delhi - 110 017, India
Penguin Group (NZ), cnr Airborne and Rosedale Roads, Albany,
Auckland 1310, New Zealand (a division of Pearson New Zealand Ltd.)
Penguin Books (South Africa) (Pty.) Ltd., 24 Sturdee Avenue,
Rosebank, Johannesburg 2196, South Africa

Penguin Books Ltd., Registered Offices:
80 Strand, London WC2R 0RL, England

Published by Roc, an imprint of New American Library,
a division of Penguin Group (USA) Inc.

First Roc Printing, July 2006
10 9 8 7 6 5 4 3 2 1

PUBLISHER'S NOTE
This is a work of fiction. Names, characters, places, and incidents either are
the product of the author's imagination or are used fictitiously, and any
resemblance to actual persons, living or dead, business establishments,
events, or locales is entirely coincidental.

The publisher does not have any control over and does not assume any
responsibility for author or third-party Web sites or their content.

for Nick

Acknowledgments

Code Noir is the darkest hour in this series and owes much to the ROR-ettes, Lyn Uhlmann, Launz Burch, Tara Wynne and Ben Sharpe (I hope we get to do this again one day, Ben!).

And as always, to Rose, Nicci and Paul.

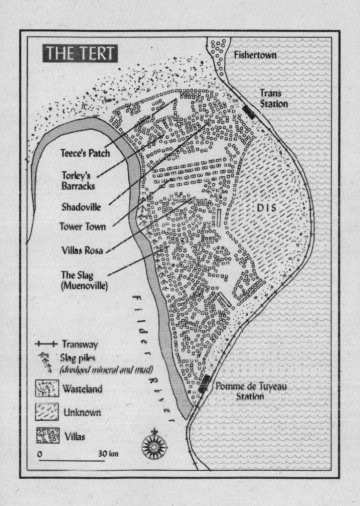

THE TERT

Fishertown

Trans Station

Teece's Patch

Torley's Barracks

Shadoville

Tower Town

Villas Rosa

The Slag (Muenoville)

DIS

Filder River

Pomme de Tuyeau Station

†—† Transway

Slag piles
(dredged mineral and mud)

Wasteland

Unknown

Villas

0   30 km

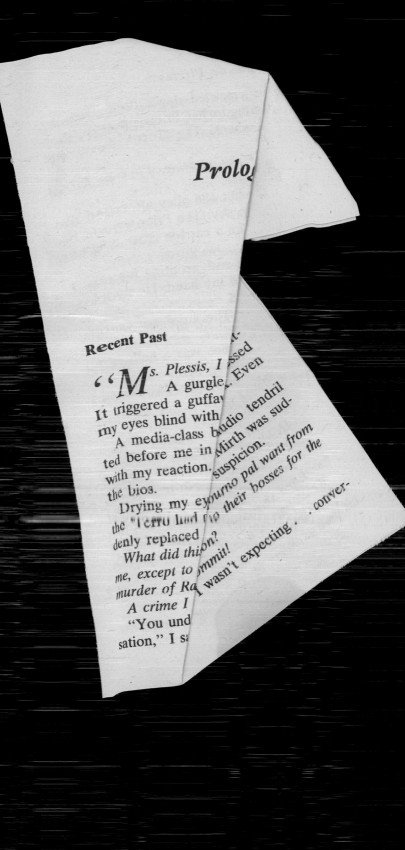

Prolog

Recent Past

"Ms. Plessis, I ... ssed
A gurgle ... Even
It triggered a guffa...
my eyes blind with ...
A media-class audio tendril
ted before me in Mirth was sud-
with my reaction. suspicion.
the bios.
Drying my e... no pal want from
the "Terro had ... their bosses for the
denly replaced ...

What did thi... on?
me, except to ... mmit!
murder of R... I wasn't expecting ... .conver-
A crime I ...
"You und
sation," I s...

Chapter One

Present

Two thin streams of water drilled into me like a needle gun. I told myself it was as good as a massage and jumped around under it like a dancing grrl in a cage. One arm, then the other. One breast, then the other. One buttock, then the—

"What the hell—" I spun around as the water suddenly cut off.

The man standing in the doorway of the san with his hand on the valve had the pleasure of my best side. He didn't look impressed.

I stepped straight out and into his face, too annoyed to be embarrassed. "—are you doing?"

"We have immediate need of your service, Parrish Plessis," he said.

Those words had become too familiar. First the Prier pilot, now this. I couldn't remember hanging out the sign that said GUN FOR HIRE.

"Our Clever Men have been taken. You must find them."

He didn't even try to make it sound vaguely like a request. But then the Cabal Coomera were like that. All somberness and threat.

This one seemed to shimmer—a dark-skinned figure with tribal scars on his bare chest and face, and an assassin's bleak, hooded eyes. His open leather jacket and titanium-capped boots were the only tangible part of him.

The ancient ceiling fan extractor of Teece Davey's bedroom—my current home—struggled to disperse the steam that curled around him.

You didn't invite the Cabal into your home. Certainly not into your san.

Behind him a couple of paces stood an identikit. Except older, leaner.

"How did you get—?"

The pointless question died on my tongue. These guys were Kadais. They made it their business to sneak around and scare the whatsit out of everyone.

Already I had a creeping urge to prostrate myself before them and beg for mercy.

Jeez, Parrish, get a grip!

The younger one slid forward without stepping— or so it seemed.

Spooky.

Legends said they once wore feather feet and sang tribal lawbreakers to their death. These days the tribes were pretty damn diluted, like all the other nations that lived in The Tert, but a flavor of tradition survived. And the Kadais were the ones who ran the hits.

He handed me a crumpled tee.

"Remember you owe us *goma*."

I struggled into the shirt, using the time to think.

Goma. Blood debt. They'd killed my ex-employer, Jamon Mondo—before he killed me. *Goma* was something you didn't reneg on with the Cabal. In repayment they wanted me to stop Loyl-me-Daac, a renegade from the Cabal, from experimenting with genetic manipulation.

I figured there was only one way to do that: execute the guy.

Simple. But there was a downside. Daac happened to be the only person in this world I had deep feelings for. Not to mention serious issues with. Either way I didn't think I wanted him dead.

"Your *goma* is . . . difficult for me," I said cautiously. Then I ventured, "He is your dirty washing, after all."

I saw a flicker of amusement cross the younger one's face.

The Cabal wanted rid of Daac. He'd strayed from their code of beliefs. For all their sinister ways, they weren't hell-bent on genetic supremacy. Trouble is they didn't want to soil their hands with neutralizing him. Or couldn't, due to some old custom.

The older one frowned a gully. "The matter of the *karadji* is more pressing. You will attend to it before you repay *goma*."

Karadji. *The Clever Men. The ones with spirit power.*

"W-will I?" I stammered. There's something about the Cabal. An aura of dignity and a cold, hard belief in what they did. It brokered no quarrel. Even from me: Parrish Plessis, pugilist and self-styled warlord.

"Four of them have been taken from us. Those remaining are in hiding. And it is not just our *karadji*. We believe others are in danger as well . . . shamans of all beliefs."

A couple of months ago I would have whimpered aloud at the thought of taking on such a task. Right now all I felt was the heavy resignation of someone who only ever gets deeper in it. "I'm—uh—pretty busy."

It was worth a try.

"When you find them, we shall return to you the research that holds the answers you seek, Parrish Plessis. This we pledge."

An answer to the Eskaalim! The creature that invaded and tortured my mind. The creature that changed me—that would eventually possess my body and soul.

My heart high-jumped at a chance to survive.

See, I was infected by an alien parasite that was working overtime on perverting my humanity. Sounded weird, but the reality was weirder. I didn't have long and I wasn't the only one.

I blamed Loyl Daac for it. My theory was that his genetic fooling had loosed this creature on the world after it had been dormant for eons. Maybe he could reverse what he'd done, except now he no longer had the splicing codes—they'd been stolen. The Cabal were telling me they knew how to get them back.

They watched me, adopting an implacable take-it-or-leave-it-and-suffer-the-consequences silence.

Find our karadji, *they said. Find them! Like that was easy? Welcome to The Tert, boys—haven for the rather-be-lost-than-found! Sanctuary of secrets and zipped lips.*

"You have Loyl Daac's stolen research?"

"We will."

I hid a sigh. It was as good an answer as I'd get. It meant I had to trust them. And for some reason I did. Call it misguided respect.

The older one did the spooky thing and slid alongside his partner, his expression bleak and cautionary. "There is one condition. If the *karadji* are not safe before the next King Tide, Parrish Plessis, the deal is off."

King Tide? I swallowed my qualms and nodded in agreement.

With the slightest swing of his shoulders he threw a dagger in a low arc. It stabbed the floor at my toe tips.

I didn't even have time to twitch.

Hotly, I bent down, jerked it free and waved it at them

Too late! The doorway wore nothing but air.

I moaned aloud, letting the built-up fear and anger stream out of me and then subside. With only a tiny tremor I handled the dagger. The hilt shone like steel-colored marble. *Polished iron ore.*

The Cabal spear that had killed Jamon Mondo had been jeweled. Opal inlaid and glittery.

I fingered the handle of this one. It felt cold and warm at the same time.

The sensation sent a shiver.

Worse than any premonition.

Chapter Two

Less than two weeks until King Tide!

I closed the screen on the cute wave metaphors of the tide tables and tried to listen to Teece, but that knowledge engulfed my thoughts.

So did the fact that the whole of One-World was crawling with meteorologists sprouking about how it would be the biggest tide in the Southern Hem's history. Close to thirty meters due to the full moon and some other tongue-tying stuff that they couldn't explain sensibly in a news grab.

It had brought the closet crazies out and given the confessed ones carte blanche. Judgment Day was getting a fair whipping. Punters had already lined the beach dunes to catch the spectacle, while others had fled to the borders of the Interior.

The Militia were busy planning how to save the supercity's inhabitants from themselves.

"You're insane!" Teece complained.

His deliberate insult finally captured my attention. I thrust out my hips, fighting the temptation to shake my fist in his face. "They're just kids, Teece. They need a home."

"*Just kids?* They make bioweapons, for chrissakes! Anyway, there are so many of them!"

The ferals that Teece and I were arguing over fell into the "Parrish protects" category and these kids *were getting a home*.

See, there'd been a war in The Tert recently. One of those weird things that the history archives will describe as "the six-day war" or "the fifteen-day war" or "the short war" or some such convenient ridiculousness that was far from the reality. In truth it went for five days, and was for the most part eerily silent and absolutely brutal.

The ferals had been part of the reason I survived it. One kid in particular, Tina, had sacrificed herself to change the momentum of things. I owed her, and them, debt beyond repayment.

I could start, though, by finding them somewhere to live that had water and power and a san. Trouble was, I cared—but I was damn likely to die or change into some*thing* that didn't if I didn't find an answer soon.

Now the Cabal had given me a glimmer of chance to see my hope through, but I needed someone to get things happening while I grabbed my chance to live.

That someone was Teece. He wouldn't do it because he believed in it. He'd do it for me. That was OK. I wasn't shy on calling favors.

"The 'goboys are mostly gone now, apart from a few stragglers. We can convert the barracks."

"What's this 'we'?" Teece growled.

I trailed a finger along his skin, above the worn nylon of his biker pants. It's not my style to play coy or use flirtation to get what I want, but Teece and I had been *close* since Jamon Mondo had taken a Cabal spear in his back.

He'd even let me live with him these last few weeks.

And maybe I was loosening up a little? He sure seemed to appreciate it when I did. This time he grabbed my hand and squeezed.

"What's it really worth?" He grinned.

I pulled away and regarded him steadily, taking in his massive wide chest, long raggedly bleached hair and faded blue eyes. Teece the original bikie surfer. A tek wizard with a sharp mind for biz.

He was looking back just as hard at me. What did he see? I wondered. Had I changed?

I felt like I had. Gone were the dreadlocks in favor of a rough cut. Gone were the outrageous nylon skintights. I was still loaded with the usual arsenal. Right this moment I packed two unconcealed pistols strapped in holsters, a necklace of lethal pins and a stack of garroting wires threaded into my underclothes. Teece reckoned it was like being friends with a human booby trap.

The Tert—the run-down villa sprawl where Teece and I lived—was as cold as it ever gets in late August, enough to keep me in a short-fringed leather jacket over matching duds. Not cold enough for me to zip the jacket up. The thoroughly dude clothes were a gift from a friend, Ibis, who said he'd picked them up in a "collectibles" shop in Vivacity. Ibis is such a girl when it comes to clothes.

But that was just the outside stuff.

Inside was where the real difference lay. The parasite was feeding off the epinephrine manufactured in my adrenals. I was its host. And to say I wasn't happy was a blind understatement.

I was pissed off.

Teece knew what was going on, but we didn't discuss it—the hallucinations, the voices in my head, my accelerated healing—and I took care to make sure he wasn't contaminated with my blood.

Blood contamination was one way the parasite spread—the slow way. And I was one of the few people in the world it was affecting—so far. My guess was that there were probably about fifty or so of us. Eventually it would take me over completely. At least that was its aim.

If I didn't find a way to stop it, my aim was to kill myself before it could.

That was something else Teece and I didn't discuss. But sometimes I'd catch him looking at me like he was in pain. I knew then he was thinking about what might happen.

You see, Teece loved me. Truly. The way people should.

And in a perfect world I would have felt the same way. But I didn't. I respected and liked and cared loads about him, but my deepest desire was reserved for someone else. Loyl Daac.

Shite happens, eh?

Teece crossed his arms like an obstinate kid. "What's it worth?"

I thought for a moment. "Remember that Brough Superior?"

"Yeah," he said suspiciously.

"I'll make good on my promise."

He eyed me for a minute. Then he took one step across and lifted me up into the air.

That was no mean feat. I was just shy of two meters tall and eighty plus kilos. Teece came up only to my ears, but then he was built like several tanks.

"Put me down, or I'll slice you," I barked, sliding a garroting filament out of my crop top. Maybe I hadn't loosened up all that much.

But he just laughed at me in his way. "Do you *really* know where to get a Brough?"

"Sure. Now, are you going to help me with the barracks?"

"Such a gracious invitation."

I'd dangled the Brough carrot before. A Brough SS1100 was one of the first superbikes ever made. There was probably only a handful in existence. And Teece was a biker from way back. In fact he ran a transport business hiring bikes out to cross the wasteland that bordered on the west side of The Tert. We were living there right now, he and I. But that was about to change. I needed action and I couldn't think of any gentle way to break the news, so I just said it.

"I'm moving on today."

Teece froze. "What are you talking about?"

"I've got some urgent business to attend and I'm going to base myself in Jamon's old place."

I held my breath, unsure if I was right to gamble on him following me.

He trembled and then took hold of himself. "I wondered how long it would be, Parrish. I only had you on loan, didn't I?"

His words stung, but then the truth is famous for being a first-class bitch.

I shrugged. "I'll lose my salvage rights if I'm not seen there. And there are some other . . . matters."

I stepped away from him, over to his comm cache, not wanting to see his hurt, and tapped in a Vivacity home code.

A plump man with pink skin and a flirtatious mouth appeared on the screen. Ibis.

"Parrish, darling? How lovely."

I smiled at him. "What are you like at interior decorating?"

"Brilliant, of course!" Then, "Where?" he asked suspiciously.

"Here. In The Tert."

His cheeks paled. For a second I though he might faint. "Are you insane?"

Chapter Three

I left Teece sulking with his bikes and ran east towards Torley's, urgency claiming me. I had to find a quick lead on the *karadji,* and Larry Hein's snoops were the best on the northside. He just might need to be *persuaded* to help me.

I reflected on my approach to Larry as I took in the landscape. From "Teece's Bike Hire" biz to Torley's stretched a jumble of conjoined villa sets, long eroded of style and robbed of any dignity. These days The Tert was a sprawl of detritus architecture. Art Crappo.

But it didn't end there. The Tert boundaries spread peninsular-style to the south of the supercity, Viva. Slick and sick Fisher Bay on one side, the ailing Filder River on the other: a despoiling one hundred or more klick strip of rabble—animate and inanimate.

It was once a massive engineering works site that got ripped down and disguised as a villatropolis—

until the locals started showing signs of heavy metal poisoning from the industrial landfill.

Now it was a weird territory for serious offenders. Every kind.

A sterile strip of wasteland like an excessive firebreak divided it from the rest of humanity.

To look at, nothing much had been altered by the short, intense war. The already patchwork human dwellings that had been damaged were now repatched and as functional as they would ever be. Not so their inhabitants.

Nearly a thousand people died in a few days. The stink had got so bad that they'd allowed the Militia in to clean up. The mass cremations happened on the wasteland near Teece's patch. Sometimes when I woke up in the night I could still smell it.

The media gave all the death a heap of airtime. One-World, Common Net, Out-World—you name it. Nothing like a stack of burning, expendable bodies to boost the ratings!

Piers—pilot/journos and their intrusive camcording 'Terrogators in fruited-up copters—supervised the whole affair, jostling their Militia lackeys out of the way for the best close-up footage. Image scavengers!

I became so desperate to lay my hands on some antiaircraft hardware Teece had practically chained me up to stop me chucking grenades at them.

I jogged until my energy waned, then I walked. Eventually I hauled my arse into a café for beer and food. Transport was around: scooters and Pets.

I'd never been a fan of Pets. It didn't seem right, riding on the back of a kid even if it was half mekan. A more pragmatic person would have said, "Yeah, but you're putting cred in their pockets." But practical isn't always my bag.

More like hyped-up gut reaction!

And getting worse.

The food was average but the beer was good. Funnily enough it was one of the few things in The Tert that always was. Humanity might be on the fast track to hell but the beer in Tert Town'd always be cold. I sipped my way through it and enjoyed being alone for the first time in a while.

Not that I was really alone here. Since Jamon went down with the Cabal spear in his back, and I'd put a bullet in a shape-shifter named Io Lang, everyone knew me. Sometimes it was good, mostly it wasn't, and some of the time I had to stop myself from hurting them.

I was carrying a load of aggression inside that wasn't entirely mine. It had to do with the needs of the parasite and the way it manipulated my body. The more epinephrine that flowed, the fatter and happier it got. The less human I got.

Most of the time I controlled it. I'd even taken up meditation. But sometimes it got me so bad anyway that I turned rabid: angry and lusting. I likened the parasite to a werewolf in the change—not that I'd ever seen one—but sometimes the need overwhelmed the rest.

I guess you could say there was a new confidence in my look now, but it was shadowed by a dark preoccupation. I'd become the sort of person I used to admire—the person no one messed with, the one with nothing to lose. It wasn't the way I expected it to be. Not one little bit.

When is it ever?

People didn't mess with me but they competed endlessly.

I slipped my hand into my pocket and fingered the little box of tattooed skin strips the 'Terro had given me. Why was King Tide so important to the Cabal? This wasn't Fishertown.

I drained my tube and asked for another. I wanted to get smashed but I didn't have time.

Eleven days!

Besides, even that pleasure was denied me. The parasite kicked in when I reached a certain point of getting stoned and annulled the effects. You wouldn't think you could crave waking up with a mother of a hangover and a mouth drier than six-month-old bread.

But I did.

One-World blathered on the bar vid. I switched sides of the booth to avoid seeing it. I didn't watch net news anymore on account of a personal grudge. Business conglomerates and politicians used to control the world. Now the steering wheel was in one set of reality-murdering hands: the media. They'd tried to frame me for the death of Razz Retribution, media hound and presenter. A capital offense. One I entirely did not commit.

I was taking that grudge to the grave.

I didn't forgive a lot.

Or forget.

For the moment, though, the media seemed to

be leaving me alone. Too much public controversy, I guessed, over the truth behind Razz Retribution's murder. Normally they didn't give a canrat's teste about the veracity of their viewing matter, but somehow enough doubt had separated the audience's collective mind. Opinion had divided into camps.

Parrish guilty. Parrish not.

I guess intrigue made a change from the overdose of LTA ultraviolence.

By forcing Jamon Mondo to confess live on the net, I'd bought myself some time. Now the media *couldn't* convict me without launching a trial, and somehow they didn't seem to be in a hurry to do that. They were milking ratings.

Though the heat had lessened, I wasn't off the hook; more like in a holding pattern. Too much was going on that I didn't understand. Like my recent tête-à-tête with the Prier. The journo had tried to warn me about something (and failed on account of Teece's trigger twitch), which left me with a case of chronic doubt and some ugly little skin flaps.

I didn't like unexplained allies.

I continued to puzzle over it all as I knocked back my second tube, until a young, slick turk came hanging around my table. I picked him straight away—competitor!

I raised an eyebrow. "Problem?"

He was lean and dark and, from the way he arched his back reflexively, on a testosterone high. Hard to say if it was natural or paid for.

"No problem," he said. "Jus' enjoying the view.

Heard you're the one that's pretty dangerous.
That true?"

I sighed heavily. Whatever tiny interest his looks
might have aroused in me dampened instantly.
"You got the wrong person."

"Pity," he said. "I been wantin' to meet her.
Real bad."

"Why so?" I asked, vaguely curious.

"Heard she could match it with anyone. Heard
she was real good at one-on-one."

"Uh-huh."

Now his mouth was geared up, there was no
stopping him. "Yeah. I wanted a piece before she
got disappeared."

"Disappeared?" *Now* he had my interest.

"There's talk," he mock whispered and winked,
sidling closer. "Someone's put cred out to bag her.
I got friends who know."

I'm pretty funny about my personal space but I
let him into the fringes of it.

My hand fell casually to my holster.

Hormone boy stopped dead when he saw what
I was packing but I had the Luger drawn in the
second it took him to breathe.

"Siddown!"

His legs folded under him, so that he just caught
the edge of the booth seat. His face flushed with
anger and embarrassment. "You are *her*. I knew
it," he cried.

He was beginning to irritate me. "Who wants
her?"

A smirk ventured across his face. "What's it
worth?"

It was the second time someone had said that to me today, only this time I wasn't feeling so charitable.

I examined him closely, my free hand fingering the collar of poisoned pins around my neck. "You could get to keep your own eyes. You might not need bone transplants. The benefits are endless, really."

His smirk transformed back to anger—and a flash of fear. A reputation could be handy.

I shifted my aim to the spot right between his legs. I expected he was keen to keep his gonads in working condition.

"Names," I said quietly.

Sweat appeared on his upper lip and his hair freeze began to thaw. "Someone up Tower Town way."

My breath caught in my chest. I leaned forward. Tower Town was Daac's patch.

Bastard!

Hormone boy saw my reaction and sucked up a deep breath like it might be his last.

I jerked the pistol, firing it off. The booth's table splintered to pieces. Vaguely I saw people scrambling away, but my sanity had waned as the parasite gorged greedily on my reaction to the news.

Somehow hormone boy had avoided the bullet and was crab crawling all the way to the door.

I let him go, flicked some credit the bartender's way for damages and got the hell out of there.

The backwash of my neurochemical reaction struck as I lost sight of the café. I went down in a heap with the barest survival instinct to get my back against something solid before the hallucination took hold. It was the same as last time and the time before. . . .

An Angel, massive, rose from a stream of blood, spraying droplets. My blood.
"The change is close, human."
I screamed my denial. A long, terrified sound.

I was still screaming as my vision cleared.

"Oya?" said a muffled, frightened voice.

A group of ragged children—ferals—stood in a semicircle around me wearing breather masks. They looked weird but harmless. Everyone in The Tert knew better. Ferals carried bioweapons. Lethal, close-range, fast-acting viruses.

I recognized one of them, a tall thin boy who had helped me once before.

"Wh-what are you d-doing?" I stammered.

The boy flicked his gaze to either end of the walkway. I could see figures moving past in the afternoon shadows.

He peeled the breather skin away from his mouth and nose. "We've been watching for you to come back. Some would harm you, Oya. We protect."

We protect.

I stifled an urge to laugh. What was it I'd said about repaying debts?

I got unsteadily to my feet, and the ferals spread to give me room. Then I touched the boy lightly on the shoulder. "What's your name?"

"Link," he said, drawing together black brows over a thin, angular face.

"Link, I have somewhere for you all to live. Pass the word. Torley's barracks will be renewed."

The boy's eyes sparked. He turned to two of the others with a quiet instruction, watching until they disappeared amongst the passing trade. Then he faced me again. He slipped his hand into the pocket of his torn overalls and produced another mask. "We stay with you. Oya's guard."

I raised my hand to protest and he deftly slipped the breather skin into it.

"You won't know we're there, Oya. I promise. Keep this close."

I sighed heavily and took it.

I didn't stop again on the way back to Torley's. Between my desire to avoid another hallucination and the knowledge that my movements were being monitored by a bunch of kids, the pleasure of being alone had faded.

Instead I ran hard. Along cracked walkways, dodging between villa sets and occasionally up and down stairs that offered shortcuts through buildings. It didn't take long for the puff to hurt and the sweat to stream. A month of inactivity with Teece had left me soft and out of condition. Contrary to what you hear, sex isn't enough.

I reached Torley's circuit by late day. Overhead, the whine of Priers made for a constant background irritation. I glared into the sky.

What were they looking at? *Who* were they looking at? What made The Tert so damn constantly interesting to the media's pedigreed vultures?

Soon a hum of a different kind drowned them out. Tert noise. The bars in Torley's ran twenty-four/seven but at dusk they assumed a new intensity. The biz end of the day.

I hadn't seen Link or his little band for a time, but I had no doubt if I wailed or had a mind flip they'd appear. Being guarded by a bunch of virus-carrying kids depressed me. My debt to those around me mounted daily.

I walked with an indifferent pose, yet my whole body thrummed with tension. Would Larry Hein help me?

Although salvage rights on Jamon's territory were mine, I'd walked away from them while I'd recovered at Teece's, a time when I should have been cementing my intentions. Some would take my inaction as a signal it was up for grabs. Maybe Larry was one. Now I had to wade back in and put my stamp on it.

Jamon had run most of the north side of The Tert. Torley's strip of bars, Shadoville and The Stretch. He didn't *exactly* pimp, but he had the power to protect the babes if it suited him. He provided most of the entertainment there was to be had. Drugs, Sensil—sensory illusion—rooms, gambling, even down to the cockdog fights.

If I got the chance, I planned to make some changes and not everyone would like them.

I'd have to do some convincing.

That thought sent me through a weapons check. I could feel the weight of the garroting filaments in the lining of my underwear. Two Lugers strapped to my thighs—show pieces—my charm bracelet of several short-range stun grenades and one gas hallucinogen (Minoj, my arms dealer, had set them to activate on my saliva only after I'd nearly accidentally blown myself and Teece away one day; I told Minoj if he sold that information to anyone I'd gouge out his few remaining teeth with a screwdriver), an oxy torch and pouch, an assortment of knives and a push dagger. The necklace of lethally tipped pins around my neck completed the package. Close on two meters of pure arsenal.

Could anyone resist a girl like me?

Well, maybe. Mainly on account of my face. One side was caved. Nose bent as well. Unsightly, I knew, but somehow fixing it never seemed a priority.

The noise and sprawl of Torley's was like coming home. Outside Hein's bar a band of King Tide crazies performed strip theater under the sulky daytime glow of a cheap advertible proclaiming "The End of the World foks."

Inside, Hein's looked pretty much the same as always—drab 'creted walls, tactile chairs, a hint of bloodstains—apart from the absence of Jamon's dingoboys. Most of Jamon's canine army had run when I'd had my wicked way. I'd heard a few of the smarter ones had hung around, hiring out as protection.

Late afternoon meant a reasonable crowd. I recognized some. They *all* recognized me. A few called out welcome. Others retreated urgently into their bio-comms, which probably meant trouble.

Larry Hein was in his usual spot behind the bar, orchestrating his servitors with a wave of his silk watercolor scarf. Larry was straight but he loved to dress up. Tonight he wore slinky, pale green lurex with slits at the side. A month ago it was chiffon. I'd have to introduce him to Ibis so they could swap fashion tips.

When he saw me, I caught the startled flash of white around his deep-set eyes.

I strolled over. "You kept a tab of what I owe you, Larry?"

He nodded stiffly, feigning insult at my question.

"Then quit looking so nervous."

He leaned forward, wafting me with his tart imitation uptown cologne.

"Where've you been, Parrish? I've had trouble keeping things tight here. And now all the nuts are nuts with this King Tide thing." He shrugged towards the door. "There's talk that you're dead. Or *changed*. Some of the 'goboys are howling that they've got salvage rights."

"Changed" meant altered by the parasite. Like Jamon and Io Lang. Lang had shape-shifted right here at Hein's in front of a room full of punters after I'd put a bullet in his adrenals. Since then word had spread through Tert Town. People knew something was wrong, that evil had been set loose.

The myth of shape-shifting had been around for as long as people had told stories. Now, though, it had become real, caused by the Eskaalim parasite.

Nothing at all to do with vampires and were-wolves.

I eased a Luger from its holster and fingered its worn familiarity. Comfortable was good, but when I got hold of Minoj, my favorite arms dealer, I was going to get him to manufacture me something special.

I propped my elbows on the bar, cocking the pistol at Larry's prize magnum of genuine malt whisky. No one who came here could afford to drink the contents, nor did he want them to. He wiped the glass religiously to keep the label immaculate and sniffed the shot valve when he was depressed.

"Do I look changed, Larry?"

He smiled like rigor mortis. "Same old Parrish," he managed.

"Just needed some thinking time. I'm moving into Jamon's old rooms. Mention it around. Things are going to change. Are you still with me?"

He considered for the time it took him to pour me a tequila. With an exaggerated sigh he gave me his answer. "Always a pleasure to work for a lady."

Chapter Four

I holstered my pistol, knocked the tequila back and put on my most innocent, amicable face.

He poured me another. "Terms."

"I'll clear what I owe you to date and add some fat as soon as I get Jamon's place sorted. On top of that you get the usual percentage to act as my broker on most things. And Hein's gets free protection. I'll even throw in a damages bonus. In the meantime I need something done pronto."

His nostrils quivered with caution and interest. Larry knew I was good for intrigue so I pushed on while I had his attention, leaning across the bar, bringing my lips close against his ear.

"Use every snitch you've got. *And everybody else's.* A couple of Cabal shamans have disappeared. I need anything you can find about it. *Anything.* This is important, Larry. For all of us."

He tensed at the weight of my tone, only relaxing when I eased back onto the stool.

With what could have been a prayer flicked in the direction of the whisky magnum, he nodded and moved away to serve.

Relieved, I stepped outside the bar. Link and the ferals appeared around me.

I'd forgotten them.

"We were watching, Oya. But we didn't want to interfere. It was good that you talk with Larry alone." Link nodded wisely.

Amusement tugged, but I pushed it away. I would never laugh at Link or his ferals. They had survived when many hadn't. And they had helped turn the war against Jamon.

Still, such pronouncements from a child were curious.

Maybe I was the naive one?

"Thanks, Link." I stared around at them. Thin, solemn faces, masks slung around their necks like bizarre masquerade adornments. "Go and prepare to move. I'll send word when the barracks are ready."

It was Link's turn to suppress a smile. "Yes, Oya, as you say."

In one accord they turned away as if they were wired together for movement.

I stared after them suspiciously. Was Link laughing at me?

As I hiked it up the stairs near Jamon's rooms, a 'goboy—canine incisors, dreads and too much body hair—jumped me from the shadows. Thankfully my olfaugs were amped up, and his dirty-dog stench gave me a warning.

I whipped a garroting wire down across his snout.

It sliced enough layers to make a flap open. He yelped and loped away around the corner.

I drew a Luger and crept towards the corner, scrying for his pal. 'Goboys didn't like to fight alone.

It turned out to be someone I'd met before.

Riko. I'd sliced his hand mostly off when he'd tried to jump my salvage claim, which meant Riko and I weren't exactly *close*.

The two of them came at me from opposite sides. I kicked the first one in the soft part of the throat. He gurgled and collapsed.

Riko, slathering with fury, leapt for me. I shot him in the leg but not before he raked me with his preternatural toenail. *Yeeuch!* Tert myth said they grafted them off dead bodies—gave a whole new meaning to false nails.

I aimed the pistol steadily at his head. "You should know better'n to do that, Riko," I drawled with calm pretence. "Who sent you?"

Beads of saliva matted his chest hair. "I wouldn't sleep if I was you, bitch. There's decent cred out on you," he panted.

I shrugged. "What's new?"

He gave me a wild, animal look. "Dead would be so much easier," he spat and dragged himself away.

I should have put a bullet in the back of his head, but I couldn't bring myself to. At this moment regret seemed a better option than murder.

I stood in the corridor, pistol raised, feeling the weight of my own peculiar morality and the significance of his words.

Dead would be so much easier.
Someone wanted me badly—alive.

Down the corridor, the door to Jamon's rooms was
unlocked. As I stepped through, the air wrapped
around me like a dirty sheet. Someone had removed his body and had been living there. Riko
maybe?

Inside, the place was a shambles of food cartons,
hair balls and dust.

I surveyed the squalor and suddenly felt at a loss.

There was so much to sort. This place. The barracks. The business.

And yet I couldn't begin the thing that would
award me the time to do it all.

The indiscriminate desire to run off searching in
villa attics for the Cabal's stolen shamans rose like
a flood inside me. I paced a few steps, pinching my
forearms with my fingernails trying to settle it, trying to make myself form a plan.

I couldn't move on the Cabal shamans until I had
some word from Larry. In the meantime I *could* get
some things in order—like this place.

I commed my newly appointed, lurex-coutured
broker.

"Larry, send your cleaners over now."

His smile was pencil thin, sparing. "Already on
their way, Parrish . . . and no . . . nothing yet."

I bit on my impatience. "Directly. Understand?"

He humphed and cut the link.

I picked through the debris towards the san unit.
It looked relatively unused. Whoever had been living here hadn't bothered to wash.

I threw my clothes into the launder slot and set the shower to full throttle. A few minutes and they would be as clean and dry as me.

When my skin felt set to blister I got out, redonned my clothes and stamped into the living room.

Four bots were scurrying around, sucking up piles of dirt and hair and spreading cleaning agents liberally over all the surfaces. One of them worked on the bloodstains in the middle of the main room. It rattled its body stiffly, as if apologizing.

I patted its display so it repeated after me. "Do what you can," I told it. "What's left will remind me."

Of what, Parrish? How to spear a man to death?

But Jamon had already ceased to be a man when the Cabal had done that. He'd been possessed—a flesh host to the Eskaalim.

Although I had no idea where they'd come from, I knew they fed on our adrenaline. They kept some of their prey as a nutritional life source; others— like Jamon had been about to become, like Lang *had* become—they transformed totally into an energy creature with a flesh exterior. A creature that could shape-change, or heal quickly, or perform conscienceless deeds.

Which one was I?

How much time? How much?

Not enough!

The voice thrummed through my body like a plucked string. It was the Angel—my own manifestation of the Eskaalim within—laughing at me.

Maybe it was right.

Following the derisive voice washed a flood of desire.

Until now Teece had been around to dampen the waves that came and went. He would be here soon, I told myself.

Hurry, Teece.

Focus.

I sat down in the middle of the room, ignoring the bots as they scrubbed away the last of the debris, and let myself drift into a meditative world of passionless calm. I was beginning to recognize a pattern in myself. Shortly after a surge of adrenaline, I was either overwhelmed by a vision or the need for energy release.

The method of release was up to me. It certainly wasn't paired with any need for emotional intimacy.

Teece had laughed at first. The reality was different.

Teece didn't like being on tap. He wanted to be revered. He wanted to be the only one. After a short time, the regularity of my faceless desire got to him.

"What would happen if I wasn't here? Would you take anyone?" he had asked.

"Maybe." I couldn't lie to him.

But if I didn't indulge the desire, it turned to anger. The anger made me less and less human. I'd slept with people for kicks before but never to assuage a violent compulsion. My lack of control sickened me.

His face had become sullen with hurt. Wariness visited and stayed in his faded blue eyes. "What about if you were with Loyl? Would he be enough?"

"I'm not with him, Teece," I'd said with stretched patience. "I made my choices. So did you."

He'd stared at me, unsure whether to be satisfied by my answer.

I couldn't help him any more than that.

Uncurling from my meditation, I instructed the bots to remove every single thing from Jamon's rooms—the furniture, clothes—and take them away. Everything except the mahogany table. Jamon had liked to dress it in candles and silver and pretend to be civilized.

I wanted a reminder of his deceit.

Just being in his apartments would take some getting used to—but I was enough of a pragmatist not to miss the opportunity for something half decent. Unlike the microchip-sized doss I'd been living in for three years.

Which reminded me. I needed to retrieve Merry 3#—my holo-comm-diary—from my old room. She didn't do a lot, but I was kinda fond of her. The tekboy in Plastique who made her had built an exact representation of me, without the crooked nose and cheekbone. Looking at Merry 3# was a vanity really. Parrish without the scars, blemishes and bad humor.

When I was satisfied that enough traces of Jamon were removed, I sent the bots back to Larry Hein. Then I did something I'd been putting off.

I entered Jamon's comm room. He'd run his side of the war from here. He'd also shape-changed here before my eyes.

Slipping a tiny, shell-shaped hard drive from my kit bag, I slotted the grooves into the wall mount. I'd taken the drive and its precious information with me to Teece's. Until now I hadn't been able to bring myself to look at it.

Torley's, Plastique and parts of Muenoville ran off reasonably reliable pirated electricity. Blackouts were common but not lasting. Brownouts were common and damaging. Teece paid a fortune to a private supplier in Viva for a steady supply to his comm cache. I'd have to look into Jamon's arrangements in that matter before someone pulled the plug on me.

I began to search his files. His virtual lock was simple enough to pick. I guess he'd figured as it wasn't networked it was unlikely to be hacked directly from his own machine.

I was no financier, but his bookkeeping icon—a set of overblown lips floating above a tastelessly naked torso—seemed happy enough to recite a clear account of his incomings and a very short list of outgoings.

The litany of profits made clear whom he provided protection for in Torley's, Shadoville, The Stretch and some areas to the west. They paid him well, and he pocketed everything but what it cost him to pay for the pirated power, to finance his lifestyle and to keep the 'goboys fed and watered. They didn't get a wage. They wouldn't know what to do with it.

One file tree had coded names with amounts listed in a column next to them. It had to be drugs, but whether they were buyers or sellers and what the drugs were I could only guess.

The lips-and-torso refused to tell me without a password, and I didn't have time or the stomach to delve into Jamon's dead psyche to unearth it.

I flicked on to another tree that contained profiles of people all in a tidy spreadsheet. Women mainly, but not only. Some I knew.

My hand trembled as I tapped through until I found my name.

Parrish Plessis. I skimmed through the physical description and went on to family history . . . *No living relations apart from a mother (addicted to NE) and a sister, Katriona, a pro-ball athlete on the Eurasian circuit.*

Known associates: Teece Davey.

Remarks: dangerously impulsive.

I flicked on to some of the others. We all had one thing in common. No strong family ties.

The last section shook me the most—pages of details on my movements and habits. I'd always known that Jamon had me watched, but the intimate details of whom I talked to or slept with, where I ate . . .

I shivered and reminded myself that Jamon was a bloodstain on the floor.

I moved my finger to delete the lot but somehow couldn't. So much information on so many people. It was stupid to lose it. Maybe I could turn Jamon's obsessive sadism into something useful.

Did that make me as bad as him? I wondered.

My finger hovered over the screen's pad. Yes? No?

In the end I erased only the segment about me and kept the rest. I told myself there were rough times ahead; it was sensible. Information meant survival.

I built a new lock on the system, a way that Teece had taught me, and tried to ignore the guilt that crawled along my shoulders and up into my conscience.

To make it go away I cracked Jamon's Tert depository cache. The larger businesses in The Tert ran their own electronic banking arrangements through illegal software managed by a numbers freak called Gigi. The rest lived off barter and kwik-ident accounts.

I transferred a wallop of credit into Larry Hein's Chained Dog business icon and confirmed the transaction.

Then I commed him again. "Larry."

He was pouring quick, successive disposable shot cups without spilling a drop on his lurex. "So soon, boss?"

I hated to admit it but I kinda liked the tag. "Just moved some credit over to your Tert account."

His surly face brightened.

My next call was to Teece.

"Where are you?" he asked.

The tight lines around his mouth told me he'd been worried. "Jamon's. My new rooms. Come see."

His eyes narrowed. "What about the 'goboys that are living there?"

"You knew about them? You didn't mention it."

"Would it have stopped you?"

"No."

"Then what would have been the point?"

"Forewarning would have been nice."

Teece shook his long hair unhappily. "Thought it might help change your mind. I don't think you should be there, Parrish. Every jerk with an itch is gonna want to take it away from you. You won't be able to turn your back on anyone."

It was my turn to bristle. "So what then, Teece? I just hide out at your place and wait until I turn into—" I stopped abruptly, fearing the line was bugged.

I had enough enemies; there was no point in giving any of them information for free. With effort I softened my tone and made my play. "Please come and help me with this, Teece. I need your smarts and your common sense."

"Yeah, well, at least I can't complain about your honesty." His laugh had a familiar tinge of bitterness.

"No. You can't."

We were silent for a moment.

"Teece?"

"Yeah."

"Come soon? I *need* you." My voice was throaty and loaded with meaning.

He flushed. "Lock yourself in. I'll be there."

I took his advice and tried to make sure no one could get in—but after my uninvited visit from the Cabal, it was token. Jamon hadn't had much security anywhere but his den; the result of too many bodyguards. I locked off the outer apartment doors and made a quick call to my favorite weapons supplier, Raul Minoj.

When he realized it was me he switched from a fake, generated image to the real thing. The latter wasn't an appealing sight. Rotten teeth and a smile greasier than a Tert shawarma. Even my onset of indiscriminate lusting failed to encompass Raul Minoj.

In biz, though, he was sharp.

"Oya, little thing. Where have you been?"

I bristled. Both those terms pissed me off. Oya was some name the Muenos had resurrected from their bastardized voodoo mythology and given to me. I didn't know exactly what it meant but it seemed to come with a load of responsibility and other weird stuff. "Little thing," on the other hand, was sarcasm, plain and simple.

If there was one thing I would never be it was a *little thing*.

"As if you didn't know, Minoj."

His spy network was probably the best in The Tert outside Larry Hein's, but his information came highly priced. He'd warned me once, for free, about Jamon. Maybe underneath it all he had a soft spot for me. He'd also agreed to support my salvage claim. Reckoned he could manipulate me.

He grinned. "I thought perhaps you'd found a nest."

My face got hot with more annoyance. He was referring to Teece and I.

"I've moved into Jamon's old apartment. I want some decent security on the place."

He nodded, tonguing the gaps in his teeth. "I have some trinkets that will impress you. For a price."

"The price isn't an issue but there's a condition."

He raised a slick eyebrow.

"You oversee the fitting. I don't want some half-baked job."

Minoj never left his compound on The Tert's southside anymore. I was asking a lot.

He was already shaking his head. "I don't—"

"You're getting my business exclusively, Minoj. I got a lot of people to protect now. Not just Torley's, but the ferals and the Muenos."

I could see the economic temptation warring with his instinct to stay safe.

"You're a temptress, Oya."

I gritted my teeth. "No, Minoj. I want to stay alive until I choose otherwise! Do we have a deal?"

A hint of sweat had appeared on his upper lip. Excitement? Fear?

He toggled back to the fake image. The hygienic version of his lips said, "Deal."

Teece must have sprouted wings. He woke me from a restless doze, a few hours later, by banging on the door. I'd kipped on the mahogany table with my jacket for a pillow. My dreams had been filled with the smell of moist flesh and a rising dark tide.

"Parrish. Let me in."

I cleared my throat and rolled off the table. "You alone?"

"Yes." He sounded terse.

I let him in and deadlocked the door again.

He looked around. "Where's the furniture?"

I shrugged. "I couldn't live with Jamon's things. Besides, the 'goboys had stunk the place up badly."

He threw a casual arm around my shoulder. A friendly hug.

But his touch was flint on my skin. I sparked inside like a fire rushing out from an enclosed space and began peeling my clothes off.

"Hurry," I ordered him, breathless.

He slipped his jacket off and looked around. "Where do—?"

I tore impatiently at his T-shirt, yanking it over his head. His chest was broad and hard. The sight of his flesh tipped me. I began to climax and took light breaths trying to stave it off. "Get on the table," I said. "Hurry."

His face was a mix of emotions. Turned on and yet not.

"Can't we just start with this?" He leaned forward to kiss me. His mouth was warm and wet, like me.

I didn't kiss him back, shaking my head impatiently as he struggled out of his pants. He tossed them aside. I clung to him, naked and shivering at the cool air on my skin.

"Your skin; it's burning."

I didn't bother to answer. I barreled him backwards and mounted him. Then I rode him into the table, my fingers clawing his chest in convulsive spasms.

When we'd finished—when my urge slid back

under the oily surface of my control—I saw the marks and the blood. I'd scratched him before. But not like this.

"Teece," I whispered hoarsely. "I'm so sorry."

He tried to grin but it didn't quite come off because his faded blue eyes grieved. "I don't care about the blood, Parrish. I care about what will happen when I'm not here. You're vulnerable when you're like that. And out of control. It turns me on. And it scares the jees out of me."

I lay on his blood-slicked chest, my face close to his. "Me too, Teece. Me too."

We cleaned ourselves up and went down to Hein's for a drink and food. Larry's menu was limited but usually safe to eat, and for once money wasn't an issue. Larry's self-satisfied grin meant he'd already checked his account.

I ducked away from Teece while he was eating. "News?"

Larry shook his head.

"Try harder."

I ignored Teece's curious glance and settled back in the booth at the south end of the bar, the one that gave us the best view. I remembered how Larry's kitchen smells had driven me crazy with hunger in the past and sent me scuttling home to my room for an indigestible protein-sub.

We'd both chosen imported meat and rice, steering well away from anything green. Vegetables grown in Tert soil tended to be venomous.

The food was satisfying and the beer took the edge off my impatience.

Teece was feeling good as well, legs apart and relaxed. He fingered his scratched chest gently where streaks of blood seeped through his shirt. "Maybe you coming back here wasn't such a bad thing. Where else can I get free food and drink, an attentive waiter and the company of *the* most out-of-control woman?"

I laughed. He was right about one thing. Larry was treating us like royalty. And so were some of the patrons. The whole bar had a different feel to it than a few hours earlier, cautious but lighter somehow.

I struggled to identify the mood, like a forgotten face or name. It came to me after my fifth tube of beer, in that small window of inebriation that I still possessed before the parasite kicked in and sobered me back to reality.

Optimism!

A warm tingle spread through me at the idea. In the last few years my life had been a matter of daily survival. Before that I'd been a kid, a child with a *hands-on* stepdad and a sadly addicted mother. For the first time in my life, desires and possibilities began to coalesce into something that wasn't crusted with semen or clotted with blood or rendered meaningless by hunger.

Perhaps I could make this place—my territory safer for some to live in? Would that be so impossible?

"Plessis?"

My agreeable daydream transformed into a sweaty scud with three arms and a body shell blocking my view of the bar. Two of the arms were flesh and held knives; the other was pneumatic and panned a firestormer across the rest of the bar.

Hein's patrons knew all about firestormers. Nobody moved to help. Nobody breathed. Especially Larry.

"Walk with me."

Bounty. I wasn't going to anywhere with Bounty.

"You must want some other girl, in some other bar," I replied.

Beside me Teece developed severe muscle spasms as the Bounty ran a knife down my cleavage.

"You give a good copy of her then. Maybe I'll take you for the ride anyway."

"Where's the ride going?" I felt strangely calm. Curious, in fact.

"I'm just working the delivery run." She jabbed the knife under my top rib. "Now move."

Shite, how I loved it when they wanted me alive!

I slapped the blade sideways, ignoring the sting as it sliced my skin. Teece grabbed her other fist between both hands, bending her wrist backwards towards her throat. It gave me time to kick her so hard in the crotch that I felt her pubic bones separate.

As she collapsed the firestormer dropped its load, melting a section of the slops tray and slagging several bar taps.

Teece got to it and pulled the charger before it cremated anyone living. I got to her . . . and shoved both Lugers in her mouth.

"Who sent you?" I still sounded calm. Too calm.

Calm enough to slide the pistols back to let her answer.

She licked her dry lips. "Hey. It's just for cred. You dig. I got no names."

"Where then?"

She took a moment to consider which loss would be greater. This job or her long-term earning capacity.

"Delivery was to be south of Tower Town. I got a compass bearing. That's all."

One thing you can guarantee with Bounty is their common sense none of this dying-for-your-job crap.

I retracted the pistols to a less threatening distance. "Take a holiday down the coast. Wait till this is sorted."

Her expression was cautiously grateful. "S-sure. Thanks."

She didn't need to thank me. I wasn't being nice. But I didn't hold grudges against people on commission.

She climbed to her feet, unable to straighten up. "153.3 long. 28.6 lat," she whispered.

I recorded the numbers carefully in my compass memory.

Teece handed her the toothless, melted weapon. "Get yourself a new piece while you're down there."

Chapter Five

I battled a vision while Larry settled things in the bar and Teece promised to pay him for new taps.

When things started to get grainy, I gripped Teece's shoulder.

Once outside, I let him steer me to the apartment and lock the door. By then, I was . . .

Swimming through blood, thick as mud. Warm, oozing blood-mud. A swell lifted me along, settling me gently on a beach. My limbs weighed heavily. I crawled forward, mouth closed, anxious to keep the taste out of my mouth.

When I surfaced back into Tert reality, I was on a foldout bed in my new digs, and Ibis was sitting at the foot of it.

"Drink," I croaked. Then, "How long?"

His plump face creased into a relieved smile, and

he handed me a beaker. "That large boy gave you a sed while you were out of it. You've been sleeping awhile."

Sleeping? I didn't have time for sleeping! "Any messages?"

"A rather elegant man in lurex stopped by with some implements."

"What did he say?"

Ibis made a poor imitation of Larry's somber voice. "Tell 'er to be patient."

Funny, Larry.

I sat up, scrubbed my face and gave him the once-over. "Nice look."

Ibis squirmed like he'd been dropped in a Dumpster and was now hoping to shed his skin. There was nothing of his usual outrageous hip about the grubby fatigues and collarless tee he wore.

"I was told if I didn't put these clothes on, he'd stuff me into them. I didn't think he meant it would be fun," he complained.

I nodded. "That's Teece. He's right."

"Yes." He sighed heavily.

I reached out and squeezed his arm. "Thanks for coming."

He shrugged. "I wish I could say it was a pleasure. But I don't think it is." He added in a low voice, "Even Loyl never asked me to come here."

Something must have showed in my face because he clucked his tongue and patted my hand. "It's all right. Really. In fact I've always wanted to . . . er . . . visit."

He made it sound like a holiday destination.

It was my turn to make clucking noises. "You should have waited for me to arrange escort. You could have been—"

A shudder ran through his plump body but I suspected it was for effect. Ibis had already proved his resourcefulness to me on several occasions. Still, this was my place now. He was my guest, here at my request. I wasn't going to take any chances.

Shite. My own growing sense of responsibility made me sick.

"From now on, you don't go anywhere without Teece, or me, or some muscle."

He smiled lasciviously. "Pat won't like it at all." Pat was his lover.

I ran my hands through the stubble of my hair. "There's something you should know, Ibis. 'Bout Teece."

He threw his hands in the air. "Hands off? Darling, you don't even have to say it." He made a sound like a punctured tire.

I nodded sympathetically. "Yeah, I know. Sucks, doesn't it?"

"Now," he said, pulling a note compact from his pocket, "before you give me any more lines to do, let's get on with this interior decorating."

I spent a short time deluging him with ideas. What I wanted done, where we might get raw materials, who would provide the labor and how we would keep the stuff safe from theft. Quality wood and clean plastic were at a premium in The Tert. Second only to food and drugs. In that race, food often ran second.

Ibis repeated things into his jotr as I talked, outlining my crazy dream to give the ferals a home.

"They're living in attics, Ibis. Like packed fish, sleeping amongst the dust and canrat shit. But they are organized. Committed to their survival as a group. They even manufacture their own bioweapons with alchemy. Wombat knows who taught them that." I thumped my hand on the side of the bed, searching for the meaning I was trying to convey. "They care about each other . . . in a way the rest of us have forgotten."

"Who, my pet, is this Wombat?"

"You pray to the Fashion Goddesses. I pray to Wombat," I said by way of short explanation.

The long explanation, as far as I knew, was funnier. Wom (corrupted to Wombat by some joker) was a nerdie-boy back twenty years who'd preached the beauty of post-humanism and the like.

He tried to upload himself into his microwave on prime-time Common Net—got electrocuted instead. His ridiculous stunt raised him to iconic status. People short on deities and big on irony adopted him. These days he was more a kinda idiom, and praying to an idiom suited my chic. It was better than believing in a god who always passed on the hard stuff.

"I can't see the similarities," Ibis said, frowning.

I nearly smiled. "Main thing is, they need a home."

Ibis glanced up from his scribbling. "You know, Parrish, you and Loyl share many of the same ideals—"

"Stop!" I jumped up, furious. "We share nothing! Community is one damn thing. Selective breeding is another. I don't think my bloodlines are better than anyone else's. I'm not prepared to use human beings as lab rats. Do you *know* what Daac has been doing?"

I bit off my tirade. Of course he knew.

Ibis sagged, upset by my attack and perhaps, I hoped, by guilt. I felt immediately contrite but had no idea how to make it up to the man. Kind words didn't come easily to me.

And what the hell was I doing bringing him here anyway? One of Loyl's oldest supporters and proclaimed member of his *gens.*

Because he'd been a friend to me when there was no one else. Because he'd risked his life for me when Daac had asked him to help. And because he could still laugh at himself.

Ibis had all the qualities I admired. All the qualities I couldn't afford.

I breathed for calm. "I must be feeling better, eh?" I laughed shakily. "Let's go take a proper look at the job."

He returned a small, troubled smile.

I hoped I hadn't just snuffed out one of the few lit corners in my world of shadows.

Teece came with us to the barracks. So did an oversized Pet.

"Gift from Larry Hein," said Teece when I raised an eyebrow. "Said to tell you he was useless as a servitor. Couldn't take orders, always playing with his weapons. Thought maybe you could use him."

I looked him over critically. Under the dirt his mek side seemed in good shape. Actuators powered by old DC motors. More degrees of freedom in his limbs than I had.

Pets came with different proportions of mek to bio. Some had mek limbs and normal bodies; others had virtually all mek with the remnants of a brain and a rudimentary set of internal organs. I couldn't even begin to guess how some of them stayed alive, what they ate, where they peed from, whether they had sex. This one looked to be mainly bio with arms and legs of titanium. And a battered cowboy hat stuck to his head.

His face was the problem. It was altogether too sweet.

"What's your name?" I didn't talk to Pets much. They made me uncomfortable.

"Roo—same as the animal."

"You like weapons?"

He gave a sly grin. "They like me."

I took in the tips of his mek digits and wondered what explosive devices or flick blades they hid. I could see the targeting hardware wired into his hat and the line of the weapon compartments in his legs. My guess was the kid made my arsenal look like toy stuff.

But did he have any sense?

"How do you afford that gear?"

"Like I said. They like me. I can make a lot of this stuff. It seems sorta natural for me to do it. I worked with Ginnopolis, fixing things, before the war. Sometimes he lets me upgrade and do maintenance."

Ginnopolis? Minoj's main competition in armaments. My eyes widened. Now *that* could be handy.

He went on. "And jus' so you know. I'm not one for older grrls. If I work for you . . . it's biz only."

I opened my mouth. Shut it again. Opened it again and managed, "Don't get in my way," as I strode inside the barracks.

The entire building smelled like kennels. I swallowed nausea and stalked angrily through each room. Ibis pranced nervously one step behind, hand over his nose. Roo trailed along more slowly, while Teece waited outside, eyeing the bystanders.

"I-it has potential." Ibis's teeth chattered as he surveyed the filth of the 'goboys' communal living— a mess and dormitory-style bunkrooms that slept one hundred or more. Then there was the fight room. Used for cockfights and settling disputes and sex and whatever else the doggie critters liked to do.

Another memory swelled like blood from a fresh wound. My initiation into Jamon's bondage had been lurid and degrading. Stamped possession.

I used my meditation techniques to soften the feelings.

"I want this room scoured and sanitized like it was a medi-lab. Then I want it turned into a rec room. These kids need some fun. No Sensil."

I had a private war going with Sensil. My mum, Irene, was addicted to it. It had turned her into a body battery that my stepdad, Kevin, had pretty well used up. With Irene in neuro-endocrine bliss, he ate her food and spent her money. The perfect arrangement. The wasted and the waster.

"That's a stupid idea," Roo commented, idly picking through his hair.

I swiveled, ready to tear chunks from him. "What makes you the expert?" I snarled.

"Can't stop Sensil. Everyone does it. E-V-R-E-E-W-O-N."

He spelled the word to me like I was a child.

My face bent into an ugly shape. I had a nasty look when I put my mind to it.

Roo seemed unfazed.

Suddenly I had an inkling of why Larry had sent him to me. Maybe I needed to hear an opinion from someone who didn't care too much who I was.

I toned down my bitch impersonation. "So what's *your* angle?"

"You stop 'em, they'll find another way. I says you can do two things. Control how often they bung in."

"Impossible. Or?"

"Find 'em something better to do."

Ibis swallowed his chuckle.

I glared at him and then at Roo. The Pet looked innocent and slightly bored. He scratched his scalp under his hat.

"Like what?"

He shrugged. "You're the boss, aren't ya? You work it out."

"You want to call me boss? Then go wash your hair and meet me later," I snapped.

"Sure, *boss*," he said and swaggered off.

Ibis followed me to the san.

"One thing, Ibis. No frills. If it looks too schmick, I'll need an army to keep the *petits* and the poachers out. And the kids will feel . . . awkward."

"Boss says plain and simple," he said to his jotr.

Boss? Was e-v-r-e-e-w-o-n taking the piss?

"Plain and simple," I echoed aloud. "Don't forget."

I dumped Ibis on Teece and said I'd meet them at Torley's. Then I headed to my old digs to rescue Merry 3#.

A babe had moved in—a pretty little piece with an extra breast. She answered the door dressed in a multi-cupped bikini that changed colors against her skin.

"I want my holo back," I said shortly. "You can keep the rest."

"Oh," she said. "You must be the last tenant. The landlord said you'd died and had no family. Said I could sell your belongings. I liked the holo, though, so I kept it."

No family! Well, she was almost right about that, with sister Kat playing pro-ball in Eurasia somewhere and Irene down and out for the mattress count. That's if Kat was still alive. Performance enhancers got all the pro athletes in the end. As for stepdad Kevin . . .

I laughed shortly. "I *am* the landlord."

"Oh." She seemed at a loss then. "Would you like to come in?"

Her accent was cultured for The Tert. So were her manners. Maybe she was lost.

I stepped across the bloodstains on the threshold—more memories of Jamon's 'goboys. I wondered if that one had regrown his eye. Inside was the same drab 'creted walls, same narrow bed.

Not so same the girlie bits—stuffed bears perched glassy-eyed on the kitchenette shelf, along with twirly-stoppered fuck-me lotions and a limp dream catcher dangling where the window may have once been.

The dream catcher spurred a thought.

Without asking I dragged a chair across and peered up into the manhole. I'd had the ceiling stuffed full of precautions—motion sensors, light sensors, every damn thing that beeped and bopped—to keep out uninvited wasters. You'd be amazed what could crawl through a Tert ceiling.

"What are you looking for?" She sounded nervous.

"You c'n sleep safe at night . . . er . . ."

"Tingle Honeybee," she offered.

I tried to say the name, choked on it and gave up. Who in the freaking Wombat would call themselves *Tingle Honeybee?*

"Yeah, well. Leave what's up there alone and it'll warn you if something's planning a visit," I said.

"But what would I do then?" She pouted.

"Buzz off, I guess."

I scooped Merry 3#'s control unit off the floor and left, stifling a guffaw until I was outside. It had been so long since I'd laughed, it hurt.

My stupid, weak joke had me sniggering all the way back to Jamon's. I backhanded the tears from my eyes and waited impatiently while Merry 3# reinstated on her new commlink. A personal organizer wasn't worth a pinch without a line to Common Net and One-World.

She shimmered into life looking pretty damn pouty. "You've been out awhile," she complained.

I ignored her whining. "I'm waiting for an important call. Anything come in?"

"Well, yeah."

"Well, show me." I dropped onto a couch that had appeared in my absence, courtesy of Larry Hein no doubt. This warlord thing had some perks, apart from the fact that every joker in The Tert seemed to be able to get into my place.

Merry 3# cleared her throat, interrupting my reverie. "Only one recent . . . and urgent."

"Shoot." I sat up, praying it was Larry.

Merry 3# snapped her fingers and a board appeared. Her clothes morphed—skintight duds to a barely bikini. Just like a One-World weather grrl.

"Fashion junkie," I sniped.

"Fashion tragedy," she retorted.

I smoothed the fringe on my jacket and vowed to find the tekboy that made Merry and get him to service her. A few weeks with Tingle Honeybee and she'd turned psychotic.

"Give," I ordered.

"Oh yes, that's right." She slipped back into her skintights and was filing her nails.

The blackboard switched to a screen. It was Teece, his face bulging purple. "Where 'n hell's gonads are you, Parrish? I got trouble."

Chapter Six

I hit the pavement in Torley's at full sprint. Teece didn't shout "help" very often. Never, in fact. He was a big boy. Able to handle himself.

Outside Hein's a mini standoff was happening. A bunch of Plastique heavies and a tiny band of masked-up ferals brandishing a vial, with a crowd of Hein's regular punters caught in between. They saw me coming, and the sea parted.

I kicked the door wide, Luger in each hand.

Melodramatic? I didn't think so.

A quick recce told me Larry had the damage meter set to holocaust. Not a drink to be seen, not a stale bread stick in sight. Nothing but some uninvited parties, Teece with a shok-rod stroking each ear and Ibis strung upside down from the overhead light grills like a pig ready to be spitted.

"Easssy," hissed Teece.

I breathed hard and fast. His look told me he

was worried about what I might do that would cause them to scramble his brain. Permanently.

The guys that held the shok-rods were my size. Skewbalds—face brown-and-white. Skin-mixed jerks with cheaply sculpted muscles. More Plastique types.

Too far from home!

They shifted a little, dragging Teece with them.

I noticed a small figure behind, seated at a table. I didn't need any introductions.

"You could have just called, Road."

He butted out his smoke and flashed me a smile. Road Tedder. Mover on the southside of The Tert, in Plastique, where you could buy anything for a price. Rumor had it he'd killed and eaten his wife when he'd lived in the burbs. Been hiding out ever since.

Couldn't see it myself. A walking cadaver with a concave stomach.

Emaciated or not, Road still stirred plenty of aggravation around here. Gave my one-time lover Doll Feast ulcers.

"Hear you're a busy girlie. Wanted to get your attention."

Girlie. GIRLIE!

Only one thing made me spit more than that term—anyone threatening my good friends. Those who cared for me got looked after by me. Period. In truth, it was all I had to give in return.

And Teece and Ibis got more than most.

I spared Ibis a quick glance. He looked terrified, but that was sham. Ibis was smart and tougher than spectra. What I couldn't work out was how the two of them got taken unawares.

"You got it, Road. But not the way you might like."

"Put the guns away. And let's see what sort of a business head you got, *girlie*."

I began to imagine what fertilizer I'd mix him with.

Not a good thought to have. The bloodlust started and the world reduced to sharp outlines. My body pulsed with revenge. I fought the sensation down with every ounce of my inner strength because the violent need kept me from doing the smart thing and got me doing the messy thing.

"What business is that?" I ground out.

"Jamon and I had a deal."

His words dampened my blood hunger better than a dunk in the Filder River. My vision cleared some.

Road lit up again and inhaled. Wet, sucking noises. "Supply and supply. Mondo supplied the punters; I supplied Mondo."

I stared stupidly at him.

In my corner sight Teece writhed a little, trying to tell me something.

Then it hit me. Drugs. Tedder moved most of The Tert's drugs.

You could buy anything from anyone around here, but the bulk procurement and sales were divvied up as tidily as sashimi.

Far as I knew, it went like this: Tedder lauded over Plastique, sold the drugs and ran the black-market trade. Doll Feast carved a chunk out of that pie and dabbled in prosthetics and body parts.

Jamon Mondo psuedo-pimped Torley's, Shadoville and The Stretch, and made sure the punters got entertained. Topaz Mueno barely controlled The Slag and a thousand knifed-up Muenos.

Io Lang—the shape-shifter I'd pinged right here in Hein's—had supposedly been *the man* in Dis, but I wasn't so sure who really lorded over the sinister heart of The Tert. According to Teece, the name "Dis" had some obscure connection with hell. Nothing obscure about it as far as I could see.

Geographical demarcation in The Tert was more than lines on a map. It was something you just knew. Usually by the look of the punters strutting the pavements, the crappo decorations on buildings and whatever the vendors hawked. The Muenos had toll points on the main thoroughfares. Plastique had toll for those that came in off the Transway.

I knew it like the classroom of my net-school when I'd lived back in the burbs.

Yet I didn't know Dis. Hopefully I never would. Hard-core crazies, hard-core heavies. Even for Parrish Plessis, warlord.

Actually I was working on another word for my current job. And the first scud who called me "warbabe" would see the thick end of my garroting wire.

"What are you offering me?"

"I'm offering to let my men come in here and distribute Lark and Speed. You get a percentage."

Lark and Speed. Basics. Not much appeal for designer shit in The Tert.

I wasn't big on chemical entertainment myself. With a body as infested as mine there was no room for extras. Left to me, I'd shoot the Lark dealers soon as I'd buried all the Sensil teks. But I'm not stupid—that was a crusade I couldn't win. Or wanted to. Just a personal preference.

One thing I did know, though. Tedder's men weren't selling on my turf. The slimy little anorexic wasn't getting a fingernail in here.

"What arrangement did you have with Jamon?"

He hesitated over the truth. "Jamon got twenty percent."

"He distributed, right?"

Tedder nodded.

"You're a liar, Road. I've seen Jamon's notes." I had, but they'd made no real sense. Tedder didn't have to know that.

I saw Teece stiffen at my provocation, wondering what the hell I was up to while he had a shok-rod inserted in either ear.

Tedder quivered, sucking deeply. "Twenty percent or nothing—a very generous offer. You can continue to collect your protection money from the bars and not worry your head about the rest."

"Forty percent and I distribute. I don't want to see your dealers within cooee."

Tedder paled, twitching. He inhaled deeply once more. "Scramble the boyfriend," he said.

My world narrowed to the space between Teece, the Plastique boys and me.

I couldn't get there in time, but if I could just get them to shift their rods a fraction . . .

"OK," I said hoarsely. "Ease off the hardware, and I'll do it your way."

Tedder smiled thinly at me. He nodded at his boys to dismount. "Watch her."

My smile was for Teece. Bright and jaunty. I hope he got my meaning.

The skewbalds released their triggers in unison, retracting their rods a fraction from his ears.

I shot them both instantly.

Teece dropped like a stone to the floor with them. I didn't look at him, whipping the Lugers straight on Tedder.

He was quick. He had Ibis as a shield, an ugly little meat cleaver jammed against his throat. The blood had already begun to trickle. "You'll regret that, bitch."

" 'Bitch' is fine, Road. But don't call me 'girlie.' And don't ever think you can play me," I snarled in reply. Blood thundered in my ears. The creep had pushed me to risk Teece's life and now he had Ibis trussed like a roast about to be carved.

Yet I couldn't let him win. Everything that had gone before would be wasted.

In some distant, removed part of my brain, I wondered how long it would be like this for me. Dealing for power. *Is that what warlords do?*

I stared into Ibis's eyes. He quivered. This time for real.

"Don't harm him, Road," I warned. "I'll—"

I didn't need to finish my threat. The hand that held the knife at Ibis's throat suddenly spasmed and fell away. The cleaver clattered to the floor, Tedder alongside it.

I pounced on it.

Tedder writhed in pain. I stamped my boot across his hand and shoved both Lugers in his face.

A scrabbling noise came over my shoulder, and

Roo crawled out from a panel underneath the bar. I heard the slight whine of his limbs. One of his digits, peeled open like starfish, had shot a dart into the back of Tedder's neck.

"You!" I accused.

His hair gleamed blond, tousled and freshly washed. Green eyes observed me calmly. "Didn't I do the right thing?"

Relief and anger coagulated in my breast, making it hard to breathe. "Watch he doesn't move."

Roo took up sentry duty and I ran quickly to where Teeee had fallen, reefing off the bodies of the Plastique boys.

He errupted from under them, a wild animal, flailing. "Jesus! *Jesus!* Frig the Wombat, Parrish. What the hell were you thinking of?" he demanded with a roar. Blood smeared his face. "I could catch something from these jerks."

He felt himself all over while I held my breath. A burn on his cheekbone, muscle spasms down one side of his face and singed hair.

"I'm alive," he pronounced finally, wiping saliva from his lips. He danced a couple of steps. Then he swung at me. The punch caught me square in the jaw and took me down.

"Don't you ever do that again," he whispered hoarsely and stormed out.

The punters teemed back into Hein's after Larry decreed the holocaust over. Seems I was good for business after all.

Larry's bouncers saw Road and his remaining skewbalds safely on to the Transway back to Plastique. It didn't pay, I thought, to damage Tedder any more, although I was tempted. The ferals went along to make sure the job got done. Seems they'd look after my interests whether I liked it or not.

I'm not sure what Larry did with the bodies, but by the time I'd cut Ibis down from the ceiling, given Roo an earful about sneaking around and rubbed my already bruising jaw in self-pity, they were gone.

My jaw throbbed but not as much as my heart. I'd killed two people. If I hadn't, Teece would have died.

Ibis glared at me from where he sat at a booth gulping his brimming beaker of scotch. His eyes were shot.

I sat opposite him with three measures of tequila lined up. As I swallowed the first, I banged the glass against my jaw and winced.

"I-it serves you right, you know." His teeth still chattered slightly. "P-playing with h-his life, P-Parrish."

Tears welled, catching me by surprise. I blinked them away before Ibis could see.

"I claimed salvage rights here, Ibis. If I don't protect them now, every no-brain in The Tert will come for me. *Me and everyone who's linked to me,*" I said harshly.

He took another sizable swallow.

I went on: "I took a risk that paid off. I'd probably take it again." My tone softened. "You can get out now. Get out and don't come back. I wouldn't blame you."

"I'm thinking about it." He glowered and waved at Larry for another drink.

Sometime later, close on to dark, Ibis and I staggered back to my new home. Roo trailed behind and I didn't mind. The visions that I'd staved off after my set-to with Road Tedder hovered like an unwanted salesman.

I hoped no one else wanted a piece of me tonight—I didn't know if I'd be good for any more conflabs with Jamon's unhappy ex–business associates.

We made it home without incident. Along with the new couch, a proper bed had found its way there. I swore tomorrow I'd chase Minoj down on his promise to fix my security, and tipped Ibis into the bed. I ordered Roo to the couch and I took the rest of the tequila bottle into the den.

Merry 3# yawned as if she'd been waiting up for me.

I made a list of things I wanted to make the place more livable and told her to send it to Larry Hein. Nothing special. Some mats, a table and chairs. The kitchenette didn't interest me much— what would I do with it? Instead I sent Larry another message telling him to negotiate a line of credit with some of the palatable food vendors. The rest I would shop for myself.

Myself? I laughed at the thought of doing something so simple. So normal.

I sat with my feet up on the PC and listened to Merry 3# gab my messages back to me.

Several from small-time sharks who'd heard I
was the new *capitán*. Two from Gigi the Cashier,
who'd no doubt seen the transfers from Jamon's
account. And one call from Stenhouse.

Stenhouse bootlegged the Sensil tekware from
the supercity corps and sold it to the movers in The
Tert. He also fixed it when it broke.

Another from The Cure. The Cure was the cute
name for a bunch of shady medics who inserted
the Sensil routes in between punters' vertebrae.

A while back one of them, who practiced under
the name of Doc Del Morte, got ambitious and
started bio-mek butchery on stolen kids as a side-
line. When word got out about his failure rate and
how he was getting his test subjects, the Cabal ran
him out of The Tert.

Even they had limits as to what they would tolerate. Del Morte left behind him forty or more kids—
Pets—in varying stages of bio-robotic decay. No
one else knew how to maintain them. Their specs
had disappeared along with their architect. They
were all dying from their condition—some more
quickly than others. Roo was one of them.

From my understanding, The Cure and Stenhouse's crowd splashed each other's boots and
scratched each other's balls.

A headache started behind my nose and climbed
up into my forehead. Frustration. I didn't have time
for all this. And yet I had no trace on the missing
karadji. Perhaps Larry wasn't the one. Perhaps . . .

I put my head in my hands and spoke sternly to
myself. Larry *was* the one. If he couldn't find a

lead, there wasn't one. Meantime I had to keep busy.

"Problems?"

The voice started me out of my chair. The blistered face and singed blond hair had me falling back into it. "Jees, you look terrible. I'm so sorry, Teece."

He ignored my apology, staring at Merry 3#, who'd flashed back, dancing to some tune in her empty head.

"Maybe she's the one I'm in love with. Someone who I think is you," he said hoarsely.

"Then you'd better go home to your bikes, Teece. Things are gonna get worse here," I said levelly. "If I can't take it, they'll get me. And I'm not ready to go anywhere yet."

I waited for him to answer.

"I'll stay around, Parrish. But you hung me out today because of your own ambitions. That's hard to forget."

It wasn't forgiveness.

"I promised you nothing, Teece. Except maybe a rough ride."

A smile ghosted his lips. "On that you could never let me down."

He went into the living room, booted Roo off the couch onto the floor, lay down and closed his eyes.

I got the hint. No sex for Parrish, and stale adrenaline aftermath plagued me, escalating the chances of a vision. The visions lingered so close to my conscious state now I feared they were becoming part of my reality.

Dread kept me from rest. So did my need to flick all this tedious housekeeping and get on with finding the missing *karadji*.

"I'm going for a run," I said and copped the beginnings of a snore in return.

Torley's at three a.m. teemed with the backwash of chemical attitudes and tragic karma. Sensil parlors. Cockdog fights. Street sex of the sordid kind. Sights that once had amused or fascinated me suddenly made me heavy with responsibility. I wore my new job like high-cut concrete boots.

But night also had a masking beauty. Even in The Tert.

I jogged past the neon replica of a chained dog on Hein's roof, along the gen-powered glittery emerald and ruby halo of The Stretch and in amongst the eerie, metallic garden silhouettes of Shadoville. An uninterrupted twenty-klick loop if you knew when to duck and weave.

An alien inner voice dogged my footsteps.

Not long, human. Not long . . .

It had wired itself into my thought processes. Sometimes it was a heavy presence, gorging on every fix of brutality. At others, when I starved it of rage, it subsided into a hard knot of discontent.

The discontent, the denial of what it wanted, was what I sought—whatever the cost. I recognized its presence in the same way that I knew a silent guard of ferals ghosted me now. Tomorrow I would elude them. But how could I elude the Eskaalim?

Would the Cabal honor their deal and give me

what I needed to fight it? Did they really know where the stolen research was?

A little before dawn I got home. Merry 3#, in niteclub undress, flashed up an incoming from Larry. He looked tired and unusually grim. Mascara smudged.

"News?"

He shrugged. "When my snitches started asking questions, one had his throat torn out and the other had his insides messed with. Looked like they were telling futures with it. Some heavy mojo."

Bile rose up my throat. Not much upset Larry. But this had.

"Your boys . . . was it anyone I know?"

He gave me a look. "Does it make a difference?"

Shame stung me. Because it did . . . and it shouldn't. "You get a name?"

He shook his head. "I got something, though. A woman's been asking about all the local shamans— where to find them. We think the same person's put up money to snatch you." He gave me a rare, brief smile. "I guess they don't know you so well."

I nodded, thinking of Riko's half-assed kidnap attempt. And then the Bounty. Somehow their acts were connected with the missing *karadji*.

"An outsider, then?"

"Definitely."

I pressed my temples tight. "Thanks, Larry. Consider yourself Plessis Ventures' newest executive."

He didn't seem to get the joke. "No thanks. You aren't gonna be around long enough for the first board meeting."

I took his cheerful advice into the den and

thought about what I'd just learned. Whoever had kidnapped the *karadji* also had their sights set on me. Playing cut and paste with entrails wasn't common, even for The Tert. If anyone could tell who had done it, it was the Muenos. Besides, I couldn't sit around any longer. The King Tide pulled.

I keyed the lock on the 'puter, told the lips-and-torso to shut up shop and went to bed, crashing, exhausted, alongside Ibis while the Angel wandered my dreams. . . .

Humming huddled sentience. Us thought. Us thought. Time spread wide, never long. Fanning the tail of the comet. Riding the diamond dust wave . . . hungry for food . . .

Breakfast was a sullen affair. Ibis nursing a hangover, Teece a bruised heart, and me hankering to cut and run.

On the pavement at Lu Chow's, a block from Hein's, we swallowed shavings of unidentifiable BBQ meat slabbed on bread, washed down with mockoff. Since tasting real tea in Viva with Daac, I'd lost my taste for The Tert's murky caffeine. The food, however, beat the hell out of the pro-subs I'd lived on for the last couple of years.

It geed me for what I had to say.

"I'm leaving soon. May be gone for a while."

Teece flinched, then kept stoically grinding the last gristle of his grill. "Where? What?" he asked, picking his teeth.

"Can't say, exactly. Something I can't ignore. Teece, can you run things here for me?"

His fork clattered down and he gave me a sharp sideways. "Things?"

"The biz. There's so much to sort. I'll let Larry know you're the man. I'll swing past Pas and get him to send some Muenos over as muscle. I'll keep in touch where I can."

Pas had just about wrested control of the Muenos from Topaz during the war. Things had quieted some since then. I knew they were waiting for a sign from me—their assumed goddess, Oya. Some people just need something to believe in, and the Muenos were big on prophecies and spirits. In any case, Topaz was on borrowed time.

"What about my bikes?"

"I've got moncy now, Teece," I said softly. "Get someone to run it for you. I'll pay them. I'll give you a cut of this. Whadya say?"

The entrepreneur in him tussled with the hurt lover. His faded blue eyes sparked up with the economic possibilities. He stuck a finger in my ear like it was a shok-rod. "Forty percent?"

I scowled and thumped him in the ribs. He'd made his point.

"What about me?" Ibis blurted.

"You're going home."

His plump face set mulishly. "What if I don't want to?" He sulked.

I wanted to laugh. When I met Ibis, I'd thought him a soft-assed neo-nu-age chump. But he proved to be smarter, more resourceful than most people

I knew. And a better friend. Not to mention he'd kept me out of a Viva quod.

Sometimes, though, his pout was pure spoiled brat.

"I don't need the worry, Ibis. I shouldn't have brought you here."

The pout settled into something less yielding. "Get on with your little errand, Parrish Plessis. I'll make my own arrangements."

I sighed. *What did that mean?*

I turned to Roo.

Bored, he flicked burned globs of meat at the passing trade.

"I want you to come with me." My conscience pricked as I said it. *A kid guarding my back! Was that right?*

It got his attention. The thought juiced him and he clacked his digits together. "For how much?"

I sighed again. Life was a lot simpler when I had nothing.

One last thing stood in the way of my leaving.

It arrived by midmorning, bad-tempered and not a little agoraphobic. Raul Minoj was *not* used to the world outside his four closed walls.

In person his skin always seemed greasier, his teeth more crooked, his breath worse than I remembered. He'd trekked across The Tert in an armored Pet, opting not to use the Trans. The Pet, modified by himself no doubt, sprouted weapons like an echidna with a hard-on.

He fussed around Larry's servitors, chivvying them as they unloaded crates of tek and hauled them to my place. "Gently, gently," he bleated. "Treat them like babies. Like babies."

I supervised the bedding in of my gun case. Nobody would be taking it anywhere without hauling the entire building along as well.

Minoj had brought a selection of rifles for me to look over. I chose around twenty pieces, sighed heavily over not having enough time to play with them and sealed them in the case.

Before I did that I took the little box with the flesh flaps from my pocket. I peered closely at the tattoos on each one, trying to decipher them. A row of decapitated symbols. Without the other segments it might as well have been hieroglyphics. I sighed and dropped it in the corner of the case. It'd be safer there than anywhere else until I figured out what in the Wombat it was supposed to be telling me.

With my newest sweethearts tucked tight in their case, I went and found Minoj.

"I've gotta go," I said.

He shot me a look of undiluted disgust. "The first time I do a personal installation in fifteen years and you don't even have the manners to stay."

"Teece will look after you," I said.

Minoj and Teece eyed each other. I'd often thought of them as kindred. Physically mismatched— Teece the oversized surfie biker; Minoj the smarmy cripple—but in biz they both burned. The cost negotiation would be a study in shrewd.

"Make sure you get this place tight," I demanded. "It's seen more traffic than a Transway station."

Minoj dismissed me with a flick of his obscenely long fingernails and went about it.

Teece grabbed my arm.

I went to brush him off and stopped myself.

His blue eyes pinned me, steady and clear. "I'll run this place for you, Parrish. Just come back in one piece."

I nodded and grinned.

Maybe I didn't deserve the second chance he was cutting me.

But hey, I'd take it!

Chapter Seven

I decided to start with Pas and see what I got. I had business with him anyway.

Along The Stretch I stopped and bought two spare sets of fatigues and some imitation Kapaluas from a rag doyen. I stuffed the clothes in my pack and donned the shades. I wasn't going on this expedition without a change of clothes. My wardrobe used to be full of dress-ups even when I had no credit. These days I'd settle for something clean that didn't attract any notice.

Roo trailed behind me, chewing on a shashlik. For a kid who was part mek, he sure could eat.

Minoj had pressed a Gurkha's knife on me before I left. I strapped it to the outside of the pack and cast a prayer to the great frigging Wombat that I'd have no call to use it.

I studied Roo as we steered through the alleys towards Mueno territory. A graceless mixture of streamlined titanium limbs and soft child's body.

Dreamy expression on a sweet face. Killer's in-
stincts. Infested hair. He'd washed it but the critters
hadn't budged. In fact they seemed happier. He
scratched every few seconds.

Note to self: *Don't sleep within bug-leap distance
of the kid.*

At the edge of Torley's we passed a building that
stopped me short and stole my breath. Ten shamans had died in there trying to spiritually piggy-
back me and seek out the Eskaalim. Their brains
had unraveled like baling twine. Vayu's death got
to me the most. A strong woman. A *good* woman.
Dead at my persuasion, and for no gain.

Now here I was searching for the other Tert shamans. What would happen when I found them?
Through the blackness of my memory a derisive
laugh echoed.

I forced myself past the building and out of my
territory.

By evening the stink of Muenoville enveloped us.
Gaudy rugs and banners decorated the villas.
Cooking smells changed from stews and dumplings
to shawarmas, beans and mesa spices. Music pulsed
into the evening from bootleg satellite taps. Latino
competing with some pretty ordinary Tert home-
bake and some antique rap.

Mostly, the anger had gone out of music. Punters
around here seemed to need *balm*—an antidote to
how they lived.

On instinct I took the shortest route to Pas,
straight through the Villas Rosa. The slums' slum.
I'd met a kid there once. 'Bout eleven years old.

No arms. No name. The no name shook me more. She'd helped me and been kidnapped by a media 'Terrogator for her pains. In one of life's bitching little twists she'd ended up adopted by the wealthy royalty of Viva. King Ban, no less. A publicity stunt. Maybe, for once, someone I'd touched hadn't come off worse.

I still thought about her.

Ibis had scried for info on her as a favor but come up with squat—other than she was alive, well and the figurehead to some spanking new prosthetics company.

When I'd met her she was surviving on the scraps the Muenos threw away, living under a stairway, trying not to get abused on a daily basis.

I'd called her Bras.

Roo moved closer to me in the early dark. I didn't blame him. If Dis was the black heart of The Tert, the Villas Rosa was the sewer.

"You been this way before?" I asked.

The neons showed his eyes wide and alert. The pavements emptied at dusk. Canrat time. "Nope. Only Torley's and Shadoville. And a while back Larry sent me to the perimeter with a sanction."

A sanction, in The Tert, was a message. One that couldn't be trusted to a comm but had to be given face-to-face. "Where to?" I asked suspiciously.

"The waste. Opp'site Fishertown."

I halted in my tracks. *Near Teece's bike biz?*

"Who was the message for?"

Roo's expression got suitably blank. "Can't remember. Sure stinks out there, though."

I swallowed my paranoia down like it was hot

food. "Yeah," I said lightly. "They cremated the dead there after the war. Blew away the odor-de-fish." *Replaced it with odor-de-burned-flesh.*

We moved on, but my edginess stayed.

Who could I trust? Really?

That got me wondering about Daac again. Twenty-odd klicks to the east was his patch. The proximity to Mr. Tall, Daac and Hormone had me sweating.

As if the nightsong in the Villas Rosa weren't enough. In the music lulls, babies whimpered and women screamed. Muenos were big on voodoo and sacrifices. I got a hollow gut every time I thought about it. Then there was the chanting: a nerve-pinching rhythm that got you taking small, tight breaths.

We crossed a parcel of space where the concentric arcs of a villa set converged. A lifeless, solitary tree poked a craggy finger through plas-sheet roofing.

I knew the place. I'd wasted bodies here. Animals who thought raping a child with no arms was sport.

I realized my mistake in coming this way. Too late—my knees buckled and the neons clotted black and gray before my eyes.

. . . I smelled bloody ichor. Felt the escaped heat of the dying bodies rising like steam around me. My limbs ached with growing pains.
Why would I need to grow? Why would I?

Roo doused me with a hatful of water.

I spluttered and coughed. "Where did you get that?"

He gestured to a puddle under a corroded downpipe.

"C-contaminated," I chattered. *Shock? Fear? Cold?*

"Didn't know what else to do. You was . . ." He trailed off, gesturing to my mouth.

I touched my chin. It was slick with water and saliva. *Nice one, Parrish. Frothing at the mouth in front of the children.*

"That happens again, you just watch my back. It'll pass."

He nodded, clearly spooked.

I stood up. "You tell anyone, Roo, I'll cut your processor out. Understood?"

He nodded again.

At least he'd lost that bored expression. But what had replaced it?

I talked to him a bit more after that, trying to gauge the effects of my mind flip. He might be a walking armory but his heart and head belonged to a child.

"How do you know Larry?" I asked, slowing until he had to walk alongside me.

"Larry's always looked after us kids. Gives us work. He reckoned Doc Del Morte must have been pasted. Reckons if he ran into him he'd shoot him."

That wasn't likely to happen. Del Morte had been chased out of The Tert long before my arrival. "What do you reckon?"

"I think I'm kinda cool." Even in the darkness I could sense his pride in his mek. "Larry's dim. He don't know what it's like to be me."

"What do you remember about it?"

"Not much. The Doc brought us here 'fore we could talk."

"So you might have family out there somewhere?"

He shook his head firmly. "Nope. My family's here." He banged one artificial arm against the other. "Get real, boss. Nobody out there would want me now. Here at least I got respect."

I stifled a sigh. I knew what he meant. There was no going back for someone like Roo.

Or me.

I wondered how long he had left to live before the interface between his mek and bio parts rotted his tissue function. From what I'd heard it was a pretty individual thing. No one seemed to know how to stop the chemical bleed, and no one cared to find out. Del Morte had invented a new type of cancer and he wasn't around to take the rap for it. Roo wouldn't live to be an adult. I was glad he was proud of himself. It was all he had.

We found Pas at home sometime after midnight. Clad in voluminous, dirty silk pants and a red sash, he sat on the steps outside his villa set holding night court over a ragged line of Muenos who clutched icons and grievances to their breasts.

Our footsteps brought knives out in all directions. But Pas seemed unfazed.

"Oya!" He gestured exuberantly as if expecting me.

Perhaps he was. Muenos watched their boundaries closer than anyone else in The Tert.

A murmur of appreciation went through the

crowd. I was famous here for a few things. None
of them particularly glamorous. I'd killed a canrat
called The Big One. Blown its testes off. I'd also
had the sacred feathers land on me while I was
trying to get the shite away from a voodoo love-in.

Somehow both those things converted into an
amalgam of their legends. To the Muenos I'd become the human incarnation of Oya, warrior spirit,
goddess of this and that, guardian of the gates of
death.

The upshot of it was a lot of bowing and scraping
on the part of the Muenos and some pretty damn
tedious ceremonies.

I'd thought about chucking in my role as the pre-
ferred deity, but Pas had been feeding the ferals.
He'd also helped turn the tide against Jamon
Mondo in the war. I found that kind of worship
useful, and damn hard to surrender.

So now we had an agreement. He got to be chief
worshipper and I got to call the shots.

Nifty, huh?

"I need to wash, Pas. Got a dose of drain water."

He waved me through his open doorway. "My
house is yours, Oya."

I lurched towards it. "Feed the kid!" I threw
back over my shoulder.

The House of Pas was much like any other
Mueno's, aside from a flashy comm set and some
not so threadbare carpet. Chicken feathers, cruci-
fixes, charms and handfuls of candles littered the
ledges. I'd been infected by the Eskaalim parasite
in a place like this.

Pas's wife, a thin, worn woman with a shaved

head, showed me to a back room and left me on a small 'crete slab with a drain hole, a hose connected to a tank and a tub of biokill. I stripped, washed, rubbed my skin with the cream and changed into the fatigues. I had no choice but let my suede suit drip-dry. The fringe had clumped and curled.

Ibis would murder me.

Pas was in the comm room by the time I'd finished. In one corner an ugly attempt at furniture crouched like a gargoyle. The Bone Throne. Last time I'd been on that I'd had a vision come on like a hangover.

"Oya." He gestured at me to sit on it.

I flicked Roo a don't-say-a-word glare, but he was busy shoveling beans and greasy pastries in his mouth with one of his flick knife digits.

Pas clapped hands at his wife for another plate of food.

I wanted her to tell him to shove it and get off his fat arse, but she didn't. I bit my tongue. Oyas didn't delve into domestic issues.

"We have waited for your return, Sacred One."

Oya I'd learned to handle, but "Sacred One" . . .

"How goes it, Pas? What news of Topaz?"

"The soft belly hides. He knows the Muenos no longer respect him. As you can see they are *your* people."

Levering his bulk out of his seat, he wound a handle. Metal shutters squeaked open. Outside, the numbers of Muenos had swelled. Most of them held candles.

"Wh-what are they doing?"

"They've come to worship you," he said simply.

I wanted to leap up and run for my life at the very thought of it! An applause of appreciation went up as they saw me silhouetted on the throne.

He closed the shutters again and I dimly registered the wink of security gizmos hidden among the swinging charms. Pas had had some half-serious tek fitted since my last visit.

He watched me keenly, like a parent aware that his youngster wants to bolt from a family get-together. "Do not disillusion their belief, Parrish. Hope is the most precious thing of all."

It was the first time Pas had ever called me by my name. His effusive mask had slipped, and I glimpsed the shrewdness underneath. It was kinda uncomfortable—realizing your chief worshipper had his own agenda happening.

I changed the subject. "There's a problem that affects all of us, Pas. Muenos, the Tribes . . . the lot. You saw the shape-changer?"

He swore and crossed himself with darting, elaborate hand movements.

I paused, deciding how much to tell. Pas had never crossed me, but we weren't exactly buddies. On the other hand, I needed him more than ever.

"Some of us believe the shape changers are the result of a parasite. The parasite changes you at the most basic level."

"What type of parasite could do such a thing?"

"Nothing from this world, Pas."

His eyes widened. Like any self-respecting Mueno, he had a straight-up awe of the spirits and things unnatural. Why else would you spend your time knee-deep in chicken blood?

"I must stop the evil spreading," I explained.

"What do you want from me, Oya?"

"My place is unprotected while I'm doing this, Pas. Can you send some of your people there?"

He clicked his fingers. "Done."

"They must speak with my man Teece."

Pas stroked plump fingers through the waist length of his hair. Mueno male vanity. Like a peacock. "I remember him, Oya. He is a man like myself. Strong and virile."

I choked back a laugh. Somehow I'd missed the similarity. "Teece holds my clout and cred while I am away."

"Your people are not familiar with our Mueno ways. There may be trouble."

"Teece will take care of things." As I fibbed I saw my second chance with Teece slipping away.

Pas seemed satisfied with my assurance. "What else, Oya?"

"I'm looking for someone. Cabal shamans are missing. When my people asked questions about it, they had their guts spilled out on the pavement and played with. I figured you would know who'd do this kind of thing."

His expression froze. His hand moved automatically to the thick hair necklace around his neck.

Pig bristles! Muenos used them to ward off evil spirits.

"I'm not sure exactly. I have . . . knowledge of a lot of practices." Pas shifted uncomfortably like

his duds had caught fire. He stroked the necklace
for comfort.

"What knowledge?"

"As houngan I perform juju, but not everyone is
like me. Some invoke the petro loa."

"Petro loa?"

He wrinkled his forehead at my ignorance. "The
petro loa want cruel sacrifice and bring much malice."

"So where would I find the people that invoke
these loa?"

He puffed his chest a little. "Those ones do not
practice here anymore. I would know if—"

Pas's wife, Minna, stepped from the shadows of
the room. Taking a quick, nervous breath, she interrupted him. "Husband. The women say—"

He punched her before she could finish.

She swayed but stayed on her feet. It obviously
wasn't the first time.

I caught his arm before he could do it again,
resisting the desire to break it. "Let her speak."

She wiped the blood from her lip and got down
on her knees in front of Pas. "I had not wished to
worry you with whispers, husband." A glance at
me. "The women say Dalatto is working with Marinette again. I can show you her place. But you
must wear this. Even then I cannot guarantee you
will be safe."

She disappeared and returned with my damp
suede suit and two pig bristle bracelets. She handed
one bracelet to Roo and one to me. I cupped it in
my hand as I shrugged into the jacket and stuffed
the pants in my kit bag.

I slid the bracelet around my fingers. It smelled of cooking fat. "How dangerous is this Dalatto?"

"No more or less than you, Oya."

Sweet!

The three of us followed her out through the back of their villa into a washing-cluttered darkness. She led with sure steps, stopping occasionally to broadcast a guttural cry into the night. Each one was answered in kind by a range of female timbres.

Back doors cracked open as an unseen audience marked our route. Mueno women, wired to the back alleys and grease-thick kitchens of their domain.

We stopped several times while Minna calmly helped Pas over rubbish-hewn steps.

More consideration than he deserved.

I was not so composed. Adrenaline and annoyance combined into a familiar mix of irritability. I didn't like my followers beating their wives. I didn't like being watched. I didn't like groping about in the dark, and I surely *did not* like visiting mojo practitioners in the witching hour.

"Move it, Pas," I muttered.

Roo kept behind me, his mek limbs coping easily with the obstacles. I didn't have to ask to know his night sight was better than mine.

Finally, Minna stopped. I heard her soft gasp and exclamation.

Pas drew her behind him. "Stay outside . . ."

She nodded, her silhouette tense and alert.

Behind me, Roo unsheathed his digit blades, and his targeting system hummed on-line. Whoever fitted his hardware had never perfected the noise suppression. Maybe that's why he'd made it into Dr. Del Morte's reject basket.

Pas took a few steps and balked. I didn't blame him. The back door to the villa was ajar. Rank blood smells radiated through it. The kind that told you the place harbored old and new death.

The stench, Pas's hard breaths and Roo lock-and-loaded fractured my nerves. Disregarding Mueno protocol I brushed past Pas and thrust the door wide, Luger in one hand, wire in the other. It was that or turn and run.

I stepped into a nightmare—the kind you were too scared to remember in the morning.

The villa was wired for vodun worship of the ugly kind, and the kitchen had been the butchery. Blood. On every surface. Spattered on the walls. Pooled on the floor.

If a petro loa had been invoked, then he-she'd gotten his-her dowry.

In three quick strides I crossed through and into the downstairs living room. Roo was a pace behind me, dry retching.

An altar took up most of the space, covered in a rich brocade cloth and crowded with candles, bottles of liquid and bead-woven objects. In the center two crudely made dolls lay squashed into a small coffin bed together, genitals intertwined. The female had short, dark hair, legs too long for its body, small breasts and a face marred by irregular features.

Guess who?

The other was male, tall and had a face like a god.

Guess who?

Parrish and Loyl in the cot.

A palpable and suffocating malice lingered around the altar, transfixing me.

Roo on the other hand scanned the room for anything that might be alive.

"Boss. Over here."

I forced myself over to where he crouched under the stairs. Something lay there corralled by boxes, barely living, fur and ears matted with coagulated blood. Large hind legs twitched feebly. Fluid leaked from a slit in its belly. Its eyes opened and rolled a little.

"A true marsupial," I said, surprised.

Roo stood by me, pale and still. "What type?"

"I'm not sure. Never seen one in real life."

He reached in to gently touch the creature. It flinched away from him and trembled.

"Boss?" His voice wavered.

I knew what he was asking. As much as I didn't want to either, I couldn't let him do it. I was supposed to be the strong one here. I sent him to watch the back door and then I put a bullet in the animal's head.

Pas joined me. He fell to his knees, crossed himself.

"Marsupial," he said gravely. "None of the signs are good."

"Meaning?"

He got to his feet and beckoned me into the room opposite.

A woman lay facedown, buried under some cushions. With sweating effort, Pas kicked the cushions away and rolled her over on her back. The contents of her abdomen stayed put on the floor.

"Dalatto." His face had turned grayer than the marsupial's fur. "I do know this work. . . . This is the work of a houngan named Leesa Tulu." Fear thinned his pudgy features and stole the strength from his voice.

"Leesa Tulu?"

His hand clung tightly to his pig bristle. "Native animal sacrifices are rare. Only two, maybe three houngan in the whole of this country use them. Leesa Tulu is the only one on the east coast. She invokes Marinette. Marinette is a fetishist—she covets certain flavors of flesh to eat. Tulu also has a reputation for disembowelment when she is being ridden."

"How do you know so much about her?"

He rolled Dalatto's body back to hide the hideous sight and wiped his hands on the nearest cushion. Then he blinked away the perspiration from his eyes. "We escaped the Merikas' borders together before the Conformist uprisings banned houngans from their practice. We came to this country under refugee status and were conveyed to the Jinberra Camp. The things she did in there . . . her style . . . attracted people in Viva . . . who bought her way out." He sighed. "Be grateful for your liberty, Oya. And your choice of friends."

My skin prickled with something that wasn't cold. Tulu had connections in Viva. "I didn't know you were a migrant."

"There is only one religion in Merika now. No one dares to challenge the creed of the White Veils."

I didn't care about the repression in Merika. The Northern Hem had dug its own grave. What I cared about was someone making funny dolls of me and spilling life in The Tert. "So where is Tulu now?" I demanded.

"I will have my Muenos search for her, though most will be too frightened." He twisted his bristle necklace until it threatened to strangle him.

Muenos frightened? I started to pace, fighting off a swarming vision. What would a Vivacity houngan with a reputation want with the *karadji*? What would she want with me?

The questions circled each other like predators. It was too hard to think . . . to breathe in this place. My scalp crawled as if it was lice infested. I marched back to the altar in the opposite room and snatched up the dolls, stuffing them in my pocket. Then I kicked over the altar in frustration.

"Oya!" Pas danced behind me, wringing his hands together. "Do not disturb the offerings."

Unreasonably, I wanted to smash my fist straight into his face. Had he known his old friend Tulu was here making voodoo coffins for me? Was his surprise genuine? How much could I trust him when it was as plain as pain Leesa Tulu scared him witless?

With effort I controlled an urge to kill him—a wrestle inside myself that I could almost see, like a shadow play.

The parasite in me swelled.

"Boss?" An insistent tapping on my shoulder. *"Boss!"*

The voice was Roo's. Sweaty fear in his face. What had rattled him so much?

"What is it?"

He looked down.

Following his gaze, I saw my left hand restraining my right, which grasped a garroting wire. My own blood dripped from the tightness of my fist.

Muscles rigid.

Jaw tight.

Motionless.

Pas had backed into a corner, trying not to cower. *How long had I been like this?*

With further effort I loosened my grip on the wire and fumbled it away. Minna appeared from nowhere, producing a rag to bind my hand.

"Thank you for sparing my husband," she whispered.

Sick realization dawned on me—how close I'd just come to killing Pas. Slitting his throat in front of Roo and his woman.

I snatched the cloth from her hands. "Go home," I ordered her hoarsely. "Roo, go back to Teece."

I turned to Pas, a worthless apology caught in my throat. "Burn this place before I get back. Understand?"

He nodded, a tiny frightened movement.

"If you find anything about her, call Teece."

Then, crawling with self-loathing, I ran.

* * *

Running has always been my way. In the burbs when I was younger and Kevin tried to touch me—before I grew big enough to dust him—I'd run.

On occasions when Jamon was still alive I'd done it as well. It evaporated the fear and the anger. I felt solid when I ran. Doubt banished.

But it never lasted.

Soon my breath rasped like grit against my lungs. I stumbled frequently in the dirty dark of The Slag, pushing myself until my muscles trembled with fatigue and my chest burned.

I dropped to a walk long enough to ease the worst of the pain and then I ran again, oblivious to the scrutiny of pavement shadows and pitiless eyes. Uncaring that word of my flight passed before me.

In the gray dawn I huddled, exhausted, under some rusted stairs, sharing seclusion with a mound of used derms and an injured canrat.

Canrats lived on the roofs, mainly, but this one had an extra spur on one leg—like a half-formed foot. It dribbled as well, a foul-smelling acid much worse than the average dog breath. Its coat had rubbed off in patches, leaving a kind of chessboard pattern of scabby pink flesh and attic-stained fur.

"You need a change of diet," I advised it. I was shaking now, with fatigue and shock and general shiftiness.

It coughed and growled a bit. Nothing serious.

We camped together until the smell of pastry dragged me out to a food stall. Curious, the vendor took my cred spike and rolled it around in his fingers.

"Just gimme the food. The cred is good."

He checked it and served me, and I retreated back to the hidey-hole with a wrapper full of hot lumps of sugary dough. By the third lump I couldn't stand the dribbling. I tossed the cripple some dough. I was no fan of canrats—the Wombat knows I'd killed The Big One—but I was still a sucker for defenseless creatures. *Hungry,* defenseless creatures—even worse.

Hunger distorts.

The canrat gobbled deliriously, then settled its miserable body with a small lick on its two and a half front paws and sighed. I saw the tremor of improved blood sugar. Knew it well.

"You're in bad shape," I said out loud.

It twitched a tired ear.

I crouched, watching it doze, letting the pastry weigh in my gut, and thought over my next move. I was on the edge of Tower Town, Daac's patch. If Leesa Tulu was carving up bodies and making voodoo dolls of Daac and me in bed, he or Mei would be the next logical ones to know something.

Going there would also give me a chance to see if Stolowski was doing OK.

Call it abundant maternal instinct!

Yet the idea of talking to Daac made me feel almost as awful as discovering I'd tried to kill Pas.

Almost.

There was also a small, treacherous part that thrilled at the thought.

I sighed. I didn't trust many people. Now I couldn't even trust myself. It gave me a sudden glimpse into complete paranoia, and I locked it up quick and hard.

I hitched my pack on my back. The canrat woke with a start and, seeing its meal ticket about to bunk out, whimpered.

No longer questioning my sanity—it was way, *way* gone—I shoveled the creature into my pack and strapped it shut.

Daac's people began tracking me as soon as I left the gaudy Mueno rugs and stink of mesa spice behind. His patch was a portion of The Tert where the villas ceased to run in concentric semicircles and stood in rows like tenements. Tower Town. Inside the buildings most of the walls were smashed down to give space to large collective rooms, biz and one well-equipped medi-lab.

Stolowski Ree and Mei Sheong had a tiny pied-à-terre in amongst it all. A place where she sat on the window ledge like a disdainful feline, sniffing her incense, sipping psilocybin tea and being worshipped by Sto.

Some women don't know a good thing when it lived with them.

Sto would die for her.

But Mei . . . looked after Mei. And when *he* wanted it . . . Loyl Daac.

My escorts picked me up a few steps into the tenements. Without speaking, I let them steer me in and out of conjoined buildings until a long stair climb clued me to where I was being taken.

Daac waited for me on the roof, amongst the sleeper cocoons and mic dishes. The view from the top was something I didn't get to see very often, filthy and beautiful in one sweep of the eye. At midday the sky promised blue and delivered less. In the far west the sea stubbed gray along the coastline; to the east, the oily brown sliver of the Filder River was a more tenuous landmark, its poisons eating into the side of The Tert.

Daac liked to come up here, a legacy from his days as press-ganged labor out on the Bitter Plains. It might have seemed like claustrophobia but for Daac it was a reminder of why he was on a one-man crusade to bring The Tert back to its rightful ownership.

His *gens*.

His place.

He had a databank of bloodlines longer than the Filder. They were the ones who would triumph. According to *his* plan. Now the register was in my possession and he wanted it back. I just as surely wanted to keep it as a safeguard. What you might call precarious negotiating ground.

I squinted into the sun, tense and aware that I stank with stale exertion, and located him standing close to the edge of the roof as if he might walk off into the air.

He probably thought he could.

Of course one little push and . . . the snipers that guarded him from all points of the compass would turn me into a sieve. I could have scried them out but I didn't bother. I wasn't going to kill Daac. Not right now, anyway.

"Parrish?"

"Loyl?"

He turned and my gut flipped about like a suffocating blowfish. How did he do that to me? Was it the 'zine-cover face? Or the too-white teeth? Or the smooth, dark skin? Or the restless energy that crackled around him?

Or maybe it was that damn evening in Viva when he'd barely needed to pleasure me. A few simple caresses and I'd prematurely orgasmed and he'd walked away from me knowing my barefaced desire for him. Body chemistry sucked. The memory sent flushes across my skin.

"You've got something of mine. Did you bring it?" He didn't smile.

I shook my head. "I think it's safer with me."

A dark flush of anger warmed his skin and I rushed on, not wanting to send him too crazy straight off.

"Actually, I've come to talk," I said. "We may have a problem."

"We? There will never be a *we* while you keep what is mine."

I gave him a deceptively airy smile. "And *I* will destroy your bloodlines register if you don't listen."

OK. OK, so much for no antagonism.

He became dangerously still. "Come, stand over here, Parrish."

The roof looked rotten and splintered near his feet. I doubted it would bear our combined weight.

"What in this universe makes you think I would do that?"

"Don't you trust me?" he asked.

Never! "It depends."

He raised an eyebrow. "On?"

"What's in it for you."

We eyed each other.

"But I can see you're not interested in what I've learned. So I guess I'll just go then," I said.

I didn't wait for his reply but retraced my steps down into the building. If that didn't get him talking to me, then nothing would.

I went looking for Stolowski, giving my provocation time to boil.

My two escorts tagged along with me. From their faintly awed expressions, I guessed they'd got the gist of my conversation. I doubted anyone around here *ever* stuck it to the boss.

I strode up and down levels and in and out of doors, acting like I owned the place—until I found a room I recognized.

Medi-lab! Last time I'd been in there, Sto was in it recovering from exhaustion, dehydration and sore feet on account of me dragging him halfway around The Tert with no shoes.

"I'm in real estate. Looking for an apartment," I told the lab's door guards. I let my hands fall meaningfully to my holsters.

One of them aimed a semiauto at my chest. "Cute," he said.

"Your boss won't be too happy about you blowing me out the side of the building. I've got something precious of his. Check with him."

The door guards exchanged uncertain looks with the trailing escort. Somewhere in the silent communing they agreed not to kill me.

I strolled on through without a quiver.

The lab had gotten larger. More internal walls demolished. Now it took up most of the floor. Before I got to even twiddle a test tube, Daac burst in.

"Parrish!" His warning rang clear as the Vivacity water. "Don't touch anything."

"See you've got all the comforts of home," I said innocently.

"Out!"

I shrugged and shouldered past him into the corridor. He hustled along behind, breathing down my collar.

"Whatever you want to say, make it quick. I have guests," he said.

Guests, eh? I heard some chanting from down the corridor on the other side and started to walk towards it.

"You can't go in there."

Can't go? Bad choice of words.

He might have been stronger and prettier than me but I was quicker in a straight line and a whirlwind down a dim passage. I'd run the few steps, shoved the door wide open and inhaled the pungent smell of mushroom tea before he could swallow.

Shaman Mei was in session, wrapped in a coat of many-fingered feathers.

I thought it a better look than her usual fluoro hip-huggers and high heels, until she casually shrugged it off onto the floor. Underneath it she was smeared in paint and oils and clothed only in a pair of grubby, woven sandals. Dimply butt, hard nipples and knowing smile.

She stared at me and snorted with laughter. "Your jacket get a fright?"

I scanned the room, resisting the urge to reach

out and smooth the kinked and curling edges of the leather fringe.

Stolowski squatted next to her alongside two scrawny femmes about Mei's age and a guy with long, beaded and boned plaits.

Against the window frame stood another femme—windows in the tenements, unlike the rest of the villas, still functioned—clad in a crimson headscarf, faded gypsy skirt over pants and scuffed combat boots. A spell pouch hung from her waist. Expensive face tattoos and a load of dangerous jewelry completed the effect. Deceptively fleshy, I decided. She could move quickly when she needed to.

She stared outside, shoulders slumped like the weight of her thoughts was crushing them.

I had a compulsion to see her face and stepped closer, stopping just short of Mei.

She, Sto and the young ones faced one another over a portable burner and blackened pan. The guy toked on something that smelled like weed killer.

"Hi, Parrish. Good to see you." Sto gave me a genuine smile.

I returned it in kind. I had a more than sizable soft spot for him.

The femme by the window stiffened at the sound of my name and turned.

"Those visions driving you crazy yet?" asked Mei.

"No more than everything else." I scowled, feeling the parasite stir inside. Maybe it remembered her attack. "You got yourself some new friends, Mei?"

Daac stepped up close behind me, uneven breath like he had a case of dirty spark plugs.

"Jenn, Lila and Crow-Call," Mei said curtly.

Crow-Call gave a lopsided, cheerful grin, wagging his finger. "Heard all about you, babe. They say you got a bad *rep-u-tay-shun.*"

He was kinda cute, which stopped me from cuffing him. An innocent like Sto.

"You forgot someone," I said.

The femme at the window stared openly at me now. The line of her body, the way she held herself, made me antsy—a don't-fuck-with-me aura. I recognized it as easily as if she was wearing my face.

Mei picked up that we were facing off. But then Mei picked up on everything.

"Leesa Tulu," said Mei. "Meet Parrish Plessis."

Tulu! The name was like a blow to my body.

In three large steps I crossed the floor and knocked her flat, my knees pinning her chest. Her head banged down hard, but not hard enough to knock the malice and the tiniest sliver of satisfaction from her face. The woman was pleased to see me—in the ugliest kind of way.

In my cornersight Loyl lurched forward, the door guards took aim and Mei pulled a knife.

I didn't care. This woman was stealing shamans and making voodoo dolls of me, and I wanted to know why.

"The muscle you sent after me was damn cheap. And the coffin . . . was way too small," I said.

She gave me a smile—the kind that froze your heart and then smashed it with a sledgehammer. With startling strength she wrenched one arm free and gestured a violent sigla in the air. Her face contorted hideously. Eyes bulging, top lip curled back.

"Orisa!" she spat.

The world dimmed. Blackness came through my skull like an ax.

The Angel reared, enormous; a giant figure of screaming data. "Don't let her in here, human. You will pay for it with your life."

I came to from the blackout with a dry throat and stilettos tap dancing on my dendrons. I stared up into a face full of Loyl Daac, bent over and prodding at me like I was roadkill. A quick glance told me I was tied to a bed.

Not any bed.

His bed.

"For freak's sake let me up," I bellowed.

"You've annoyed me again, Parrish."

Is that so?

He went on before I could spit my thought out. "Leesa Tulu is a powerful, respected shaman. She is *my guest.*"

"Reach into my pants pocket," I told him.

He stopped short and stiffened. I *never* gave him invitations like that.

"It's not booby-trapped. There is something in there you have to see."

Cautiously he felt around my pants.

I couldn't stop an involuntary wriggle. His breath fanned me and his eyelashes were altogether too close for rational thoughts. I forced myself to breathe shallowly, not to get muzzy on his scent, and looked about for my pack. With a tiny wave of relief I saw it dumped by his comm.

Like Jamon's place . . . my place . . . Daac's comm cache took up a fair chunk of his room. Unlike mine there was not much room for anything else. A narrow cot in one corner, a tiny cooka and frij and a built-in with no door. Boots, socks and underwear tumbled out onto the floor. I felt embarrassed at the sight of them, like I was spying into his mind.

Finally he stood back.

I risked a glance.

He stared blankly at the crumpled dolls, connected obscenely by their genitals. "What—who are they?"

"You and me. I just came from the Muenos. You ever hear of Dalatto?"

He nodded. "Mueno shaman. Doesn't practice much anymore. Bad stuff."

"Well, she just came out of retirement. Briefly. See, she had a guest too, same one as you got now. Only together they invoked some evil bitch called Marinette who likes flesh to eat. End result: Dalatto disemboweled, tasteless little dolls of you and me in bed together."

His face tightened. "You're saying Leesa Tulu made these?"

I nodded. "Leesa Tulu made these. I just don't know why. Now untie me and let me get my hands around her throat."

He hesitated. "But she knows where Anna is."

I took a steadying breath and tried to locate the logic attached to that piece of information.

Dr. Anna Schaum, aka Loyl's most devoted admirer (that's if you didn't count the three thousand or so disciples who ate, slept and copulated at his word) and part-time grrl, was the scientist who'd accidentally unlocked the Eskaalim parasite. His precious, pale, pedigreed princess had then panicked and bared her guilt-ridden soul to Io Lang. Lang'd stolen the research and nobody had seen Schaum since.

If Tulu knew where Anna Schaum was, did that mean she knew who was behind Io Lang? Connections met and married in my brain.

"Have you asked yourself *how* she knows where Anna is?"

He studied me before he answered: liquor-black eyes without a trace of fanaticism in them, warm and drinkable. I'd been suckered by them before. "She's clairvoyant."

"Sure. Or maybe she's just a homicidal liar."

Mouth grim, he abruptly loosened my bonds. "You'd better be wrong, Parrish."

I wasn't.

Mei's crew of spiritualists were out cold in an untidy circle around the billy. Too much weed killer: not enough real *caapi*. If they were communing on a higher plane, I was a . . . a hottie.

Stolowski was gurgling face-first in a puddle of blood that I hoped wasn't his.

I rolled him onto his side and wiped his airways

clear while Daac bellowed up the corridor for help. He then tried to rouse Crow-Call.

"Where's Mei?" he demanded.

Crow-Call crawled onto his knees and vomited a little.

I stretched my leg out and poked one of the others with my foot. Jenn or Lila? I didn't know. "Where's Leesa Tulu?" I demanded. My voice wasn't quite steady.

Her eyes stayed closed. "N-not sh-shure. Sh-she put some shit 'n the tea. Said it was g-good for the spirits. Thatsall I 'member," she whispered thickly, and drifted out of it again.

Daac hauled Crow-Call upright out of his own sticky mess. "Did she force Mei to leave with her?"

Crow-Call made a choking noise and went slack in his grasp.

Dead. Like that.

Overdosed.

Forget the weed killer; this was something else.

A minute later a couple of medics were on the floor at my feet, working to revive Sto, Jenn and Lila.

I got up and stared at the bones in Crow-Call's hair, feeling pissed off at the cold injustice. The harmless ones always got it. By turning up here, I'd unwittingly forced Tulu into making a move. Crow-Call had gotten in the way. So had Sto.

Daac wrapped his prosthetic fingers around my wrist like a handcuff. "If you know something, Parrish, now's the time to speak."

"Ditto."

"I've told you all I know."

"Friends called by, said their shamans had disappeared. I asked around and it got a few people messily dead for it. When I followed the messy dead trail it led me to Dalatto. The dolls brought me here. I wanted to warn you. Looks like I got bonus points."

"Who are you out hunting missing shamans for?" he asked sharply.

"I'm not being paid." It was true. I was the one paying. Paying off a debt. "*Remember,* Loyl, I also have a vested interest in the spirits."

He unlocked his fingers and I rubbed the circulation back into my arm.

The stench of vomit and blood made me claustrophobic so I moved to the window and watched as his people combed the alleys below. I also couldn't look at Stolowski lying there gray as death.

Minutes later the medics pronounced Jenn a survivor. Lila would live as well, but with brain-fry. Sto was still only a maybe.

Two out of four for Tulu. If Sto made it three, I'd hound her beyond sanity.

I helped stretcher the bodies to the medi-lab and waited until one of Daac's men came back to report. He narrated a bunch of sightings and plenty of speculation. I sidled around the edge of the lab as he talked.

Daac's eyes had begun to kindle with something I hated to see. Fervor. Fanaticism. Mr. Mild and Conciliatory had gone walkabout. Mr. Somber and Merciless had come to call.

When somebody messed with Daac's *gens*, they brought themselves a problem. It was the one thing he and I had in common. Loyalty.

Except mine didn't depend on racial birthright.

Time to move. There was only one thing I needed to know and I'd heard it straight off. Tulu had Mei with her. And they were headed southeast, towards Dis. I was down on the tenement pavements and running before Loyl could swear.

I'd never been as deep in The Tert as Dis, and to tell you the truth I rattled at the thought. I didn't even know how to get there, exactly, so I set my compass implant to record my movements and altered my direction slightly more east.

All up, The Tert sprawled over a hundred or more klicks from north to south if you could do the straight-line thing. But you couldn't. Apparently, the closer you got to the center the worse the crazies.

Whereas Torley's, Plastique and even The Slag relied on some outtown trade—it had to be halfway safe for the punters to try and buy—Dis was another story, and, if the rumors were true, another world. I had no idea who lived there or how they survived. Up until now I hadn't really cared.

I ran on until my chest got heavy and tight. Until my skin slicked with sweat. Then I walked, cooling down, and scried for a half-decent place to eat.

The straps of my pack ate into my shoulders. The darn thing had gotten so heavy and I couldn't figure out why. I knelt down to rearrange the balance and scared myself half to death.

The forgotten four-and-a-half-pawed canrat was snugged up and dribbling on my spare duds. The shaft of daylight woke it up and it licked its wrinkled chops hopefully.

I tried to dump it out on the pavement but it scrabbled back in, legs working like paddles. I went to grab its neck but it bared its remaining teeth and growled.

Damn!

I didn't fancy being bitten by anything quite so fetid, so I closed the flap and ordered shawarmas with extra meat shavings on the side from a vendor on the edge of the tenement spread. Then I found myself a quiet corner to eat.

I set the meat shavings on paper, enticing the canrat out of my pack. It sniffed the air, crawled out to gorge, and in a happy fugue limped off to find water and take a piss.

Relieved of its company, and my guilt, I wandered back to the vendor and bought some damper.

"You heard of Loyl Daac?"

The woman with gray-streaked hair and studs for eyebrows crinkled her lined face and rolled her eyes.

"Sure. Who doesn't around here? He's one man I'd like a piece of every night."

I hid a sigh. Did he have that effect on everyone? "What's his story?"

She pointed to a nearby stall. Daac's face glowed an unflattering tinge of green on a damaged advertible tethered above it. Despite the color, his presence dazzled. Behind it the tenement walls swore graffitied allegiance to him.

"Where you from, girlie?" She wagged a finger at me. "That man's gonna make things how they were here. Give us back what's ours. Get rid of the filth. Make us healthy people again."

He could start with her food. But I didn't like to mention it, seeing as her tongue was loosening.

She leaned in close, like I was in her deepest confidence. "There's bad things happening around here now. Shape-changers, bloodsuckers, spirit shit. I hate that spirit shit."

You and me both, hon.

With that off her chest she went back to hacking ragged lumps of meat from a homemade rotisserie. "You should get your face fixed. You'd scrub up OK."

I choked on my mouthful at the beauty advice, and changed the subject. "You seen a couple of women? One wearing a colored skirt, headscarf and face tattoos, the other a Chino-grrl in . . . er . . . feathers."

"I been asked that twice already. Told them what I'll tell you. Yes and no. No, I ain't seen if you can't pay. Yes, I seen 'em if you can." She paused expectantly.

I took the cue. "How much?"

"Three thousand."

Three thousand. I didn't even have a quarter of that on hand. "You planning on opening a bank?"

Her face closed over. "That's the price of things around here to snoops and strangers. Pay up or go home, girlie."

I should have shaken the info out of her, but she was on Daac's turf, one of his protected species, and I had enough to worry about. She'd seen them, there was no doubting that, which meant they were headed in the same direction as me.

As I trudged on, I started thinking about my face. I hated pretty. In fact I loathed all the crap that went with beauty. It didn't mean I didn't appreciate it on others. Hell, Loyl was pretty, handsome and gorgeous in one tidy skin.

I just didn't care to change the way I looked— love me or leave me alone, preferably the last. Most of the time, anyway. Occasionally I caught myself in a princess daydream. Usually I wanted to kick her arse.

Human beauty got in the way of things. Changed things. Muddied people's minds. More precisely— it fucked with the truth.

On the edge of Tower Town, I heard a sickly mewling behind me. The canrat, unbalanced by his extra foot, was covering twice as much distance as he needed to. He struggled toward me in a roundabout way, copping an occasional sideways kick from passersby just for being there.

I guess no one saw a deformed canrat as much of a threat. More like sport.

By the time he got to me his tongue lolled with exhaustion. He flopped across my feet.

Loser!

Irritated and guilt-ridden again, I picked him up and tossed him into my pack before anyone could see. At least no one knew me here.

Eventually the tenement landscape gave way to the concentric villa mishmash I was used to. Excepting that the thoroughfares narrowed and every way south became a blind alley or a pathway that turned back on to itself.

Too many mods on the buildings. Even the old villa monorail had been wrecked and converted.

Daac's face haunted me on walls and crummy advertibles, and his voice resonated out of villas broadcasting Common Net. As I roved in and around, forced more west than I wanted, I saw less transport. Few Pets and no bikes. Only fuel'n'food 'peds. And people.

Gen sets purred constantly. Solar panels glinted dully. This part of The Tert sucked energy in its own fashion from hybrid sources. Only lucky ones like Loyl could afford poached mains power.

I turned my thoughts to Roo. Hopefully he'd gone home with the Mueno contingent.

That got me thinking 'bout Teece.

I found a public comm with a dinged plasma interface and spiked a call to him. He came on quick like he'd been waiting for me.

"How's it?" I asked.

"I can hardly see you."

"Sick comm. Are the Muenos there?"

"Larry's not big on chicken blood. Or the prayers."

I laughed. "Sorry, Teece. Knew you could handle it."

He made a sound like a tiny explosion. "*And* you sent Roo back. He said someone had been making mojo dolls of you and some guy."

"Loyl." I tried not to look sheepish.

"You with him now?"

"I'm not *with* Daac now, Teece. But I may run into him again."

"What do you mean?" he demanded.

I groaned. "It just seems to happen a lot. Look, I'll be away awhile longer. Business is taking me inwards."

Even in the dimness of the display I could see his face pale. He knew what I meant by "inwards." "Can't you trust me even a little, Parrish?"

"I do trust you. That's why it's better you—"

"Don't patronize me," he snapped.

I put on my most appeasing smile. "Do me a favor, will you?"

"Another?"

"There's a bim living in my old room. Drop by and check the security in the roof. I'd hate anyone to get in there thinking she was me."

He sighed heavily. "Nobody could be like you."

"I'm sure that's a compliment."

I cut the link and walked through the rest of the night, notching enough sightings to tell me Tulu and Mei were still out there ahead of me.

Around dawn I caught some sleep in a communal laundry until the women woke me coming in to wash. They surrounded me with an assortment of knives and sticks until I reassured them that I worked for Daac.

At that news they erupted into smiles and sly giggles. The younger ones demanded to know *how* well I knew him. The older ones went about their washing and pretended not to be listening.

I took the opportunity to bargain for information: the dirty lowdown on Loyl for a more solid ID on Mei and Tulu. They sent the word out among their own and came back with a confirmation—heading *inward* still, traveling by 'ped.

So I gave them a close-up account of their pin-up boy, his beautiful face, toned body and his lightning switches from easy charm to brooding maniac. I told them how strong his prosthetic hand was and how he'd cooked breakfast for me once. I even described the inside of his room with only a couple of embellishments. Then I made a show of sighing hard.

"The thing is . . . don't spread it around but he's . . . y'know . . . impotent," I lied.

The older ones scrubbed angrily at their dirty clothes. The young ones groaned in disappointment.

The whole thing seriously cheered me. I mean a grrl's gotta get even somehow!

I left them, hiding my immoral grin. It might have stayed on my face for the rest of the day if Tulu hadn't gotten away from me.

Late in the morning the sound of prop chop sent my pulse dancing. It sounded like an air raid on the listless breeze, but a quick scout of the sky told me it was just a solitary flier—an ultralight, coming in to land.

I ran after the sound until I met a wall of discarded poly pipes blocking the end of an alley. Dumping my pack, I burrowed awkwardly in amongst them, searching for a crack to look through. The crack that showed promise was crammed with debris. I poked my fingers through it and paid severely for disturbing an ants' nest. Time wasted as I slapped the biters away and gauged their home out.

When I had cleared enough to scope through, the peephole revealed a Tert *anyways*—one of the precious expanses of space at the hub of dozen villa sets. This one had contained a bunch of different-sized swimming pools. A "water park," Teece called the one in Plastique. Now the pools were filled and plascreted over and turned into a make-shift runway.

My spyhole revealed Tulu strapping Mei to the back of the UL. Lucid memories of my own buzzsaw experience over Viva sent my stomach weightless.

I stuck the pistol through the hole and fired. It missed. I shot again. This one went wider and pinged the cabin.

The UL pilot revved the engine. Tulu threw herself aboard as it hopped off down the short runway. For a second it careered wildly off path and then steadied.

I scrambled out of my hidey-hole and tried to climb the wall, but a pipe slipped free and sent me tumbling downward and under. I rolled away just as the whole thing collapsed, spreading down the alley. By the time I got up from the pummeling, the UL was disappearing east.

As I logged its path in my compass memory, a priority icon flashed in my right eye. The Bounty hunter's coordinates blinked up alongside it. This was the exact spot the Bounty had been told to deliver me to.

Crap!

I climbed over the mess and walked down to the runway, kicking pipes around in frustration.

My annoyance hadn't even begun to drain away when a Prier swept belligerently into my space, blasting air downward as it hovered low over the runway.

I dived for the nearest cover and ran a frantic weapons check. Ally? Or enemy?

Or maybe the two were interchangeable.

Had the media finally decided to come and get me? Or were they chasing Tulu?

I tugged a charm from my bracelet. A stun might work on the 'Terro, but not for long. My best chance was to toss one inside the Prier's cab when the 'Terro dispatched, which meant getting close enough to see the pilot. At the moment I couldn't see anyone through the reflective cabin bubble that resembled a set of oversized, outdated mirrorshades.

Adrenaline spread like a cold knife scraping my skin. With the charm clenched in one hand, I waited for the Prier to make a move.

But it didn't land. Or show any interest in me. In fact it lifted higher and headed east, leaving me relieved and indignant.

Double crap!

When I got over still being alive, I went in search of my pack. Loser—the canrat—had slept through the whole thing. I woke him and tipped him out to piss and gum bits of damper. He stuck close by in case I had abandonment on my mind. Funnily enough, though, I was starting to think of him as company. He was sure less demanding than most I'd had around me lately.

When he'd finished his chow I packed him back in the pack and set off, doggedly following the UL's bearing.

By evening, I noticed a decline of people noise and an absence of people light—an eerie trailing off of life into the encroaching darkness.

It forced me to use my headband to light my way and turned me into a walking lighthouse. I spent the night with my hands on my guns, squinting into the shadows. By morning my fingers were cramped and clawed and my eyes bulged from strain.

I wanted to lie down but two things kept me walking: the knowledge that Tulu was way ahead of me now, and the fact that the villascape had radically changed.

A mutated rain forest had sprung up around the empty villas. Upthrust roots nudged already subsiding buildings, and sharp-suckered vines pierced the porous walls. Brown-blood-colored ground cover clumped like fungus over pavement cracks, and ugly, squat, spiked date palms threatened to impale me if I brushed too close. Overhead Alexandra palms towered too thickly together. Even in the mild breeze they sloughed off boat-sized, empty seedpods and heavy bundles of orange berries. The berries littered the ground, making it slippery, the scent of their decay more pungent than a spilled bottle of tequila.

Not wanting to be clouted by a falling pod, I got

a neck ache from craning upwards. I'd never seen palms growing so densely or so tall. I didn't like what it said about the state of the soil.

The recent war had touched most parts of The Tert. Not so here. Here there were no people to fight, no one to hurt. Only buildings covered with bug-infested vegetation and the warm, clammy fingers of an early spring northerly eddying through.

My ignorance astonished me. Only klicks from where I lived was a complex, bizarre jungle, and I'd had no idea it existed.

Did I say empty villas?

Several canrats appeared and began to stalk me along the plant-strewn pavement. Large, mismatched fur—canine and rattus—chiseled fangs and long skinny tails.

I tried to lose them by entering a villa and climbing up into the attic. Mistake. I discovered a fresh cemetery—layers of bones and fur of other mammals filling the ceiling in between joists.

The canrats herded me from behind and I found myself backed into a low corner, overpowered by the stink of dograt fur and foul dog breath. One scrape of one incisor and it would be all over.

I slipped my pack off and braced against the sloping roof. As I drew my pistols, the rotten tiles crumbled away. I slipped, clawed and finally fell down two stories of derelict villa, landing flat on my back.

My head thumped so hard I saw comet tails. Every instinct urged me to get up and get running while I had a few seconds' edge, but my arms and legs declared a flat, inarguable "time out."

I got my eyes open.

Mistake. This was worse. Much, *much* worse! If I had breath I would've screamed, but my lungs hurt so much I suspected they'd herniaed out between my ribs.

Looming twice the size of a canrat, with a jaw that could dislocate wide enough to swallow my face without a belch, was a bungarra.

The Big Country'd always been a place for lizards but this ugly reptile made the spiky mountain devil look as pretty as a porn star.

I stared up at the thick ridges of its neck.

It took two steps and perched astride me like I was a handy rock in a gully, its long claws stabbing into my shoulders, tail down over my face.

The shoulder pain took over from the one in my back and lungs. A noise escaped from my lips. A whimper-grunt.

Above me, I heard the canrats complaining. The bungarra was thieving their meal.

In answer it hissed and *caark*ed at them. Entirely primitive. Entirely pissed off.

What now?

Fok knows.

Body hurt scrambled my brain. The world got grainy. Then it got black.

Sometime later it came back.

Monochrome first. My shoulders ached but the nauseating drill stabs had ceased. One half-opened eye told me I was no longer the bungarra's pet rock. I rolled onto my side, coughing and spitting phlegm.

A noise assaulted my eardrums. A few body

lengths away the canrats crouched, snarling and growling, tails stiff as erections, hackles raised.

I propped onto an arm. The bungarra stood between us, motionless. It eyeballed me as if cogging whether I was worth the fuss.

One, two, three heart thumps . . .

Not! A *caark* and it leapt off in the opposite direction.

The noise stirred Loser, who emerged from my pack, groggy from the fall, drool stringing from sloppy lips. I could smell his mange.

I struggled unsteadily onto my feet and looked for my pistols. They lay close together on the ground near the biggest canrat. As I contemplated how I might get to them, the big one forced its way past the others and stalked towards me.

Loser stunned me by issuing a blood-clotting growl and leaping straight for it. They met and rolled, teeth hooked into each other's abdomens.

Loser raked his extra foot across the canrat's face.

The bigger canrat fell back, keening with pain. His tongue swelled and within seconds he was dead. Poisoned.

It worked a treat on the others. They vanished as if they'd never been there in the first place.

Loser staggered over to me, wheezing like he had asbestosis. I shook my head in awe. He managed to look smug and pathetic all at once, rattail swishing.

With a shaking hand, I hooked the stun I'd been ready to use back onto the bracelet. I stared at his extra paw and made a mental note never to get too close to it. Even though he'd probably saved my life, I suddenly wanted to put a lot of space between myself and the Borgia dograt.

But tenacity was Loser's only virtue and he pursued me like a disease. By late afternoon, not able to stand his pitiful shadow, I—carefully—threw him back into my pack.

We walked another few hours, without incident, into a light, annoying drizzle.

I saw plants that resembled animals, animals whose names I'd almost forgotten, including three species of venomous snake: a red-belly black, the squat, gray ugliness of the death adder and, worst, a western taipan.

I trod heavier after that, giving them plenty of time to hear me and go about their biz.

Soon I'd had enough of Loser's snoring and his weight on my back. I dumped him out onto a clear patch of pavement, gingerly stretched my shoulders and thought how comfy the ground cover would be if the place wasn't so infested.

Loser weaved off down the side of a villa set, hissing like the feline he wasn't.

More snakes?

My hand fell to my pistols. I slipped the pack back on and edged along in among the shadow-thick vines, following him.

Should I unstrap the Gurkha? It might be more use than a pistol if it came down to a snake and me. When I found Loser, though, his beef turned out to be something else altogether.

I smelled it first. Saw it soon after.

Thick, oily and ruined.

Chapter Eight

The forgotten canal lapped heavily: a disruption between worlds.

Like the strip of rain forest jungle, I'd never heard of its existence before, but it explained a lot. Even though it was the heart of the villatropolis, Tert punters whispered about Dis as if it was in some way isolated from the rest.

I saw now that it was.

Once this water would have sparkled. It may even have boasted fish. The only life I saw now were oversized barnacles clinging to the walls like cankers.

The canal wouldn't take long to swim, but I didn't need a chemical analysis to know swimming was suicide. Already my nose and eyes streamed. Whatever the canal was excreting into the air was pure toxin. It burned the back of my throat like a flaming shot of alcohol.

Only there wasn't any fire—just a thin, almost dissipated trail of smoke low in the sky.

I felt a tingle. *The ultralight? I'd damaged it?*

I checked it against my compass bearing. It read a steady east. I was heading in the right direction.

"Now how do I get across?" I asked no one in particular.

Thick, unnatural colors swirled sluggishly along the surface of the water. I recognized the brilliant blue of copper sulfate. Pure and deadly. There must have been a copper smelter nearby in the early days.

I backed off a few meters and looked around.

The other side lurked across the short distance like malice. It must have been home to the wealthier of the villa dwellers—separated by this thin strip of water that signified status amongst the low-set high-density living.

Loser hunched on the bank like he was pondering world decline, indifferent to the smell and my dilemma.

Keeping a small cushion of distance from the water and its stink, I trudged west, looking for an overpass. Several klicks and too many snakes later, I found an old monorail bridge—or what had been. Hard to say if it'd been torn down deliberately or eroded by the toxins flowing beneath it. Only the uprights remained: rusty spiked pylons, eaten at the base by the acidic water.

There must be another way, I reasoned. Human traffic always maps a path.

But there was no human traffic this way. Not anymore.

Even the snakes kept a respectable distance from this water. I watched a couple slither out from buildings and veer sharply away as they reached some invisible mark near the canal banks.

Whatever they knew, I wished they'd share it.

As the dark flowed in, I peered at the other side of the canal with frustration. The landscape smudged. No life.

I crouched down in exhaustion and pain and let my eyes drift. In the distance, a luminescent arc of neons caught my eye.

I wanted to go home, tell the Cabal I'd lost Tulu. That Dis was closed to tourists.

But someone *was* living over there.

Deeper in.

I knew.

I also knew that Tulu had nearly killed Sto and had kidnapped Mei. She was collecting shamans, which meant the *karadji*. Going home was premature.

I walked back to where I'd left Loser for no reason other than I didn't know what else to do. All the way back I stayed close to the river, using the breather mask the ferals had given me and risking the use of my headband light to stop me falling into the noxious soup.

I found him in the same place, still and dejected as a grave-robbed statue. He uttered a series of yowls, which sounded like the last seconds of a catfight, and I wondered if Loser's hybrid heritage had caused a crosswire in his dograt brain.

I dropped down next to him, leaning against

what might have been a mooring post. Mask over my face, Gurkha in one hand, pistol in the other; blood on my clothes.

Glamour puss Parrish! I was glad I'd left Merry 3# with Teece. I couldn't stand the bagging.

I turned my mind to my problem. How to get across? I needed a raft but my stomach ached so hard with hunger I couldn't think. Next time I went on a walking holiday in the enchanted jungle, I'd remember to pack lunch.

I worried over a whole lot of things while the night got old and a bungarra *caarked* threats and paced up and down the borderline.

In the early light it relinquished its pacing vigil and dragged a small, empty palm pod down to the water in its jaws. It leapt aboard and let the sluggish current drift it across in a diagonal to the other side, where it jumped off and shook its scarred feet dry.

I'd considered the pod shells already and dismissed the idea, but the bungarra's jaunt got me scratching around until I found several that were large enough to sit in. I dragged them to the canal and one by one tested their buoyancy. A couple sank; some stayed afloat. I put my pack and armfuls of berries in the largest one until I thought it approximated my weight. It bobbed low and uncertainly but stayed afloat. After a few minutes I emptied it.

With more than serious doubt at my sanity, I climbed in. If I didn't breathe or move too much, it might not even leak. Loser took the cue and scrambled in after me. Immediately we began to sink. I tossed him out onto the bank and the canoe steadied again.

I couldn't take him with me and make it across. The realization was kind of a relief.

Loser didn't agree. He stumbled determinedly back.

I used the Gurkha to push off out of his reach and endured terrifying minutes as the pod rocked. Loser howled with distress.

Water seeped in one end, puddling closer and closer to my feet. I shrank into the smallest area possible and paddled frantically with a smaller pod shell, trying not to watch the water eating its way toward me.

A bit longer . . . just a bit longer . . .

When the pod bumped into the bank on the other side, I gave a terror-fueled leap up and out of it. As I fell onto the bank, the front end sank below the waterline, followed quickly by the rest.

I ran a couple of steps to the cover of a villa before adrenaline poisoning took over. In a vine-crossed doorway, away from the putrid water, hands over my ears to block out Loser's aggrieved coughs, I fell asleep, too exhausted to slap the bugs.

A foul, burned taste woke me. It coated my teeth and nose, and rubbed at my skin.

I forced myself up and on. The rain forest strip didn't extend to this side and I walked into a more normal villascape.

Did I say normal?

If the night noises of the Villas Rosa spooked

me, then there were no words to describe what I heard during that day. Inhuman crackling, sizzling, popping sounds and grinding. Every hair on my body stood rigid enough to snap in a puff of wind.

I crept from one alley to another, seeking the broadest paths, trying to sketch a mind map. The villas here were double the size of those in the outer Tert—luxurious in their time.

Now each one carried a deformity of some kind. A cankerous lump attached to a roof, fleshy wall-length scars, crucifix window frames rough with sharp spikes. Every klick or so a glistening tower shape erupted from a crater in the pavement.

The sidewalks had altered as well. They'd buckled and warped in places and often led directly into blank walls, like someone had plucked the path up and shifted it, or plonked the building down there at random.

I felt like I'd crossed into another ribbon of existence.

Grubby and wasted as the outer Tert was, families lived there—noisy, abrasive groups of humans that bothered with each other in some peculiar way.

Where I journeyed now there were no cooking smells, no family arguments, no crying babies and no showy street sex. After a while punters appeared on the pavement as if they'd been hiding, checking me out. But something was wrong. Something vital.

Derangement seeped from them. Some chattered and laughed to private dialogues; others emanated the heavy silence of contained venom. In every imaginable way, I was deep, deep, deep in the nutter zone.

I worked my way close to one of the mysterious towers and discovered they were bundles of fiber optics torn from underground and frozen in a glass haystack. Some pulsed with dying light; others jutted upwards in blackened shards, leftovers of a one-time communication system that threaded underneath the villas. Something had eaten away the plas casings and forced the bundles upward in a series of bizarre towerlike structures.

Compelled, I reached out to touch one and couldn't pull my hand away. A sting to my finger, and my blood sprayed finely out from the tip. It pulsed up the length of the nearest fiber and glowed into life.

Heart racing, I pulled a knife and forced it between my finger and the glass, shaving my skin to do it.

Suddenly I was free and the fiber dimmed to a faint red glow.

I became aware of people around me and shoved my hand in my pocket. Pushing past them, I kept on, averting my eyes from their half-faces and bodies. Not like the Pets, but something less wholesome. Like living tissue grafted onto dead bodies. Conjoined creatures—only one of them perceptibly human.

Or was it me? Had the Eskaalim distorted my world so totally I could no longer see reality? Hadn't I sworn on the Wombat's name I'd shoot myself before I got this crazy?

I started sneaking glimpses of my reflection in

windows. I *seemed* sane and real. Short hair, off-center nose, caved cheek, tense mouth, eyes stark with dread.

My paranoia—the need to keep stopping and checking my reflection—scored me several hits from behind. I swiveled each time, chasing the source, and found only blank expressions and bent heads. I choked back my retaliation instinct, ignoring the barely heard sniggers.

Forget your reflection, Parrish! Keep moving!

Clots of people jostled past now. Hands felt me, some sexually, some searching for more than that. My hands clamped rigid to the Lugers.

Humidity seemed worse here, like the season had catapulted ahead into greasy summer heat.

My thoughts got spacier by the heartbeat. Not helped by the knowledge that someone was tailing me. Someone with more than a passing interest.

I rubbed the prickling on my neck and, glancing around, shifted the weight of my pack. If a direct attack came I planned to make my retaliation as quiet as possible.

I slipped a wire from my crop top and held it loosely.

Three days of walking, little sleep, nervous bites of grub too long ago and a near miss as dograt chow was turning Parrish into a paranoid grrl.

And that was without the claw marks and aching ribs.

I felt like everyone around me was breathing in time, waiting for the attack, lusting after some type of spectacle, looking for leftovers—the crumbs of a violent death.

Sweat made my hands slippery. I slowed down, tilting onto the balls of my feet, pretending to look into the doorway of a bar. Quick and quiet was what I wanted. No fuss. Leave the pickings for the nutters.

As the hand reached for my shoulder, I let the wire uncoil. I swung around, whipping it in neat loops around the attacker's wrist. My fist came up hard the other side, connecting with meat and bone.

"Parr—"

Loyl. My fist kissed his chin but I pulled the sting from the punch. I released the wire, but I'd already cut him.

"Stay still," I hissed. With shaking fingers I unwound it. His wrist bled but I'd missed the artery. "Quick, bind it before someone decides you smell good enough to eat," I panted. "How did you find me this time?"

Last time we'd been together in a strange place, it was because he'd duped me into carrying a location finder.

"You leave a trail a mile wide, Parrish. It wasn't a case of how I'd find you—just when. Following you is like slipstreaming the end of the world."

"Don't joke about the end of the world in this place."

His eyes were bloodshot. "Don't you ever sleep?"

"Only when I have to. You should know better than to sneak up on me," I growled.

Despite myself, I was pleased to see him. Even Loyl passed for a friend, right here, right now.

"Didn't think you'd want me calling out to you," he said, wrapping his hand with something from his pack.

"Next time . . . approach me from the front."

He gave a curt shake of his head. "Next time . . . look first."

I stared at him. "Are you kidding? Look around."

"Yeah," he said softly. "And the place is crawling *with wild-tek.*" He gave me the benefit of a strained smile.

Any smile from Loyl was like a present. White teeth, dark skin, black-juice eyes. How did anyone stay looking so beautiful living in a joint like this? It had to be unnatural. Or a sin.

His skull had a prickling shadow of hair now, the baldness all but gone. His fatigues were crumpled but unstained—not like mine. Only the barely concealed zealot's glitter in his eyes kept me from hugging him.

"Wild-tek?" I shivered. I'd heard talk of it but figured it was romance, like the mystique around the Cabal. The closest thing I could relate it to were the Pets. But they were an intentional creation. One person's design.

This place looked like the results of biowarfare. "You mean nanos?"

"Nuh. Nanos are mostly used for building and repairing. Viva's literally crawling with that kinda thing! That's why it's so damn clean," he said.

Viva! I flashed on the broad, immaculate streets and the shining cityscape, the fragrant smell.

"This stuff's something to do with the pollution

in the soil. Molecular changes. Things have gotten creepier and uglier." He took a deep breath. "There used to be some underground tek manufacturing here, in amongst all the other industrial 'gineering stuff, back before the villas ever got built. Maybe the two got crazy together. . . ." He was as fascinated and freaked-out as me, talking quickly, eyes flicking around. I wasn't used to him being afraid.

"You knew about this place? What it was like?" I asked.

"Rumors. Never had any reason to find out until now."

I gave him a sharp look. "How did you cross the canal?"

He shrugged. "My grandfather used to make boats from palm pods. Simple enough."

Naturally.

He clamped his prosthetic hand under my elbow to steer me.

I winced.

"What hurts?"

I shrugged him off. "Had a small dispute with a bungarra."

He laughed. "I saw him. We used to get them out at Bitter Plains. Mean and mammoth, some of them."

"Did you catch the canrat convention back there?"

We'd fallen automatically into a walk, like we knew where we were going. Standing still got you into trouble. I'd learned that much.

"I heard the noise. Figured something was up so I skirted wide of it. Never had any problems."

Is this what it was like for saints? I wondered. Wandering through hell—oblivious and untouchable.

"Why? You run into some trouble?" He twisted my wrist, forcing me to walk closer to him.

I pulled it back. "Yeah, I ran into some trouble."

I didn't bother to tell him how I got out of it. It sounded too weird. I also wasn't going to share anything I didn't have to with my fiercest competitor.

Brain flash! *That's what he was. A competitor.*

Putting him in a mental box felt a whole lot better. I could deal with *competitor* where *lover, saint* and *hero of the people* burned holes in my psyche.

We were competing for the right to fashion our own vision of the future in The Tert. Right now that meant who found out what was going down in crazy town.

It occurred to me that he might have seen me in trouble back there amongst the canrats. Perhaps he'd even left me for dead. I thought I could read Loyl some of the time, but predict him, never.

"You know where you're going?" he asked.

"Do you?" I countered.

"Mind if I follow you?"

I shrugged. "Wouldn't be the first time."

We walked on in tenuous accord, shoulder to shoulder, like rival cops into a riot.

"Leesa Tulu's mine, Loyl," I whispered.

He grabbed my sore shoulder. "No."

Despite the pain, my body hair warped at his touch. I suddenly wanted him. Desire rose in the back of my throat like vomit. How could he do this to me? How could anyone do it to me? In a place full of nutters, my head loopy with visions, and some serious shit to deal with, how could I want him so bad?

I shook his hand off. "You're a zealot, Loyl. Zealots don't help people; they use them."

He smiled. "You see, Parrish, you and I have so much in common."

Not much was said after that—apart from agreeing to stop and share a watch so we could both get some sleep.

I tried to fathom the scene around me. Bars, food stalls, smoking and shooting dens—regular things that weren't regular. For starters, each stall dished out the same food. Pies and something I took for coffee.

One lit doorway we passed advertised a garish pink "Kleen Beds and Air Con" neon, and a bunch of warty growths hung under the eaves.

It had to be better than a night out on the pavement.

Didn't it?

We stepped into the entrance hall: a guest lounge on one side, a small desk unit on the other. Unlit stairs promised bedrooms.

Underfoot the floor crunched. An albino girl/thing perched on a stool behind the desk, her bare legs adhered, literally, to the plas of her seat.

"Howsitgoin'?" Her voice was sweet like sugar-switch, but her accent was broad—archaic almost. "We gotta beeee-uutiful room for youse."

Australians had lost their twang sixty-odd years ago, along with their nationality, when refugees from southern Europe, forced away from their own contaminated territories, flooded their borders. The refugees tried Afreeka first, but the Freekans had their perimeter tied up tight with some advanced defense. Their conscience didn't blink at a horde of white Euros in trouble.

Couldn't say I blamed them.

Down here, we'd always thought the man-flood would come from the islands to the north, Indo and Malayland and the rest. But they'd got smart and cleaned up their countries.

Although I'd never known the Australia of before, the albino's accent flooded me with curious nostalgia. Like genetic coding.

Loyl-me-Daac, on the other hand, seemed excited by it. I hunted his face for traces of fanaticism. No way was I sharing watch with this guy when he flipsided into his I'm-on-a-mission-for-myself persona.

"What happened to your skin?" he asked her.

I elbowed him hard, figuring personal questions were not the way to stay unnoticed around here.

The albino girl/thing rolled her eyes.

They were black like Daac's. Not true albino.

"Skin-stripped," she said. "How d'ya think I'd afford this place?"

I stared closer. Speckles of blood seasoned her arms like finely ground red pepper. Raw bleeding meat covered in a translucent synthetic skin. I didn't understand what she meant. Didn't want to.

"You seen a woman go through here? Scarf, boots, face paint?" I asked instead.

The nearly albino girl/thing chewed on a fingertip. Some plas skin came away in her mouth and she spat it onto the floor. I suddenly knew what made it so crunchy.

Beats nail biting, I guess.

"Nope." She watched the blood well on her fingertip, licking it like an ice cream until another skin grew.

"Putcha print 'ere. Same on the door lock. What've you got to pay for it?"

Loyl and I exchanged looks. We held out our cred spikes at the same time.

She stared blankly at them. "Fingerprints buy youse a shower. No bed. What else you got to barter? Skin, hair, sperm, hormones—though me sampler's on the blink. I'll have ta use me big glass. It's all good in Mo-Vay."

Mo-Vay? "What do you do with the samples?"

She frowned at the question. Bemused. "Sell them to Ike," she finally answered. "What else?"

"Who?"

"That'd be God to you," she said.

I couldn't think of what to say next, so I stood and waited to see if Daac would lop off a finger or spit into a jar for her. I sure wasn't going to.

Maybe he was thinking the same thing about me.

The albino girl/thing began to tap her fingers on the desk. One of them left wet, pink smudges.

Eventually I scrabbled in my pack for something of value and came up with a fistful of Loser's fur.

I plonked a pile of it in front of her. "Body hair," I lied.

She stretched backwards and pulled a magnifier over her head. It didn't do much for her look.

Blood-specked white girl/thing in brightly lit plastic bubble.

She studied the hair expertly. So much for the broken DNA sampler. This little girl didn't need one.

Daac sent me a what-the-fok-did-you-give-her frown.

She answered him before I could. "This is canrat. Not worth batshit, usually. But this one's got dingo innit. None left around here no more."

She flicked off the light and jerked the bubble back, beaming a grin.

"How long youse wanna stay?"

I followed Daac past the guest lounge towards the stairs.

Did I say guest lounge? Try locked ward. I knew lots of punters in The Tert suffered from the effects of the heavy metals, but I'd never seen the worst of it.

Until now.

Some of the occupants *lounged* connected to pumps, their uncontrollable shaking, warts and rashes testament to their particular poison. Others were vocal and hallucinatory. One—a woman, I think—smiled soft, bleeding gums at us. Her toxin-darkened skin reminded me of Stellar, Jamon's ex-squeeze.

I turned away, sick to my stomach.

We climbed three flights of rotten stairs and risked the corridor. Daac reached into his pack and produced a skin glove. He slipped it on and touched his fingers to the keypad.

Nothing happened.

After a moment he kicked the door and it sprang ajar. Peeling off his glove, he dropped it. In a minute it had shriveled into something like the albino girl/thing's fingertips. "No need to give anything away for free," he said.

The room sported a half-window view of the pavement below and the stink of urine in the san. Richly colored mold stains formed a dizzy pattern across the ceiling—a tripper's paradise. One bed, a low chest with single drawer and a hard-backed chair. The air con wheezed in asthmatic spurts: freezing blasts—then nothing.

"You sleep first," he said. He dragged the chest across in front of the door and the chair to the window. Then he pulled a Sprag semiauto from his pack.

I'd never seen Daac with a weapon like that before.

He felt my curiosity. "Just a feeling," he muttered.

The pillow looked risky, so I set my pack under my head and stretched out on top of the cover. My hands rested on the Lugers for comfort.

"Don't shoot yourself," he said.

"Never." I yawned, wanting and not wanting to sleep. "Plenty of practice."

He slung himself down onto the chair so he could recce the window and the door. With half-light and half-closed eyes I feasted on the sight of his face. My thighs itched, so I rolled away.

Could I trust him? For half an hour, surely, I decided, and crashed.

I didn't have dreams anymore, only dark shadowy spaces of dim consciousness. The Eskaalim's gluttony filled me like a bloated carcass.

I wallowed in thick, red, river-warmth. It washed into my mouth and across my breasts, pouring down my body. Spreading my legs for it, I came high and wide like a summer sun.

I sweated myself back to proper consciousness, fist clenched between my thighs as I shuddered to the end of my orgasm. Thankfully my back was still turned to Daac. Had I moaned aloud? *Please, no!*

I lay still, waiting for the moment—and the embarrassment—to pass.

But the heat wouldn't leave me.

Hadn't left me for a while. Since The Slag, my tee had been wet under my arms and around my neckline. I sweated all the time, like I had menopause or some other shitty female affliction. My neck ached from leaning on my pack.

At least Loser isn't in there, I thought. How would I have explained him to Daac?

Daac! I sat bolt upright. *Where was he?*

Chair empty. San empty. Bed empty. Chest back in its place. Door ajar.

Relief came first. He hadn't witnessed my lust. Then fury.

Bastard left me unprotected! If the Cabal wanted him marinated, garnished and barbecued, I'd be more than happy to do it.

I slipped my pack on and stumbled to the window.

He was out there on the sidewalk, under neon, in deep discourse with a stranger. He handed a pockmarked guy something and then slipped back toward Chez Nutter.

Forgetting my relief that he hadn't seen my night-jinks, I sat on the chair, pistols drawn, waiting for him.

He came quietly into the room, replacing the chest.

"Friend?" I asked.

He jumped and then located me in the dark.

"Parrish?"

"Unless you left someone else here asleep and defenseless."

The smallest of grins. "You? Defenseless?" Then he ran his hand across tired eyes. "I shook you. You wouldn't wake. It was important."

"What was?"

"Biz."

"Out here in Mo-Vay?" I drawled.

"We could spend forever looking for Leesa Tulu. We need information or we're wasting our time. My last sighting was back on my place—a vendor who said she'd seen Tulu and Mei. Since then I've been following you."

"What vendor?" I demanded. "Don't tell me . . . gray hair, eyebrow studs, food like rat vomit."

He gave me a stare. "How did you know that?"

"Never mind. How much did it cost you?"

The stare became quizzical. "Cost? Why would it cost me anything? She just told me."

I suddenly got a bad case of gnashing teeth. Life

sucked. "Why are you here, Loyl? This isn't just about Mei and Sto, is it?"

He sat down on the bed. "You first."

"I've been hired to find Tulu," I said truthfully. "I told you that. Attempted hijacking and voodoo dolls made it a bit more personal."

"And your employer would be?"

"Client privilege."

I watched him carefully now, the neons outside strobing pink and sickly yellow stripes across his face. Maybe it was fatigue—the Wombat knows he'd been traveling hard and fast as well—or maybe he'd held on to the sane, gorgeous act for too long, but fanaticism had begun to transform his face into something much less attractive.

"She's an experienced medium. I might be able to reach the Eskaalim through you, Parrish. With her help."

"Why me? What about the others who have been infected?"

"We've tried. They didn't survive," he said flatly.

"So it's about attrition, is it? You happened to kill the others and I'm next on the list?"

He frowned, missing my sarcasm, missing everything that didn't fit with his skew on the world.

"You're stronger than the rest, Parrish. You've already survived two attempts at contact. If somehow I can harness this creature through you . . . it could be useful."

I exploded. "Harness it! For what? What are you thinking? An army of shape-shifters to fight your wars?"

He didn't answer me directly. He didn't have to. I saw the truth of it in the glittering calculation of his eyes. "We *will* have our place back, Parrish. Our land. This will all change. I'll rid it of the scraps."

Scraps! The Tert punters? Sure, I guess. But right there was where Daac and I had a *fundamental.* When I said The Tert is full of human scraps, I meant it fondly.

He meant, *torch 'em!*

You see, I'm pretty big on live-and-let. Unless you try to stick a gun at my head or a knife to my throat, in which case I'll turn you into dog food. To my mind the world had a history of carnage that could be summed up by arguments over who thought they had the right.

Most people still didn't get it. *We all had the right. And none of us had the right.* How simple could it be? How we fucked it from there on in was an individual problem. The thing I hated more than anything else—more than stone-cold crazies, fakers and pretty dresses—was manipulative zealots.

And yet my hormones squealed every time this particular one came near me.

Well, hormones or no, I wouldn't let him use the Eskaalim to make foot soldiers for his cause. But I wasn't going to tell him that just yet.

Just tag along, Parrish. Play the game. Come from behind.

I calmed myself with that plan. "So where is Tulu?"

"Won't know until morning. When they come back to get paid." He yawned and slumped down on the bed. "Wake me at light."

I watched him sleep, and stewed—several hours of a bitching internal war that alternated between wanting to leave him and wanting to lie next to him. Moral disgust versus fleshly temptation, while his jaw fell slack and he snored softly.

By dawn temptation had a foot on the home stretch and my pelvis was doing a funny crampy thing. I shoved him awake with my toe, avoiding flesh contact, in case the crampy thing turned into another orgasm and I died from mortification.

"Let's move. This place is making me scratch."

He rubbed his eyes with his flesh hand and stretched, pulling his tee tight, flashing rib flesh. I turned away, willing the heat to leave me. How could anyone look so innocent one minute and act so rabid the next?

I got one flight down and the stairs stopped dead. "Loyl?"

He looked past me, slipping the Sprag loose from the straps of his pack. A wall of pale membrane blocked our path.

I touched it. "Feels like a thick sorta web. It's warm."

He pulled me back, frowning. "This'll be noisy."

"I like noisy."

"You would. Back up in case."

I climbed back to the top of the stairs, marveling at how we slipped from enemy to ally so easily.

Daac sprayed fire directly into the membrane.

No ricochet. When the vibrations stopped he stepped down to feel it. "Holes are there, but closing up already."

Claustrophobia was on me. "Let's look around."

We marched down the corridor, taking one room at a time. All the doors opened easily like ours. They were empty. About six in all.

Back in our room, Daac pointed onto the street. "Fancy a climb?"

I reached to open the window, eager to get out. "Sure."

The window was fastened shut, nothing unusual in The Tert.

"Watch out." He swung the chair at it and nearly flattened himself as it bounced straight back at him. He touched the window. "Same stuff. Transparent though."

I pulled a knife from my boot and stabbed at it. The "window" barely dented and within seconds the surface smoothed.

"Parrish!" Daac had that tense, throaty tone.

I knew what he meant. Add "trapped" to my phobia list.

I ran from room to room, checking the ceilings. Dirty but smooth. No manholes? Why hadn't I noticed that before? The only gap I could see anywhere was the air-con breather vent at one end of the corridor.

"Look," I shouted.

"I think you'd better look," he called, "here." I ran back to him. Through our window the gray-pink dawn lit a swarm of activity. He pointed to a quad-runna. Around it roved a guard of naked, painted-up young turks armed with kit rifles and fast-twitch muscles. Their movements were swift, exaggerated. And arrogant. A confidence you got only when you believed you were untouchable.

"The web stuff doesn't seem to be covering the vent. Otherwise the air con would have blown," I said.

"How big is it?"

I glanced meaningfully at the width of his shoulders. "Big enough. Just. You should lose some weight."

He jerked the Sprag. "I'll cover the hallway. You get the damn thing open."

I didn't need to hear any more. I grabbed the chair and ran back down the corridor.

With my push dagger I pried around the edge of the vent. No go. I stabbed and hacked with each of my knives in turn. I couldn't even dent the metal.

For a run-down piece of crappo architecture, this place sure had some interesting extras.

My hand strayed to my dagger belt. It brushed the Cabal knife. *Maybe?*

The black metal sliced through the grating like cheese. "Loyl! Come!" I bellowed.

Back near the stairway, the wall began to harden and become brittle. The youth army was spraying it with something from the other side.

Loyl stood there transfixed.

I shouted to him again. *"Now!"*

He ignored me, dropping to his knee in the corridor. The Sprag sprayed its own message, perforating the membrane.

He was buying me time. Only I didn't need a hero. That was my job.

Annoyed, I holstered the Lugers and hauled arse up into the mouth of the vent.

I've been in chutes before. Well, once, anyway. But that was laundry and going down. This was air con and going up.

Dusty and slippery.

My upper body strength was pretty good for my size, but that's the problem. My size. The effort of getting my entire body plus pack up into the hole nearly did me in. Only the thought of what the small army of jacked-up pubescents was planning on doing to us got me up over the first lip.

I squirmed around and hung an arm down for Loyl.

"Come *on!* Grab it."

A second later he was there. He stretched to meet me.

I saw restraint probes snake out, fixing on his neck. Flat-ended suckers delivering tiny paralyzing kisses.

Too late!

He gargled and flopped to the floor.

I should have gone down there after him. But the sight of his paralysis terrified me. Jamon had done the same thing to my legs not so long ago. Then he'd tried to rape me.

Rewind on the hero thing.

"I'll find you," I yelled consolingly at his unconscious body and contorted up around the first kink in the duct and along as far as I could squeeze.

I lay panting. Below I could hear voices. Shots bounced around the opening of the vent. Any second I expected web stuff to come crawling up the sides. My muscles screamed with exertion; my mind screamed with dread.

So much noise.

In the end nothing and no one followed me.

I lay wedged there, fixated with guilt and worry at leaving Daac behind.

Leaving him behind? Who are you kidding, Parrish? You're the one stuck in an air-con duct.

Stuck was the word. I tried the caterpillar thing and went nowhere. Ahead of me the duct narrowed away into a thin tube. My feet paddled and slipped on the smooth interior. Because of my pack, I couldn't go backwards either. So I lay, arms pinned to my side, wondering what it might be like to mummify. Fingernails of panic clawed at my belly.

A few minutes later freezing air blasted through the pipe, over and under my clothes. Forget flooding the rat from the sewers—these scuds were trying to freeze me out!

Soon my teeth were chattering.

The cold must have frozen my brain because it took an age before I remembered the Cabal dagger. Or maybe it was just that it began to dig a hole in my groin. With difficulty and a lot of wriggle, I slid it from inside my knife belt.

I gouged in a small, laborious circle. Slowly it punctured the metal. Every now and then I stopped and poked a finger through. Encouraged and warmed slightly by the effort, I worked on. The layer of insulation wrapped around the outside of the tube was easier to sever. Soon the hole got big enough for my hand and arm, then my shoulder and finally my head.

With relief I squirmed out of the duct and into the ceiling. I rummaged in my sack for my head-band light and slipped it on.

Fashionless enough to make Merry 3# gag—but effective.

The light illuminated the usual rafters, cobwebs and dust. No one had crawled through here in a while. I remembered the intricate mold patterns I'd admired in the room and wondered if they were connected in some way with the creepy mesh.

I checked my compass implant and got a bearing. Bent over like a hunchback, I ran through my options.

Most Tert villas had cut-thrus into the next set. This one had been blocked off with scrap and chunks of plas—no signs of the mesh, though. The roof above was intact, which meant I either hacked my way out onto the roof—time consuming and noisy—or I removed the rubbish.

I didn't fancy climbing around on the outside of the roof waiting for a canrat, or a whatever, to pick me off, so I went for the cut-through option.

A minute later I was dust coated, fingernails torn and bleeding from scrabbling and scraping, face and the insides of my nostrils caked. On the bright side, the Cabal knife was a freaking miracle of cutting power. When I found out what it was made of, Raul Minoj and I were gonna make a killing on the open market.

I hacked a rough circle in the plas bricks and put

my boot through it with a couple of big heel kicks. Those sambo lessons I'd traded for karate had been worth every bruise.

I didn't wait to check what was on the other side but crawled through, headfirst, hands out to break my fall.

Mistake. I touched something alive. Tilting my headlight downward, I scoped a dazed python, curled up tight for the winter.

Well, it would've been—if I hadn't disturbed it.

It stirred sluggishly like it had a hangover. Pythons weren't poisonous but their bite hurt and was filthy. Septicemic in fact.

On instinct I grabbed its throat before it had a go at me and then I tumbled the rest of my body through the hole. By the time I got upright, it had roused itself and begun to constrict around my arm and shoulders.

I shuddered and sucked in a deep, steadying breath. I didn't want to kill it—there were few enough native animals left in this country, and these guys kept the rats down—but I *was* in a bit of a hurry. With difficulty I unwound its heavy body.

Now what? If I put it down, it might bite. Maybe if I tied it *really* tight in my pack it might come in handy. Not many people could think straight when you waved a snake in their face.

I stuffed it in awkwardly, strapping the flap down hard. After a minute or two of frantic gyration, it went still.

I sighed. I'd have to stop collecting things; a Borgia canrat, now a diamond python. Anyone would think I was the animal kind.

I rechecked the straps several times before I levered the pack on my back, trying to shut out images of the python getting loose and throttling me.

Maybe it wasn't such a good idea. As soon as I got back on the ground, I'd dump it.

Taking a settling breath, I looked around properly. Now that I'd broken through the wall of plas bricks, cut-thrus ran in all directions. I chose one randomly, keeping to a generally south direction, taking care to avoid any more sleeping creatures.

Twenty or more villas later I risked coming down. Even then I squatted for a time over the manhole, remembering my last roof crawling excursion. Stolowski and I had found our way into a Mueno living room. Considering I wasn't even Oya yet, they were pretty chilled about it. If my hunch was right, that was the time I'd been infected with the parasite. That'd teach me to get splattered with sacrificial human blood.

Blood! A surge of desire for it welled up in me—breathtaking in its strength. I bent it into anger and self-pity.

What the hell was I doing chasing Leesa Tulu around this place?

My head ached with the intrigues in my life. Everyone had an angle. And for some reason they all seemed compelled to use me to work them. Daac wanted to manipulate the Eskaalim, the Cabal wanted me to find their *karadji,* the Muenos wanted a real flesh goddess and Teece wanted a woman who would stay at home helping him make money off black-market tek and motorbikes.

But what did I want?

I wanted to stay alive.

And I wanted Loyl Daac to stay alive. In that order. I cared about him. And that I *really* hated!

Forward was the only way I'd get those things.

Sighing, I hauled the manhole cover off and took a recce below. For once I caught a break. Empty—apart from small vermin and ankle-deep small vermin shit.

I dropped down and waded through it with big, impatient steps, stamping my boots clean when I hit the pavement. Then I checked my direction log.

Dawn had deserted and the sun already radiated onto the tacky plas overhangs with a new intensity. I felt the sudden change of season, a declaration that winter had pissed off. It got me jogging the return route with fresh determination. King Tide was only a couple of days away, and I hadn't found the *karadji*.

I recognized the villa set soon as I turned the corner. The "Kleen Beds and Air Con" neon was dead, but it was unmistakably Chez Nutter. The quad-runna had vanished from outside, along with its legion of twitchers.

Panting with exertion, I took my pack off and squatted down next to it, wondering what to do next. Nothing came to me except the desire for food and a comatose sleep.

I only sensed the set of tampering hands when my pack got up a fair wriggle. Wheeling, I found a *petit* crim—spotted with bleeding, cauliflower-shaped hives—draped in a gray-green python.

I grabbed the snake's neck as it fanged open to have a taste. "Get your fingers out of my stuff, or I'll let go."

The *petit* choked and coughed, waving his hands frantically in front of me.

"What do you want?" *Petits* didn't bother me much. They were usually after food, sometimes drugs. Often they poached just for the sake of it.

This one had a curtain of limp, thin hair that did little to hide the bloody sores on his face and neck.

"Did-youse-come-in-on-the-quod-copt? Youse-gotta-be-from-outwhere-cos-they-speak-different-so-slow."

I wasn't surprised he thought that. He gabbed quicker than a cheap advert.

As I looked closer, I thought I recognized something about him. With a foot anchoring my pack to the pavement, I unwound the snake from his neck and wrestled with its tail.

"You did biz with a friend of mine yesterday. Big guy with dark skin."

He nodded, being careful.

I glanced over at Chez Nutter. "He ran into a problem."

The *petit* nodded. "Clancy-uses-Crawl. Spread-quick." He glanced across at the lifeless neon almost bitterly. "Epox-can-afford-it."

"Clancy? Grrl at the desk?"

"Uh-huh-that's-her."

"What's an epox?"

"Epoxyed-to-whatever. You'll-see-more-of-'em." His face closed up then like he'd said too much.

People were the same everywhere when they didn't want to talk.

I wasn't going to let that happen, so I leaned down heavily on him. "First, who took my friend and where?"

He squirmed a bit. "Hey-my-words-ain't-free."

I'd really had a skinful of this *how much* thing, so I loosed my grip on the python.

It obligingly constricted around his neck.

He gargled like baby, "Get-it-the-fok-offa-me-can't-talk."

I figured he could talk underwater, strangled, with burst lungs, but I relented and recaptured the snake. Why did everyone in this damned world want to be paid?

He rubbed his neck uneasily, glancing down at my pistols and back at the python. "Ike-took-him."

"Where?"

"Ike's-place."

"Is my friend alive?" Considering the karma I'd attracted on my journey this far, it seemed a reasonable question.

"For-a-while-depends-how-long-it-takes-to-strip-him-down."

Strip him down? "Who is this Ike?"

"The-manufacturer."

"What do you mean, 'manufacturer'?"

He gave me a considered look, as if to gauge whether I was capable of understanding. He even spoke slowly, so I could take it in.

"We call him God."

Chapter Nine

"Oh," I said. *So God was in manufacturing.*

"We-trade-body-stuff." He thumped his bony chest. "Me-I-carry-the-sebar-virus. Me-I've-lived-longer-than-all-the-others. Ike-says-me-I'm-a-fokin'-miracle. Get-all-my-food-for-free-now. S'long-as-I-turn-up-for-swabs."

Sebar virus? I'd never heard of it but the sores on his face told me enough. Ike—God—sounded fully uncool.

I delved into my pack for some of Loser's hair and flicked it to the *petit*. "Here," I said. "It's part dingo. Worth something around here. Buy yourself some health care."

He gave a confused look.

I slipped the rest of the hair away into my pack before I lowered the python back and strapped it in.

Damn me if the little creep didn't whip a magnifier and light gizmo out of his pants to check the hair out. What was with these Mo-Vay people? Was everyone a lab geek?

His grin broadened into something almost pleasant. "Go-to-the-pies-a-couple-sets-down. Tell-'em-me-Monts-says-you-should-have-the-floater."

Monts? I gave him a look.

"'S-cool. 'S-not-on-the-menu. Strictly-on-the-house-for-friends."

Friends? What was the little creep thinking?

I bared my teeth at him and moved on.

My stomach growled incessantly as I jogged southward, but innate paranoia told me not to risk eating from Monts's recommendation or any other of the food vendors. Apart from the hygiene questions, I seriously did not take to the locals.

I thought I'd seen every type of aberrant living in The Tert, but Mo-Vay punters were something . . . other. Not sicko so much as sick . . . ailing in mind *and* body. Crusted lesions or wet scars marked their skin like they were living with a permanent, oozing toxicity. Certainly nothing you wanted to get physical with.

How did they get like this? Where had they come from?

Urgency forced me to stop and ask questions using the canrat fur as lubricant. Straight up they knew I was a stranger. I was outsized, my skin was too clear and I talked too slow to be anonymous in this place.

Everyone had a fancy magnifier or a portable DNA analyzer and a sample scoop. I imagined the scoop gathering sloughed-off skin cells or catching exuded moisture droplets, and found myself holding my breath as I waited for them to answer.

I approached twins (or one person split—it was hard to know) who had only one set of arms between them. They camped under the old monorail track in a lean-to made of cracked roof tiles. Up close their congenital abnormality was less alarming than the sticky, lumpy texture of their skin and their infected eyes.

"I'm looking for someone." I waved a finger of canrat hair in their faces and described Tulu and Mei.

I got no response.

"What about an ultralight? You seen one fly over?" I tried.

That got them laughing. At least that's what I think it was. When they spoke to each other, it fell somewhere between a dialect and a cleft palate.

Pretty soon, though, I got their joke.

By late morning the sky was busy with air traffic—droning unmarked cargo 'copts and buzz-saw ULs swooping in from the east. Each one circled low before disappearing into the same spot. Due south.

I tried talking to a young epox who looked like Clancy. This one was gummed to a short-board on nifty all-terrain wheels.

I showed her my dwindling tuft of canrat hairs.

"What's all the action with the 'copts? What's in them?"

She opened her eyes wide. "How-else-do-youse-get-here? Wern'tcha-reborn?"

Reborn?

I suddenly got cowardly on that conversation and

changed the subject to the quad-runna and its escort of Twitchers. On that topic I got nothing concrete—just enough to know south was a safe bet, and that the Twitchers were trouble.

By late afternoon the villascape altered again. I waded into a dense, impenetrable morass of plaster, plas and planks. The pavements narrowed into endless culs-de-sac. I had an unnerving image of myself as a bug at the narrow end of a funnel web. All paths leading down, and around, and in.

My compass told me I was circling. No matter what I tried I couldn't seem to go any farther south or east. Sweating freely, light-headed from hunger, mouth watering constantly, I lost direction like a compass affected by magnetism. Only sheer stubbornness and an unhealthy dose of fear kept me upright and moving.

Space dwindled to tiny pockets of pavement and gaps between villa walls. Figures scurried between them and disappeared into buildings.

I dared not follow them inside and found myself swaying, sucking in large gulps of air as if the oxygen quotient had dropped away. The air reeked of incenses and decay and unholy secretions—a head-spinning mix.

My skin prickled with paranoia.

Am I being followed?

Unfamiliar hesitancy crept through me, turning my thoughts gloomy and muddled and leaden. The parasite was taking hold of me the deeper I traveled into Mo-Vay. Stealing my hope.

I tried to concentrate on what I knew, to think my way through a wave of despair.

Tulu had brought Mei to Mo-Vay. *Why?* Daac had been taken alive. *Who by?*

Wild-tek was rampant here. *Did the Cabal know about this place?*

I wallowed in a trough of unanswered questions. Apprehensions turned into hard lumps of worry. As the evening shadows lengthened, so the shadows darkened my mind, suffocating me in the worst kind of hopelessness.

I found a partly boarded-up recess—an old cylinder housing—and slid my pack off. As I loosened the strap, the jolt stirred the python. It slithered out and away from me.

I watched it. Wanted it to go. Until an intolerable vision of it turning up in some sort of pie pressed me to follow. On automatic I chased it to the door of a shabby villabar where it wound itself around the neon like a string of broken party lights.

"Come 'ere." I reached up a shaky hand.

It surrendered meekly despite my clumsiness, curling around my arm.

I dropped it slowly back into my pack. "This is no place for you," I whispered, fumbling with the flap. "Or me."

Yet exhaustion coaxed me inside the bar. I asked the barkeep for a jug of whiskey, water and some privacy. He pointed to an orange glow coming from a cubicle at the back of the main room.

"Private booths cost."

I scraped around for some of Loser's hair.

He dropped it in his analyzer and nodded. "One night only."

"Enough," I agreed, and waded through the jumble of patrons. I might have been hallucinating but punters seemed to reach for me without touching. Conversations about me seemed to happen behind hands. So did shrewd, avaricious looks.

I felt the strain like a psychosis. Did everyone know I was a stranger?

I managed to fumble the shutter across on the booth and take several, lengthy, breath-denying swigs before I passed out. Oblivion had begged a dance and I gratefully accepted.

The swigs turned out to be half of the jug and I woke up a few hours later—around midnight, I thought—with a swollen tongue and a fetid mood that didn't welcome the racket in the bar.

Pushing the screen aside, I took a blurry-eyed look. Most of the patrons were up on their tables throwing things; the rest were backed up to the door or haunching it on to the bar.

Head thumping and faint, I squinted into the near dark.

The python stretched lethargically along the bar. The lump in its neck suggested the successful quest for a decent-sized canrat. Or a small human.

Maybe even part of a human.

Sudden unease made me glance back into the booth. My pack had been rifled. Flap open, clothes scattered. I slapped my hand to my holsters.

Empty.

Wrist check. *Charm bracelet?* Gone. So were my pins.

Knife belt? OK. Cabal dagger sheathed and pressing into my belly like a prayer book.

I'd slept on the Gurkha.

I grabbed hold of it, thinking to help the python out, when a figure caught my eye.

I fell back in the booth and shut the screen to a crack.

Leesa Tulu scanned the crowd. She was dressed in the same headscarf and boots. Her metallic eyebrow studs glinted, and luminous beads glowed at her throat and waist.

She made violent hand movements, rubbing something brittle between her fingers, chafing it to dust as she mouthed silent words.

A draft spilled across my overheated body, and a memory of how easily she had laid me out in front of Loyl and Mei with her power.

Blowing the last of the dust from her hands, she swept the bar with her gaze. It settled on my booth. I told myself she couldn't see in. I *knew* she couldn't see in . . . and yet . . .

A moment later she disappeared through a back door.

I stuffed my clothes quickly into my pack. My new fatigues looked like they'd been through several wars and a zoo insurrection, and I hadn't even worn them. *Crap!* Mourning the loss of the Lugers, I went after her.

The door led to a filthy corridor. I tried all the rooms along it. Mostly, they contained beds. Some even had bodies in them: stoned or comatose, smelling worse than a Sensil parlor.

The last door fed into a dark closet under the stairs. With enough room for a small, hunched-over adult, it led down rough steps to a makeshift cellar filled with unevenly stacked kegs and a neat, new still belching pure ethanol.

I unsheathed the Gurkha and waited for my eyes to adjust to the dim light, then I searched the cellar for another way out.

Nothing.

I moved in between kegs, barely daring to breathe, expecting Tulu to slam me.

Nothing.

A creak on the steps and I froze.

The barkeep stamped down and poured two large flagons straight from the still. Maybe the python had bitten someone? After a kill they were usually too torpid and lazy, but the barkeep carried enough whiskey to numb the entire bar—or serve as antiseptic.

He left a few moments later, sloshing drops.

I crouched, face pressed against the cool plas kegs, and waited. A tiny draft caught the attention of my fevered body. The smallest sigh of air that diluted the reek of hops and grain alcohol and served notice on my body hair.

I hunted for the source.

There. Had to be. Obscured behind a wall of crates, another set of stairs leading upward to a small hatch.

I crawled up them to investigate.

The hatch was open less than a thumb's width. In The Tert hatches were usually sealed like tombs. You never knew what was behind them. Or what might come in through them.

Me, for instance.

I shoved this one open and climbed through.

Chapter Ten

Like switching Sensil mid-program, disorientation gripped me. Soil crunched underfoot. Moist breeze licked me all over like an eager dog.

Absence. Of . . . what?

I peered into the dark, trying to make sense of the lights flickering in a crisscross pattern above me.

Veiling. Electrical impulses used to create a mirage.

I'd heard of this type of thing, never seen it before. Teece said Southern Hem drug barons had invented it and sold it to the Militia. An efficient disguise if you were hiding from an air recce. It worked like a one-way mirror, and from underneath the grid I could see the starry night sky—not a thing I was at all comfortable with.

I trembled.

The Tert got you like that if you stayed there

long enough. It overfed you with people and place until you felt hungry and bare without it. I felt bare right now looking out into so much space. The hungry went without saying.

Eyes adjusting, I realized I'd come up on the other side of a vast wall erected along the backs of the villas. On this side it ringed a perimeter of space. I roughed its distance at maybe a klick wide and several long. Tall enough to obscure the rooftops.

Out towards the center squatted several buildings flanked by an array of shadowy, upright statue shapes and a large canopy over the top. White light leaked out of the windows of one of the buildings.

A faint crackle and a whiff of ions came to me. I twitched up my olfaugs and breathed in the smell of av-gas, corrosives and electrical energy. Av-gas could have been the heavy copter traffic—there was enough space to land—

I suddenly lost my train of thought. Cries of celebration resonated from the bar. Something had just happened in there, and its consequence carved up my insides and messed with my head.

I couldn't remember why I was here. Or what I wanted to do. I knew I should go and explore the darkened buildings, but my sense of purpose was gone. When I should have been buying in, I bailed.

Breath short and panicky, I scrambled down through the hatch, jamming it shut behind me. Stumbling down the stairs, I paused only to scrape some milky corrosion from my boots before I made my way back to the private booth.

Shuttered against the world, I swallowed what was left in the jug. The whiskey further unwound my mind and body.

Something had lowered my resistance, and the Eskaalim swooped in like a vulture, stripping the last of my self-confidence with a carrion cry.

Feel me, human. Feel me make ready. Feel me take you down . . .

No! A shred of denial got my legs up and moving. I stumbled through the bar and towards the outside as if I could outrun it—past the barkeep passed out in the drip tray and the remaining patrons scattered in a tangle of bodies on tables.

The grainy light spoke of predawn and the world teetered on the wrong side of reality.

As I pushed opened the door, the python's lifeless body slapped me in the face. It had been nailed to the doorframe like a trophy. Right there on the doorstep I vomited up whiskey. And guilt.

I wandered—stoned, possessed, fully deranged. How many names were there for it? My appetite had deserted me though it had been several days since I'd eaten. Mouth dry, senses altered.

A recurring wail and a light drumbeat echoed off the gutterless roofs and crumbling walls. I clung to the sound and followed it. Anything but this emptiness . . .

At the narrow end of an alley I found the wailer crouched, crying like a grief-stricken bird, her face daubed white and red in the manner of shamans. As I approached she raised a warding hand. Her coarse, dark hair was knotted wildly around a jumble of bones and painted beads. It framed accusatory eyes and a worn face.

Yet her power emanated like a storm.

"You've abandoned your familiars. One lost, one passed back to the spirits."

"What familiars?" With energy my words would have tinged hysterical; instead they rasped hollow and dry.

"Your safe passage through the Belts and into Mo-Vay. You think it normally so easy? You were granted protection by your guides. Now they are gone. Betrayed by your selfishness when they would have showed you the path to the healing you so desire."

"What guides?"

She made an undulating movement with her arms.

The python?

Followed by the growl of a feral animal.

Loser?

I struggled to remember something of shaman practices. I knew their drugs of choice were distilled fungi, cactus and vines: mushrooms, peyote and *caapi* if they could get it. Here in The Tert, though, it was more likely to be datura or morning glory.

They said it got them to the higher places

Mei Sheong had talked to me once of her familiars, spirits who guided her through the treachery of these planes. But they were illusory creatures, drug induced, not real animals like Loser and the python.

And yet the cynic in me was running on a dry tank. Right now I was way too vulnerable to all manner of possibilities. Hadn't I ended up in that particular bar because I'd followed the python? In there I'd found Leesa Tulu. The coincidence of it unnerved me.

"I didn't know they were guides," I croaked. "How could I know that?"

She restarted a beat on her small drum. I felt my heartbeat slow to match its rhythm. As dawn stole in, she seemed to waver and fade before my eyes.

"She calls the power of Baron Samedi and Marinette. With them she will suck you dry."

Tulu? "What do I do now? Tell me . . ." I reached out a tentative hand to her. "Please . . ."

She stood and hobbled away, despondent as me, out of the alley until she was lost in a jaundiced Mo-Vay daybreak.

I stayed crouched in a huddle of misery, unable to find any reason to move. Had this happened to the other shape-changers? The breakdown of beliefs. The loss of purpose.

What was next? Total possession? How long before the cellular changes became irreversible? How long before the Eskaalim had its way?

I had no will to fight. Nor any idea how to atone for the loss and deaths of my spirit guides. I didn't even know if I believed in them.

Tremors racked me instead of tears. I had no tears.

Only blur . . .

Small furred hands tugged and tapped insistently at my knee. With effort I forced my attention and focus to a child's face. Like a distant observer I saw coarse, bristling hair on her chin, forearms and the tops of her bare leathery feet. Her head was almost bald. Her upper arms bled from deep scratches.

"Food. Pay with hair," she pleaded, pulling at the few remaining tufts.

I shook my head, dimly wondering why she used the hair on her head as currency instead of the unsightly body hair.

She gave up on me and moved on to ferret among the rubbish heaped along the sides of the alley, slipping happily among the waste as if she was harvesting flowers.

I watched as she felt her way around a pile of broken furniture, first putting everything to her mouth like a baby. She stuck odd useful bits into her pockets.

I lifted a hand and tried to call to her but was defeated by my own inertia. My energy depleted in that one small movement.

A gang of thin-shouldered bigger girls came trolling the alley. Almost asleep, I took in their prepubescent hairless bodies and the checkered pattern of tattoos and raw, healing skin on their nakedness. Tattoo grafts.

One of the gang seized the feral child, tipping her upside down. She spat back at her tormentor, beating her with wild, desperate hands while the collection of oddments tumbled from her large pockets.

Dumping her into a pile of refuse, they pounced on it, pilfering their fancy: a used derm, a clump of hair, and a near-empty container of blue fluid.

Afterwards one of them kicked her and another

tried to set fire to her arm hair with a Zippo. Another spat on her and doodled her fingers through the saliva. Another pulled her top up and squeezed her tiny, immature nipples cruelly.

Pulse-quickening excitement steamed into me as I witnessed the torment. The parasite raptured.

Savor it . . .

No! I fought back from somewhere deeper than the Eskaalim could ever burrow.

You can't deny me . . .

I can! My conviction grew as I twisted the tainted energy into something else. Slowly . . . so slowly . . . it grew.

The parasite shrank from it.

As the girls passed by me, laughingly callous, I sprang from nowhere like long-buried grief.

"Back," I rasped. "Give it back."

They spread automatically in a circle, producing shok-sticks. For a bunch of preadolescent Mo-Vay scum, they had a more than tolerable arsenal.

Dizziness came and went over me. My heart thumped painfully to meet the sudden muscular demand. Part of me wanted to kill them outright. The other part cogged some pity for their strange, wretched lives.

I wavered between the two.

Wise enough to keep some distance, one of them threw a live shok at my head. I batted it away, almost welcoming the pain—anything to dispel the numbness.

With the other hand I unsheathed the Gurkha, glaring at her. "You could be that kid," I said.

She stuck her finger to the tip of her nose in

contempt. Her gratts looked so fresh they might bleed. One of them was a man's face. Someone familiar.

"She's a ma'soop. You see any rug on me?" Her feral-green pupils dilated with disgust.

"No. But I see someone who could be her sister."

"We got no famlee in Mo-Vay," she said.

They chanted in practiced accord, *"Famlee's a dysfunc'nal kustom. It's got no use in pos' humanity."*

The crude recital sounded like it had come straight from the mouth of an idiot prophet. But which idiot prophet?

"Here's my prophecy." I lunged to my right, hauling the nearest girl into my arms, twisting her arm up hard and pressing the Gurkha across her throat. "Leave her alone or I'll separate this one's tonsils."

"No!" shouted the shok thrower.

The others joined in with a screaming protest.

I smiled tight and tense at the abhorrent noise, feeling deranged as all fuck. "See, you do know about family."

I shoved the girl away into the arms of her gang. In seconds they scarpered, yelling obscenities at me.

I sank back onto the pavement, weakened with the effort of speech and the confrontation. I must have dozed because the hairy kid woke me, tugging on my arm.

"Youse can't stay here during the daytime. Youse'll get it. Lemme show you a place to sleep."

Grateful for a reason to live a bit longer, I struggled after her into a villa and up a homemade ladder into the roofs.

She told me her name was Glida-Jam and pulled the ladder up behind her. Though there was no resemblance, she reminded me of Tina, the feral child who had taken out fifty 'goboys with a bio-bomb in the war—a single act that had shifted the momentum of things in the favor of me and away from Jamon.

Glida-Jam and I crawled through a warren of cut-thrus. She chivvied me along and waited patiently every time I faltered.

My body ached unendurably, wasted by too little food and its recent saturation in raw, potent booze. My compass implant told me we moved south and east in a kind of semicircle.

Finally we stopped in a heavily boarded-up attic where slivers of light lanced through the dust from roof to moldy ceiling. On her assertion that it was safe to stop, I collapsed on a raft of planks and slept.

When I woke, Glida-Jam forced a broken beaker of fluid into my hand.

I took it shakily, wondering if the other equally hairy kids, crouched in the darkened corners of the attic, were real.

Glida forced some heavily sweetened bread on me and more of the salty, mineral-bitter water. I sucked greedily at the bread. My tongue swelled after the water, but I felt faint fingers of hope revive along with my blood sugar.

"I saw you in Splitty's," she said.

"Splitty's?"

"Splitty's bar," she said impatiently. "Not safe for us. Too close to Home. Roof is wired."

"Home?" My mind felt heavy.

She frowned, stroking the hair that bristled out from the back of her hand. "Where we was reborn. The flying angels brought us there and let God remake us."

That word "reborn" again. I tried to make sense of it, but the meaning slipped away and I dozed.

The next time I woke stiff all over but better able to concentrate. She gave me more water and bread, and with it my mind got sharper. I saw rather than sensed the small, furtive creatures gathered at the fringe of the light.

"How long have I been asleep?" I asked.

She made a hand motion. One half of a circle. A full day. I was running out of time.

"No more bread," she told me.

I chewed the last mouthful slowly, smiling to show my appreciation. "I'm looking for a shaman named Leesa Tulu. You know her?" I asked.

The girl shook her head. "Not know that one. Only know Home." In frustration she started plucking at the hair along the top of her feet, twisting it into tiny plaits.

I rubbed my eyes and nose with the back of my hand and tried another tack. "Tell me how you get there. To your . . . home."

She shook her head. "Youse crazy if youse go there," she pronounced.

"Yes," I said. "Tell me about it. I can't pay you. But if you want, afterwards I can take you away from here."

She stared at me in disbelief. In the shadows, the others gave a perceptible murmur. "Can youse take me to the city? Torlee's?"

"How do you know the name Torley's? I'd never heard of Mo-Vay. Where I come from, we call this place Dis."

She blinked. A flush crept up her hairy neck and into her cheeks. "I'se met someone from there."

"Who?" I snapped, immediately thinking of Loyl.

"He's'll come here soon. Youse'll see."

Chapter Eleven

Glida gave me a muddled idea of the physical layout and the distances around Home. When I tried wringing more detail from her, the feral couldn't explain it.

"Youse'll know—when youse see it," she said.

"See what, Glida?"

"How it is."

"How is it?"

"Youse'll see."

I gave that up and tried working sideways. "How come you never left here?"

"I never heard of no other place now the monsters have taken over."

"Monsters?"

"On the other side of the water."

"Those are just animals. Lizards and canrats." *The monsters are here.* "Who's that hiding in the shadows, Glida?"

She made clicking noises, interspersed with single words. I'd heard some weird lingo before and could speak some pidgin myself, but this patois . . .

<click> *show* <grunt>, she uttered.

Half a dozen children crept forward. Like Glida-Jam, hair covered them in places usually reserved for bare skin. Unlike her, they closely resembled ugly monkeys. They smelled like them as well. Several of them dragged primate tails.

Shock made me recoil.

"This is my . . . what'd youse call it? . . . My famlee." She gestured grandly.

"How did this happen?" I cried.

Glida frowned, confused. "What'd youse mean? They's belong to Ike. We's all do. Only they's didn't work."

Didn't work? I took a breath. "Where I live, some kids have mekanical parts. We call them Pets. Medics fooled around on them; is that how it happened?"

"Just one medic, boss."

I swiveled where I crouched. "You!" I accused the darkness.

Roo picked his way across the cut-thru and balanced on the beam in front of me. He scratched his hair under his hat. In the other hand he carried a pack. "Yeah. Me."

"What the—"

"Teece told me to tell you that if you send me back, he's quitting his day job."

"That's blackmail!" I growled.

"Yeah."

Glida crept up to him and put a small, furred hand tentatively on his arm.

"She's . . . jus' like youse said," whispered Glida. "Nuts."

I felt annoyed—and pleased beyond words—to see Roo. "How did you find—?"

"Him." He un-Velcroed the sack, and a mangy canrat poked his head out.

"Loser!" I felt like the moon had suddenly risen on a pitch-black night.

"That what you call him?" said Roo. "I've been trailing you since back before the canal." His eyes widened. "How's that dinosaur?"

"Lizard," I snapped. "You mean you watched all that happen and didn't lift a damn finger to help me?"

"Teece said not to interfere unless you was frigged. I figured you could handle it . . . mostly."

Mostly!

Roo was scratching again. "Beats me how he fixed up that big canrat."

Loser scrambled out of the pack and onto the ceiling floor. I stared hypnotized by the mangy creature scratching its balls with its extra half foot. "Charisma."

"Car-what?"

I sighed. "Never mind."

"I lost you for a while after that but he found me near the canal. He was barking so hard I guessed you must have dumped him. Anyways he jumped on the raft I made." He held up corroded digits on his left hand. "That water bites."

"Copper sulfate," I said automatically.

"He sat on my head the whole way across. Then wouldn't let me touch him. I guess you two got some special . . . y'know . . . bond."

My mouth opened and closed, suffocating fishlike.

"I found you again near that bar. She came along while you was drinkin' and I was waitin'." He nodded to Glida. "She was stealing food. While I wuz watchin' her I lost you again. She showed me some safe place to sleep."

His injured hand tightened on Glida's furry arm in gratitude. Glida grinned at him, and the flush crept back onto her face.

Not to be ignored, Loser limped over to me, panting like trouble. Unable to stop myself, I scratched his matted, vermin-riddled hide. The movement sent energy and certainty flooding through me. Whether Loser was my spirit guide or just a filthy piece of fur, I didn't care. I wouldn't dump him again.

Inside I felt the shrinking Eskaalim protest at the sentiment.

"You look different from the others, Glida," I said.

"That's cos my hair is worth somethin'." She rubbed her mostly bald scalp. "They don't get as much for theirs."

I noticed the ma'soops had tufts missing here and there. Nothing like Glida's.

The abusiveness of it fired my boosters. These children had been crossbred right here in Mo-Vay.

Why would anyone want to do this? *Who* would want to do this?

I thought of Loyl Daac. What he was doing wasn't such a large step away. His genetic mods might not be as dire as these but his notion of breeding selectivity was.

In a single heart wrench my resolve was restored.

Over the next few hours Glida and Roo showed me a dozen different ways down to the street, safe access between conjoined villas and a couple of routes to Splitty's bar, including an attic cut-thru. I logged them carefully in my compass memory.

Glida described food vendors whose food might kill me and those that wouldn't. Then I told her to wait until I'd done what I'd come here to do and that afterwards I'd find her, and the ma'soops, and take them with me.

I took Roo aside. "If I'm not back by tomorrow, I want you to take Glida and the ma'soops back to Torley's without me."

He gave me a look. "But Teece—"

I stared him down. "Who do you think needs protecting, Roo? These kids? Or me?"

His young face hinted at warring emotions, his eyes straying to Glida as she played with the ma'soops.

He sighed. "OK, boss. But if you get killed or anythin' Teece said he'd pull my implants out. That wouldn't leave me much."

"Nice type, that Teece," I consoled, hiding a grin.

I left the ma'soops jumping and somersaulting in excitement and nervousness at the idea of leaving Mo-Vay, with Glida growling parental warnings about the brittle ceiling and Roo shyly watching her.

She went to tug out her last knot of head hair and slip some of it into my hand.

I stayed her hand and patted Loser, sloughing off a handful of his instead. "He's good currency," I said. "Look after him until I get back."

She blinked at me, unsure of what to say. "If youse come back."

"I might need you to help some others. Keep a watch over Splitty's. If you see some people come out of there that aren't from around here, show them how to be safe until I get back to you," I said.

She rolled her eyes. "More like you?"

I grinned. "I've been told there's *no one* like me."

I wasted precious time finding someone who'd trade for a Zippo and information. As the day got old, I risked food and water from one vendor on Glida's recommended list. The water swelled my tongue again, but my stomach toughed the food despite its peculiar taste. That was one puzzle I hadn't solved. How did they get food in this place?

As far as I could tell nothing came in from the rest of The Tert, which left Fishertown bay.

After I'd eaten I found my way back to Splitty's. The python still hung from the doorway, flies buzzing, mouth in mortis as the afternoon switched to evening.

Tears stung my eyelids and I pushed down a resurgence of misery. I sent a mental plea for forgiveness to the snake—along with a picture of some serious arse kicking.

Then I marched into Splitty's, a knife carelessly loose.

I stood in the middle of the room with my back to the bar. "Who killed the python?" I demanded.

Most of the patrons turned their backs. A couple headed for the door. I hustled over to stop them.

"No one leaves until I know who killed the python."

"What's it to you?" said the barkeep. I saw him whispering into his bio-comm. How long until the Twitchers came? No turning back now.

"What about it?" A thickset man at a table, tattooed like the kids in the alley. Pig-faced and belligerent.

He wasn't the only one. Belligerent didn't get close to describing my mood.

"Take the python down and bury it," I told him.

He turned his head away and kept on drinking.

"TAKE IT DOWN!"

He slammed his beaker on the table. "Fuck you."

In two steps I was on him, letting his blood. I forced him from his chair and across to the door.

The rest of the bar froze into uncertainty. Who was I? What would I do? Everyone waited for someone else to act. I kicked the door open and yanked his hand up high on the frame. Then I stabbed the dagger into it with all the force of my anger. He hung there, crucified by one hand and still screaming.

Not a good feeling, eh, scud?

In minutes, glistening-naked Twitchers swarmed the bar.

I busted outside, using my logged memory of Glida's knowledge to lead them on an elaborate chase. Several times I doubled back over their heads, climbing in and out of attic cut-thrus. They got easily confused, sparking fights amongst themselves.

An hour or more of exhaustive dodging and I circled back using another of Glida's cut-thrus to get back into the ceiling at Splitty's. With steady hands I disabled the movement detectors, smashing the heat sensor into shards against a beam with the butt of the Gurkha. I let myself down through the manhole and into the corridor. Half a dozen steps to the closet and I was in the cellar.

Like a berserker I kicked the stills over and unscrewed every keg until the place was awash with grog.

Then I scrambled up to the hatch. This time it was wide open. Moonlight spilled in. Half a dozen Twitchers had climbed through in a hurry.

One hadn't.

I catapulted straight into her arms—a close-up of a savagely hormonal face, down to the wildly dilating pupils, pussing acne and a gaping, ugly neck jack. Ike's army came complete with anger, skin complaints and programming plug. But something was wrong.

I tilted my headband down the length of her body. Her genitals were grossly overdeveloped and her muscle mass was huge. As if someone had flicked the puberty-on button and jammed it.

She banged my thigh with her shok for peeking.

My leg buckled, but I compensated. When she moved to shove it into my stomach I was quicker, and much, *much* madder.

I brought the flat side of the Gurkha's blade around, a semi open-shouldered swing that should have knocked her unconscious. All it did was send the knife ricocheting out of my hands, clanging into something nearby.

A fast squint spotted the outline of a quadrulma with outsized mudguards and alloy wheels shining, parked against the wall. Just like the one outside Chez Nutter.

The Twitcher staggered backwards but steadied, a stupid grin on her face. I'd given her my best whack and she was laughing. My strength came from hard work and some good genes and the occasional use of stim; hers had to be from a total endocrine jack-up.

I couldn't beat that.

She uttered a guttural, totally meaningless sound, which I interpreted as *Now it's your turn, baby.*

I jumped away as the first punch came, but it caught me on the jaw, slamming me hard into the wall near the hatch.

Somehow I stayed on my feet. I fumbled for the Zippo.

Back inside the cellar I could hear the cavalry slopping about in the grog. Splitty's bar would remember my visit for a while. Not only had I staked a regular to the doorframe, I'd also smashed up the booze cellar. There wasn't much worse in the Big Country than a pub with no beer.

I ignited and jammed the Zippo and dropped it back through the hatch, flattening against the wall as flames spouted out and engulfed the Twitcher.

The taste of burning flesh clogged my airways as I vaulted onto the quad-runna and gunned it.

The glow lit my way towards the buildings.

As the wind cooled my skin, I started to come down from my fit of rage. The aftermath left me distressed at what I'd just done and more than a little horny.

It was better than the numbness of the last day.

Whatever the next few hours brought, I just hoped I didn't end up alone anywhere with Daac.

I knew he was still alive. The sky hadn't fallen.

Not to say that it wouldn't.

Which led me on to Ike's private army. Was their age and hormones their only qualification?

And what the hell had he done to them?

I gave up brain-straining over it and took up eye-balling what was out ahead of me. The outcrop of buildings I was coming up on was ringed by a smooth, glistening expanse that could have been a lake.

The buildings looked neglected—dilapidated roofs, buckled window frames, rusted pylons, and above it all a huge darkened canopy. Underneath one end of the canopy stood the litter of small rectangular objects that resembled statues.

Light seeped sideways from one of the buildings and like a suicidal moth I winged towards it. The sweat that drenched me set off a shivering fit. My neck prickled with the possibility that other Twitchers might jump me.

As I reached the glistening lake, a musty smell wafted my way. It made me want to sneeze. I reined in the quad near the edge and examined the surface. It was coated in a mottled, vaguely luminescent, dry mold. Quad and 'ped marks crisscrossed everywhere, declaring earlier traffic and a solid base. It gave me confidence to nose a wheel out. The mold filaments crunched like thin ice, but the quad's tracks gripped on to something hard underneath. I revved up and shot out onto it amongst the crazy confusion of old tracks. As I threaded between the eerie maze of statues, I noticed that the front of each one had broken plas panels and defunct displays. Some even had hoses attached like long, flexible arms.

What in the freaking Wombat were they?

I got as close to the lit building as I dared before I powered down the quad and settled it snugly in behind a statue. Boots crunching, it took me a lifetime to creep the rest of the way, and another to decide the building was empty and safe to enter.

The door was unlocked. Obviously Ike was short on uninvited guests.

It took me moments to comprehend what was inside. Hundreds—thousands—of petri dishes growing cultures sat on rows of old supermarket shelves. I threaded amongst them, whispering the labels aloud.

" 'Zygo-my-cota,' 'Bas-idio-mycota,' 'Asco-my-cota.' " I didn't need the sci-speak to know they were fungus: brilliant but creepy colors and textures.

A popping noise drew me to the back, where I

found a bank of upright refrijerators containing vats brimming full of viscous muck, each with a skin across the top like two-month-old hummus.

The frij labels read "Pysarum polychephalum."

What had Monts called it? Crawl.

Voices suddenly interrupted my snoop. Two figures entered and stopped by the first row of shelves. One began checking the dishes.

I dropped down behind the last row of shelves and peeped along the aisle.

"—set fire to one of the bars," said a male voice. "I can't spare you any more people. I've got a drop coming in."

That had to be Ike.

"What if it's Plessis?"

Tulu! I could see enough to know.

The maybe-Ike figure straightened up and swiveled towards her. He wore magnifying glasses. Not just shades. The real thing! I mean nobody wore optical glasses anymore. Nobody *made* glasses—corrections were as easy as scoring painkill or Lark. And shades were used only for . . . style.

Beneath his glasses I imagined rather than saw a set of wide, crazy eyes. His body was encased in a top-shelf, matte-black exoskeleton. I'd heard about them, dreamed about them; never seen one. They bulked you up; gave enhanced endurance, speed and recovery.

A fine black web grew out of the back of the suit and attached into his neck and bald head. Color coordinated wetware. His head looked like an exorcism—his body looked like a graphic novel. He reminded me of someone, but I couldn't quite nail it.

"Yes, Plessis," he observed. "Why this obsession with her?"

"I admit an interest. And so should you. According to the Chino she's the only one able to resist the change."

Mei! Wait till I get the scrawny little— But Tulu hadn't finished.

"I have other reasons, though. Plessis may be useful barter. I've tried to get to her before, but she's crudely unpredictable. She has a lot of people watching her back. In the end it seemed simpler to get her and Loyl Daac to hunt me."

"I'm impressed by your thinking. But what does an erratic hothead like Plessis offer as barter?" Ike picked up and gently handled the top of a dish. "She's what you might call sociopathic trash."

I swallowed hard at the personality analysis and leaned farther out into the aisle, risking discovery. This I had to hear.

"Let's just say I have to have her. You understand?" She picked up a dish and rattled it.

"Put it back," he said coldly. "I don't tolerate blackmail. Besides, now that I have Daac she'll come for him. Anna tells me they have a . . . bond of sorts."

A bond? With Loyl Daac? I wanted to shriek. Eavesdropping was more mind-blowing than any trip. *And who was Anna?*

I moved back behind the rack to let out a deep, indignant breath. Too deep. A set of aluminium dishes clanged against each other.

"Someone's in here?"

"It's the frij," said maybe-Ike. "The *polychephalum* are stretching its ability to cool."

"Why do you have to keep the filthy stuff cold anyway?"

"It reproduces rapidly above fifteen degrees. That's why it's so effective as a containment field if you possess the dispersion emulsion or some way of cooling it."

I could almost hear his voice shine with pride. The devil was a geek.

"What did you want with Daac?" Tulu's question sounded casual but I could tell it was far from that.

"He's the Cabal's heir apparent. His contacts go deep into Viva. I can't risk him upsetting my projects. You see, he's the one who commissioned Anna to do the original research when he realized some of the inhabitants of the Fishertown slums were displaying immunity to the heavy metals. He knew what he was doing when he involved her. Her intellectual pedigree is impeccable. But she can be so . . . unimaginative."

Schaum! She's alive. And she's here? The two thoughts simultaneously elated and depressed me. I peeked around the shelving again.

"What will you do with him? Didn't the Cabal run you out of The Tertiary?"

"You *are* informed." Ike's exoskel practically swelled in reaction to his anger. "You say you want Plessis as barter. I wish to use the Cabal's prince for the same purposes. But it can wait until she's taken the bait."

"If I don't get her, our agreement will be at risk."

Maybe-Ike studied her hard, as if he didn't trust her. "I am allowing you the use of equipment and a trouble-free environment to work in. So far I have seen very little return on my investment. You put me at risk with my providers."

"I brought you Loyl Daac. My primary end is fulfilled. As for the other matters, I need Plessis and I need time."

"Anna has nearly finished her contamination process on the Trophins. I'll send more of them out for Plessis—after the drop. Meanwhile, stay out of sight. If you are seen, *our* arrangement will be fatal for *you.*"

Finished contaminating what?

"Keep your promise to me. I know a lot of people." Tulu's voice lowered to a dangerous timbre. She raised a threatening hand to him but he batted it away with a wheeze of his skel.

The air filled with the sound of heavy blade traffic just as I thought they might hurt each other.

Shame.

"It's here." He turned and walked out.

Tulu stayed behind. She ranged down through the shelves, bringing her closer to me.

I crept across to the nearest frij door and slipped in between two vats, squeezing behind them, hoping she couldn't pick out my chattering teeth from the indigestion of my gelatinous companions.

She stopped and stared into each frij cabinet as if she could sense something.

I willed myself to think serene thoughts. Like how I would like to stick her potion pouch down her throat and tape her mouth and nose up. Choking to death was memorable.

She uttered some words I couldn't hear and sprinkled a pinch of something from her pouch.

I suddenly wanted to run out past her. It came on me as an intense, unquenchable craving. In desperation I pressed my body hard against the steel of the vat. My muscles bucked and twitched but my flesh stuck where it contacted the freezing metal, and the sensation short-circuited the compulsion.

I felt rather than saw her go—the draining aftermath of her voodoo.

Cursing and crying, I peeled my skin off the vat and crawled out of the frij. It wasn't until I thumped the circulation back into my legs with the backs of my bleeding hands that I realized I'd picked up a passenger.

A dribble of PP suckered enthusiastically at my ankle. I pulled out the Cabal dagger and sliced it clean off, along with a hunk of my pants. It fell to the floor and writhed.

With a shudder I made for the door. All I wanted to do was go home, but I still had to find Daac and the shamans.

And now there was the small matter of Anna Schaum. This was where Lang had brought her.

Lucky grrl.

My toes itched. If there was one person in this whole goddamn world I desired to put the fear of all things bad into, it was that little babe. Looks like I needn't have bothered; she'd done it herself.

The quad was where I'd left it, and I gunned across to the next building, hoping the noise of the 'copts landing covered the engine.

Outside, the near-full moon hung behind a dross of gray cloud, leaving a dull illumination. I re-parked the quad and in my hurry to get under cover tripped over the concrete lip and crashed against the doorjamb.

It would have been nice to lie there, maybe sort my love life out, but the moon was only a night off being full. No shamans by tomorrow night, no cure.

Seemed like everyone had plans for King Tide.

I got up and wobbled inside.

The door sucked shut behind me, climate con-trolled, cool and dry, belying its dilapidated facade.

Squinting around, I wished I had nightsight aug-mentation. I could see less in here than outside, so I found a wall and shuffled along it. I'd made it a few meters down the west side when I tripped a light sensor.

A section of the building blanched into surreal shadows. I took me moments to make sense of it— the surfeit of fancy metals, hydraulics, molds, tables of 'tronics all in catalogued order. Around the edge of them sat tanks of human body parts, tissue parts and other organic bits and blobs. Dotted among the tables were small aquariums—lots and lots, containing the weirdest, most inert fish I'd ever seen.

They say reality bites! Well, this reality bit, chewed, gobbled and hawked. I'd found Ike's shop of post-human lunacy.

It shouldn't have been such a surprise. I mean,

I'd met the ma'soops. I'd got close and personal with the Twitcher army. I'd already witnessed plenty of his walking leftovers. But something about seeing the raw materials assembled under-neath one roof was like opening the garbage on the butcher's off-cuts.

Vomit burned the back of my throat. I ducked to the nearest window and pressed my nose against it to stop the spin.

Outside a legion of unmarked cargo 'copts had settled on a brilliantly lit slab. Twitchers climbed about their gizzards, unloading crates of all shapes: long flat boxes of weapons, chillers of foodstuffs. I now knew how Mo-Vay's punters were getting their food and probably everything else that kept this sick little burb fermenting along.

I also knew that for once my timing was immacu-late. It would be all hands on deck while the drop was on. Hopefully the Twitchers would be kept busy while I finished my snoop.

I peered along to the other end of the slab. A UL sat there, composed and at home—the same one I'd seen at the water park.

And next to it a Prier.

Pieces of information played tag in my head. I wanted to sit right where I was and have a first-rate cog, but behind me someone moaned.

I hit the floor. A punter was in trouble, but that didn't mean he was on my side.

I crabbed underneath the workbenches, racing the sound until the moans got louder. Peering through coils of wiring, I saw clear-plas partitions.

I crept along, peering through them until I found

the moaner under lights, strapped on to a surgical table.

Loyl!

He was naked apart from bedfilm, and the hussy in my heart beat an excited tattoo. "Loyl?" I whispered.

No answer.

I tore the partition aside, charged over to him and began loosening the immobilizers. The one that adhered his hands to the inside of his thighs gave me some trouble. I tried not to look.

In truth though, I was more worried whether he was still paralyzed.

As I pared away the last restraint, he opened his eyes. Blinking once, he rolled sideways and kneed me hard in the crotch.

Call it shock, but I staggered, straightened and punched him right back.

The momentum of my hit knocked him onto the floor. He got up slowly.

I didn't help.

"What the freak was that for?" I whispered fiercely, cupping my pubic bone.

He held his jaw with a shaky hand and flashed me a look of relief. "One sure way to know if it was you."

My breath caught in my chest. That could mean only one thing. *Shape-changers.*

"Brilliant timing for once, Parrish."

Hadn't I just been telling myself that? "Why so?"

He gestured to a robotic arm with a thermal scalpel attached. "They've been prepping me for a total skin strip. Seems they wanted to take my skin off in layers. Some heavy copter traffic started up and suddenly they all disappeared."

I flung back the plas partition and looked squeamishly out at the aquariums with the strange floppy fish.

Not fish . . . but skin.

"There's a supply drop going on outside. Mainly weapons, by the look of it. We've probably got a bit longer," I said. "What is this place?"

He ineptly tried to make a sarong out of the bedfilm.

I slipped my pack off my back and fished around inside. One pair of fatigues and a tee left. I didn't turn away as he squeezed into them.

The tee was too short and left his stomach bare, but I could live with that.

He talked fast. "It's the old depot. Where the 'gineering factories got their fuel. The underground is littered with huge fuel storage tanks. The dirt was so toxic here even the villa developers didn't dare build on it. They walled it off instead."

"Some secret garden, eh?" I muttered.

He gave me a funny look and shrugged. "He's converted the buildings to a bunch of labs."

I whistled under my breath. "Seems to be the thing."

"Yeah, and this makes it easy." He pointed to a humming machine with a perceptible haze over it. "It spits motes into the air. With them you can create a sterile environment on a two-day-old corpse. Any science geek with enough money can set up."

My gaze ranged over the host of mobile modules wedged between tabletops. They resembled kitchen appliances but their labels read "autoclave," "centrifuge," "thermal cycler" and "spectrophotometer."

"This is more than pocket money."

He rifled through a neatly stacked shelf under the bed and grabbed a derm. Checking the label, he whacked himself with it. "Someone from outside's propping up a mini economy here."

"Yeah, I figured that." I twisted nervously towards the door. "What else?"

"The loon who runs this show calls himself Ike. I think I know him or at least . . . know who he was. Used to call himself Wombat, among other names."

"Mr. Microwave!" Amazing how the real wackos always survived.

"Yeah. He was *the man* when I was a kid. His cult was pretty big here. It died out when he supposedly did—but somehow his name stuck. He used to have a saying. Something like 'evolve or eff off.' I didn't go for it anyway."

"You wouldn't need anyone else's religion. You've got your own brand," I threw back at him over my shoulder. Call me dogmatic, but I just couldn't let a chance go by on that particular topic.

He ignored me. "Where's Tulu?"

"She's with him. They've got some deal going between them which included suckering you and me to the happy house of horrors." I pointed out of the cubicle to the far end and another set of doors. "What's through there?"

He brushed past and wrenched a two-handled pincer from a tray of evil-looking instruments. "Let's find out."

I squeezed between tables after him. "There's something you should know. I overheard Ike talking to Tulu."

"And?"

"Anna Schaum is alive. Here."

He stopped dead and turned. I watched a play of emotions flicker across his face: pleasure, satisfaction and relief.

How did she warrant that when all I got was a kick in the crotch?

"If she's here, then there's a chance the splicing codes are as well."

My mood lifted with a jolt. Had the Cabal known that? I wondered.

"So we just have to find her and Mei." *And the* karadji. "Give Tulu a hiding, then get past the Twitchers and the hell out of here."

He glanced at me. "Twitchers? You mean the teens? He—Ike—is bringing them in from supercity quods and mucking with their hormones. His idea is to prolong and augment puberty. Something to do with the release of gonadotrophin. Gets some fierce results if you want aggression." He smiled grimly. "You'd understand all about prolonged puberty."

Snap, matey. But before I could get all snarky, he held a finger to his lips and gestured me on.

We crept down a long corridor that linked buildings, through three sets of heavy plas partitions and up to what looked like soundproof doors.

Daac cracked them open enough and scoped two

Twitchers lounging nearby. One was squeezing her skin lesions. The other mimed humping Anna Schaum as she bent over a scrub station.

I knew her from the blemish on her face. It stood out starkly under the lights, like a mask. Other than that she was unrecognizable, worn dangerously thin. Her blond hair hung clumped and matted and her body sagged in the manner of someone who'd rather be dead.

She finished her scrub and collapsed onto the makeshift cot next to the trough. Alongside that a mockoff jug and a pile of used foam trays were stacked on a microwave. Looked like she hadn't been doing a lot of sightseeing or restaurants.

Daac's arm muscles flexed and trembled in anger. I forced myself to stay next to him when all I wanted to do was move to stop his skin touching mine.

My line of sight drifted across the room. I grabbed Daac's shoulder, the touch of his flesh suddenly forgotten.

Rows of warm, horizontal bodies lay before us.
Shamans.

He moved before I knew what he was doing—a couple of steps and he whacked the zit-squeezer across the back of the head with the pincers and stabbed her in the chest.

It didn't take her out. She buckled and recovered, jerking a spear up from her side.
Shite.

I was a second behind him, garroting wire whipping the air. I sliced her hand to the bone before she could impale Loyl.

With a foot to her chest he yanked the pincers free and jabbed them down her open, outraged mouth. They missed the spine and pierced straight through the back of her neck.

No, Loyl, don't . . .

He turned away, but I copped the spurt of blood in the face followed by the tidal wave of nausea that sent the world spinning.

Blood . . .

The other Twitcher bellowed with rage. I swiped my vision clear as he threw his spear and ducked but it was Daac who took it in the side.

Anna Schaum screamed.

I fumbled for a knife and chucked it.

It caught the second Twitcher in the shoulder. He barely noticed it as he dropped and charged me. Somewhere between Anna Schaum's coffee table and the nearest shaman body, he *changed*.

Just like Jamon had. Only this was from human to . . . not so human . . .

Beastlike. Unexplainable.

Terrible.

I felt automatically for the Cabal knife and met him head on. The thump jarred every part of me. As I bounced sideways, I stabbed the Cabal dagger into his abdomen, right about the adrenals. The Twitcher flopped backwards over one of shamans, dead. He regained human form as he hung there.

I went under again with appalling relief that I hadn't killed an innocent teen.

There are many of us here now. Many, many, so many . . . we disseminate . . .

It was absurdly quiet when I came out of it.
Then Daac moaned.

Schaum spread over him like an epidemic, sponging the blood away, padding up his wounds, derming him with painkiller, kissing his face and whispering, "I knew you would come" over and over.

What, no thanks for Parrish?

I got up slowly and turned my back on them, repelled by the tender reunion. Hauling the dead Twitcher off the shaman, I retrieved my knives and wiped them clean, giving my hands time to steady. The shaman had a cobweb of bio-ware feeding from a device that led across into her skull. Her eyes rolled constantly under her lids. Tiny whimpers escaped worried lips. Whatever the hell she was hooked up to was sticking pins into her while she dreamed.

I glanced back at Daac, questions tripping over themselves to pass my lips, and saw him pushing Schaum aside to get up and search among the unconscious bodies.

"Mei's here," he said.

I stumbled to the scrub station and sluiced myself down, then I started searching for faces as well. *Karadji* faces.

I met Daac somewhere in the middle of the room. Bruises were beginning to color his skin and he hunched, favoring the spear wound. His eyes, though, glittered like ruin.

"What are they using them for, Anna?"

Schaum came to his side and rubbed her weary eyes. Her face was pale beyond pallor. Darkness was tattooed in and under her eyes. I had no time for her, but I understood the depth of her exhaustion.

"Ike—h-he thinks *this* is post-humanism. He's brilliant and passionate about it but he's . . ." She trailed off as if she couldn't find the words to explain herself.

"Crazy?" I offered.

"No," she insisted. "Misguided. The animal woman is crazy. She believes she's harvesting neurochemicals."

Misguided? Her defense of Ike told me something. They'd gotten to know each other well. Too well. I understood the darkness in her eyes. I'd carried the same look when Jamon was alive, but Anna had gone one step further.

"Neurochemicals?" I asked.

"She thinks if she can distill the chemical essence of their spiritualism—the alpha waves—and infuse it, it will make her a more powerful shaman. The bio-ware is analyzing and sweeping their blood while they're in a trance state. It's rubbish but he's indulging her because she promised him some things."

"What things?"

She looked at Loyl. "You for one. But there's more. Ike is being paid to contaminate the Tertiary sector. They want the whole place infected with this . . . discovery we made. In return for spreading it, he continues to get what he needs to run this place."

"Tulu's one of them?"

"No. I—I don't think so. I think she's working

for someone else who wants what Ike knows.
There's some kind of struggle going on in Viva. Ike
is smart. He knows that. I think he's trying to play
both sides."

Hearing my suspicions so brutally confirmed was
in no way consoling.

"Who are they—who wants to contaminate The
Tert?"

She shrugged as though it wasn't important, as
though she didn't care or know, her eyes on the
shamans.

"I tried to make them comfortable," she said in
the drained voice of someone who'd long forgotten
any reason for ethics.

"What about them?" I gestured to the dead
Twitchers.

"You know they can't think for themselves. He's
mutated their cognitive functions and he's got them
wired for his simple, direct orders. They were normal enough when they got here. Just criminals—"

I interrupted her before the crack in her voice
got any wider.

"What have *you* done to them?" I asked.

"He forced me to . . . I've put them through
the same process as our original trial group. The
change . . . it starts with something piggybacking
on the polmayse messenger. I've never encountered
its like." She spoke only to Loyl now, as though I
wasn't there.

"Is it alien?" he asked.

Her eyes widened with a fascinated horror. "I—
I don't know how to explain it. It's definitely para-
sitic," she said slowly. "It constructs another set of

DNA and then causes the body to flood with an immunosuppressant to survive the changeover. The pituitary becomes hyperstimulated and the hormonal release is astounding. It shouldn't be possible, Loyl, but I've seen it."

"I know," he said flatly. "So have I."

"So all the Twitchers are infected?" I could hear my voice edging to hysterical.

Loyl grabbed Anna by the shoulders and shook her. "Where's our data?" he demanded.

His self-interest in the face of her revelations made me sick.

"Here." She pointed to a small bank of hardware on a tabletop. "We can take it but I can't access any of it without him knowing. He's got an identical set of data in his exoskel's processor and wireless connection between the two. While he's alive and in the skel, he can destroy this set and retain his own."

"While he's alive . . ." Daac echoed.

His face said the rest.

Schaum blinked and looked at me properly for the first time. She shuddered. "Everyone we trialed the splices on will suffer the change. You weren't one of the original group, yet the Chino shaman says you carry the parasite."

I nodded. "I swallowed the blood of someone who'd already changed."

"That would explain—" She looked quickly at Loyl to satisfy herself she had cleaned him well enough.

"Can you reverse what you've done?" I interrupted.

She blinked again, this time with a spark of clinical interest. "Not once the change has occurred. For you, though, maybe gene silencing is a possibility. Or even gene replacement. Although the fact that ingested blood is the transmitter makes it likely that it is too late . . ."

I tuned out the rest of her speech. *Options.* I just needed to know there were options—otherwise everything changed.

I turned my attention to why shivers had begun to turnstile down my body.

Daac noticed too. "What is it? What's wrong?"

I dashed spittle from my mouth, unable to put it into words.

The door crashed wide and a 'Terro came for us like sudden death.

Chapter Twelve

Daac let go a wholly animal moan. I didn't hold it against him; he'd been tortured by meks before. He grabbed me so hard against him I thought he was going to say something sexy.

"You deal with it," he gasped.

Wrong. Wrong. Wrong.

I didn't know who I was more pissed off at—me for hoping for something, or him for saying the wrong thing—but I tackled the 'Terro low, right on its knee, aiming to buckle its knee actuators and cripple it.

It toppled onto me.

"Go on then, get outta here!" I gasped from underneath it.

Why was I doing this?

Even worse, he didn't need a second invitation, disappearing out of the door, dragging his precious medic along.

I wrenched my leg free from the 'Terro and

rolled away, but it caught me in a bear hug as I scrambled after them toward the door. I pitched forward deliberately, tumbling us both onto the floor, and clawed at every protrusion, stabbing my fingers into its camera sockets.

It couldn't get upright without letting me go. When it did, I rolled away on an explosion of adrenaline.

I was on my feet and lunging for the door again when it got me.

Crap! Crap! Crap!

It bundled me under its arm and stalked through the maze of shaman zombies, dumping me next to something labeled "chemical analyzer" and resembling a fancy still.

With any luck I'd get mainlined with tequila.

As it strapped me down, Leesa Tulu's face filled my vision. I wanted to smack her satisfaction away.

"Why do you want me?" I demanded.

"You'll work that out for yourself . . . eventually. Meanwhile I get to play with the rest of you—"

I didn't hear it all. The 'Terro slammed a mask over my face. A fine dust invaded my lungs.

Smart dust.

Reporting on my vitals. I tried not to breathe it. Useless, I knew. But hey . . .

Hot pinpricks of flesh-questing bio-ware pierced my skull. The real world ceased to exist.

It wasn't like waking up. More like dreaming just under the surface of wakefulness. I could see and think but had a nagging feeling there was more to it.

And what could I see?

Nothing comfortable or familiar, just blur.

For how long?

Slowly my focus sharpened.

Campfire. Flames licked in shadow tongues across low, dense scrub. Starless night sky. A solitary figure sat cross-legged, sucking a pipe. Rainbow skirt, scarlet headscarf, jackboots, junky bling.

Marinette wishes to mount you. Leesa Tulu raised a jealous gaze to me. *She likes your flavor.*

"What are you about?" I shouted.

She flung an arm wide. *She believes you to be a stronger host than these.*

I squinted into the dark, to the scrub perimeter. A circle of translucent figures stood inside the bushes. I'd looked straight past them before. Dim outlines of bodies with faded visages and subdued, pulsing lights within. As I stared longer, I somehow knew them. I sensed the *karadji* emanating their hot, earth-red light. With each pulse they faded a little.

Scanning quickly, I recognized others—all shamans. One I knew better than the rest. Mei's light pulsed an angry orange, bright and defiant alongside diminished grays and browns.

Instinctively I looked down at myself. My being flowed violet beneath my gaze with the energy of an electrical storm.

Spiritual essence. Tulu tongued her upper lip. *Eau-de-life.*

Anger shot through me, translating into a streak of brilliant red amongst the throbbing violet. I felt undressed, utterly transparent. With that thought came a pink flush.

I glanced nervously towards Tulu but her eyes had glazed over, shining in the firelight. Her body began to twitch, arms flapping like bird wings. Her head rocked unnaturally on her neck. She hooted and cawed. I heard drums without seeing them.

Marinette was coming.

The night sky spun, the campfire distorted. I found myself pulled to the outside of the circle to take my place amongst the other shaman.

Get out of here! the Eskaalim commanded.

Coherency faded. I felt my self-control ebb and let out an almighty roar. *"Mei!"*

Across the circle Mei's fiery orange light contracted into a tight ball like a collapsing sun. With a ferocious tenacity it began to enlarge. I reached out for her, desperately arcing my energy like a supernova, plundering the boundaries of her psyche. Our mingled essences skittered around the circle, empowering the others. An explosion rendered me into a thousand shards of light. I tasted tea with sugar. And thought how "enemy" was a relative word.

This time I did wake, hiccupy, but in a reality I knew and at this moment loved. My entire body burned on the inside, a fire that wove through my muscles and flamed along my blood. I breathed lightly for fear of fanning it.

"Be quiet and drink this."

The voice was raspy and low, but I knew it.

I opened my eyes. Loyl Daac. His face was blotched with lesions. The only time I'd seen him less than wonderful. Part of me wanted to cheer. Another part bemoaned the loss of perfection.

Next to him stood Mei Sheong looking like two-week-old chow mein.

He freed her first! Next thought: *How long has it been?*

"Where's Tulu?" I managed.

"Hurry. Anna's detaching the others."

I didn't like his tone. "You've done something?"

He nodded. "I burned some things."

"What about the vats in the frijs?"

"Uh-uh. I cut the power supply and opened the doors. They should burn too."

I shook my head, knowing that didn't sound right. "I don't think you should—"

But he'd already moved away to join Schaum.

"You're one careless piece of work, Plessis." Mei bore down on me before I could pursue it. "You could have killed us all. You breach another sha-man's boundary like that and their spirit leaks away. No spirit. No person. It's called death, Parrish."

"Oh," was all I could offer. "So what happened?"

"Tulu invoked a bitch loa, but the loa was angry because her sacrifices weren't what she wanted. Marinette likes her chickens plucked alive. She wanted to mount you instead but you slammed her." Mei's whisper held a trace of awe.

"I slammed a loa?"

"I helped," she added sullenly. "Tulu got distracted by something. It gave your guides the chance to show us the way back."

"My guides?"

"Yeah, you got three of them. You had some scrawny dograt thing and a python. There was one other but I couldn't see it properly. Most of us get only one guide. How come you're so lucky?"

Lucky? I didn't think that was the word for it, but relief swamped for no good reason. Maybe Loser and the python had forgiven me after all. Except, of course, I didn't believe in that crap.

Around me shamans were sitting up, starting to help each other. I pried a cup of water from Mei's fingers, swallowed some and smothered a cough as it went down the wrong way. I wanted to ask Daac how long I'd been here, but he was bent over bodies in the middle of the room, his thigh rubbing against Schaum.

I stood and staggered a little. The stink of unwashed bodies—including mine—made me gag. My knees wouldn't bend when I told them to, nor would my back straighten properly. I felt at least two thousand years old.

I lurched over to the happy couple as they stood reviving the four *karadji*. The Cabal shamans lay head to toe like body batteries. I looked into their faces to memorize them.

Two of them were muscular and lean, indistinguishable from the Cabal warriors except for an absence of scars on their faces and torsos. A third, older one gasped softly as if he was having trouble breathing. The three were naked aside from filthy denim cutoffs. The fourth, though, was overweight and flabby, like the soft, city cousin come to visit. He even wore the remnants of an expensive three-piece and sneakers.

Daac spoke to them in a dialect I couldn't understand. Telling them what he wanted them to know—that they owed him their souls, no doubt.

I sat by the older, gasping one and held the cup to his lips.

He took a sip and moistened his cracked lips. "You burned like the sun," he whispered.

"No," I corrected. "That was Mei." I pointed to her.

He dismissed my reply with a steady blink over opaque, aged pupils. "She is strong, that one. But *you* . . . glowed like . . . creation."

Loyl glanced sharply at me and I looked away. I did *not* want to have this sort of conversation. Not now. Not ever. *Ever!* Oya was bad enough. *Creation.* Euchh! What a word.

The old *karadji*'s hollowed cheeks quivered. "You must help us in the battle."

Battle? Deep inside I felt the Eskaalim strengthen on that word. I laid the old *karadji* down and moved away from yet another conversation I did not want to have.

Schaum began handing out glucose tabs and fluids. Daac hurried her along.

I itched to cut and run. My choices had multiplied and I didn't know which way to jump. It left me restless. I sidled closer to the flat stack of hardware and ran over my options again.

Should I bolt with the stack and risk Ike nuking the lot when I tried to access the data? Or should

I help get Schaum out of here and trust Daac to help me? What about my deal with the Cabal? Could *they* be trusted to meet their promise now the information was in Daac's hands?

My head hurt with the frustration of not knowing the answer to anything. I moved away from the stack and went and grabbed a handful of glucose tabs from Schaum.

"I'll scout out some transport," I told them.

Mei gave me the narrow-eyed treatment. "You gonna split now, I s'pose?"

I rewarded her with pure Parrish belligerence. "If it suits." I had no intention of it, but Mei—like Loyl—brought out the worst in me.

"You know them?" She nodded over at the *karadji*.

"Do you?"

"Don't mess with them, Parrish. They suck wannabes like you up through a straw."

I tried to keep my voice down, but it had its own ideas. "And I got some advice for you . . ."

She cocked a smudged eyebrow.

"Don't mess with *me*. I skin backstabbers."

OK, OK, so we had some old issues. And this wasn't the time. It's never the time for issues. They just sometimes force their ugly way to the top. Like scum floating out of a sewerage outlet.

Or was the fact that Loyl kept rubbing his hand across Schaum's back the reason for my aggro?

Mei's eyes glittered. I could see her casting around for a weapon. Maybe she had a bit of her own anger displacement going on as well.

"This is about Loyl, isn't it? You want him," she said in a shrill whisper.

"No. This is about something much more precious. Trust. You sold me out, Mei. Back in the beginning and now—"

She leapt, hissing like a mad cat, claws extended.

I flicked her away with one heavy swipe, but she was back a second later. We grappled, crashing over cots.

She scratched me under the eye. As I recoiled, she pounced, wrapping herself around my throat and shoulders. We lay together on the floor locked in an untidy impasse.

A furious voice interrupted. "Parrish, you'll bring them!"

I craned my neck to see Daac. "Get—her—off me," I rasped.

He obliged, scooping Mei up like she was a kitten, and with the other arm steering Anna, he headed towards the door. They both instantly cuddled into him and I wanted to chop them all into little pieces.

"Enemy" is such a relative word.

Twitchers materialized before he could get through the door. They jumped him, knocking Mei and Schaum from his arms.

He tripped one up but another whacked a shok against his ribs.

As Daac went into muscle spasm I sprang up from the floor. The Twitcher bared his teeth and beckoned me with the rod like it was candy. I nodded, smiled, stepped over Loyl and threw the Cabal knife from point blank. He keeled over at my feet.

Stop, Parrish.

The command was a thought, not spoken. Behind

me the *karadji* had fanned out in a line, crouching on unsteady legs, chanting.

The Twitchers circled them, becoming submissive as the strength of the chanting increased. One by one they sat down, tranced like they'd jacked cold into one of Irene's neurostims. Schaum scrambled into action, whacking each one of them with all the seds she could lay her hands on.

"That's a handy tune." I knelt down next to Loyl. "Where are the rest of them?"

"They are all that's left," he said. "Ike's gone. The invasion's begun."

I beat everyone to the door. Outside it was dusk. I couldn't see the veiling grid but something told me it was down. The air smelled different. Fewer ions. The pad was empty of 'copts. Even the UL and the Prier had gone. A huge full moon was rising. I'd lost too much time coupled to Tulu's juice extractor.

"By morning it will be King Tide. This place will no longer be safe," pronounced one of the *karadji*.

Daac pushed alongside me into the doorway, leaning on Mei and Schaum. They weren't exactly adequate as a prop for someone his size—but I wasn't offering. His body still tremored but his eyes were hooded, almost like an attack of fanaticism but not quite, because I also glimpsed fear. When Daac really went off, there was no fear. Only belief.

"What is it? What invasion?" My heart pumped like a hydraulic ram.

"The Cabal have come to take back the Heart."

Chapter Thirteen

That was it! Enough!

I thumped Daac on the chest. "Outside, Loyl—you and me."

Outside was the three-by-three concrete lip that served as a doorstep, but I hauled him out there and slammed the door in the others' faces.

"Make it quick, Parrish."

"That depends on what you've got to say. First a room full of freakshow. Next a room full of spirit-sucked shamans. And then there's the small matter of a 'Terro being here. Now the Cabal are the newest breed of colonials. Which bit aren't you telling me?"

I watched his face twitch as he sifted through what he would reveal. At this stage I'd take anything. "The Cabal used you."

I let out a snort of disgust. "Something I *don't* know would be better."

"They needed a distraction to buy time, but

when Tulu kidnapped Mei and injured Sto, it got personal for me. I couldn't stand back and wait."

"What I don't get is how you know what the Cabal are thinking and doing. You're an outcast." *Yet hadn't Ike called him the heir apparent?*

This time he did smile.

Despite everything, I felt like my insides had been X-rayed.

"You look for a straight line through life, Parrish. There isn't one. The cord that binds us is cut and knotted in many places. You can't be part of something like the Cabal and then not. It's a family."

At last he'd admitted his connection with them, but it told me nothing. "But they say they want you—" I broke off, shutting my traitorous mouth.

"Dead? No, I don't think so. Maybe they're telling you that."

Well, actually, yeah . . . My brain felt seriously crosswired. Who to believe? How many lies had I been fed? If "enemy" was a relative word—where did that leave a bendy little concept like "truth"? Truth seemed to be the invisible line that nobody but me was interested in walking.

"The Cabal knew what I was doing with Anna and how the codes were stolen by Lang. When the *karadji* went missing, they knew it had to be connected."

"So what happens at King Tide?"

He glanced around uneasily at the rising moon. "I'm not sure exactly. So many of our myths have been distorted over time. Whatever is predicted, the Cabal have hung their invasion on it, so we need to move. Get this data and Anna somewhere safe. Are you in?"

Was I in? I certainly wanted to help Daac preserve the data. But there was the small matter of the *karadji.* I'd agreed to deliver them to the Cabal by King Tide—only a few hours away. With the Cabal nearly on the doorstep, maybe I could still fulfill my deal.

Did I need that deal anymore? I could go with Daac now: he had what I wanted.

But what about the other shamans and the ma'-soops? They'd never make it to Torley's without me.

I put my conscience on the scales. It was freaking heavy. "I don't know," I said, because I didn't.

He brought his hand around from behind his back. It held the Cabal dagger. He'd pulled it from the dead Twitcher. "Will this help you make up your mind?"

I stared in fury. "Give me the knife."

He moved it away from my reach. "This is sacred. How did you get it?"

"How do you think I got it?" I snapped.

I seriously considered taking him then and there. If it came down to hand to hand between us, I wasn't confident I'd win, but his arrogance and his baiting had pissed me off enough to give it a go. The trouble was I might still need him to get out of here. "When I made a deal with the Cabal," I said, "they gave it to me."

"They gave it to you," he echoed.

"Surprised?"

He raised his eyebrows. "I thought you'd stolen

it. Tell me why you agreed to work for them, Parrish. What do you owe them?"

"You must know that." I stared down at my worn boots, filthy clothes and scratched and bleeding arms. Then, finally, back at him. "Such as it is, I owe them my life. I pay my debts. What's it to you anyway?"

He blinked. "I care what happens to my people."

My people. Those two words stopped my heart. He considered me one of his people. What gave him the right to do that? And why, perversely, did the idea make me want to thread myself through him like macramé?

I pulled the door open. "You and I got a bit of a problem with definition, Loyl."

"We got more than that."

Chapter Fourteen

The quad was where I'd left it. We ferried the first few shamans across the poison dirt, leaving Mei and Schaum to watch the rest. Mei sulked openly and that improved my humor.

Smoke from Daac's arson adventures made my eyes itch and weep but the flames helped to light our path. I wondered what the heat would do to Ike's *polychephalum.*

When we reached the wall, I had my answer. The hatchway, destroyed by the cellar fire, was now covered in a thickening layer of Crawl that glistened strangely in the moonlight.

I held out my hand. "Let me use the sacred dagger on it."

He refused and began carving into the Crawl like it was a fresh carcass. "You know what this dagger represents, don't you?"

I shrugged, watching. He was going to tell me anyway.

"*Goma.* Blood debt. You can never repay *goma.*"

I stiffened. "What's that supposed to mean?"

"You owe *goma* for life. You can't buy it back."

I narrowed my eyes at him. "You're lying."

He stuck his fingers in and sloughed bits of Crawl off. The hole was big enough to open the hatch, but the Crawl was already resealing it.

"Quick." I gestured to a small Polynesian *kapna* called Ness, and a young boy with startling blue eyes and feathers implanted in his scalp instead of hair. "Cover your nose and mouth; the smoke is still strong in there."

"Where do we go?" Ness asked.

"Go up through the basement and out of the bar. Look for a bald kid with long hair on her arms named Glida-Jam. She'll be watching out for you. Stay with her until I find you."

She nodded and pulled the boy down after her.

Daac stared at me, fascinated. "What is it about you, Parrish? You collect people."

"No," I corrected. "They collect me."

I wheeled the quad around and heard a clunk. Daac peered under the rim, then reached down. "Pretty."

The Gurkha! I'd lost it when I'd played gladiators with the Twitcher. Somehow it had lodged under there. "That's mine," I said.

He scraped it clean on the faring and rested it over his knee. "Let's get moving. We'll negotiate over it later."

Negotiate! Who was he kidding? I twisted around, reaching for it, but he held it away with his prosthetic hand.

Note to self: *Chop that damn hand off one day.*

We repeated the journey and the hacking three more times, freeing ten shamans. That left another eight, plus the *karadji*.

Smoke thickened and the flames plumed as the sample shed collapsed. The smell was putrefying, like burning bodies.

I gunned the quad back to Ike's building. Mei waited at the door, hopping from one foot to the next.

"There's something growing on the roof," she said. Her more than usually jaundiced skin was dotted with perspiration.

"They call it Crawl. It's wild-tek," I said. "We've only got one knife that will cut through it."

Schaum joined the conflab. I wondered how Ike had mistreated her and what effect it had. She already carried a galaxy of grudges. The only thing that remained of Daac's precious lady scientist was the dress that hung loosely on her emaciated body and the cold eyes harboring their own-brand sanity.

Daac shifted impatiently. "I'll make this trip. You stay back this time, then I can fit one more," he said.

I shook my head. "No. It's better if you stay with Mei and Schaum."

He looked doubtfully between us all. He didn't trust me not to hurt them. Good!

"All right." Reluctantly he passed over the knife.

As soon as it touched my hand, I relaxed. Six of us crammed on board and set off like a circus trapeze act. One thin Indian shaman with a tattooed face clung on to my shoulders. The rest tucked around us. That left four behind with Mei, Schaum and Daac. Too many for one last trip—Daac and I being the equivalent of two bodies each.

I put that worry aside and forced myself to concentrate on the present trip across the waste. We reached the wall without toppling but the quad motor sounded sick. The cutting was tougher, as if the Crawl was resisting.

Two shamans leaned elbow deep into it as I tried to find the hole beneath.

I got ready to push the Indian through. "Reach your hand back; you might have to pull the others through. It's growing quicker than I can keep it apart."

He nodded.

I repeated the bit about finding Glida-Jam. "Wait for me when you do. Mo-Vay's no place for strangers."

"We have protectors," said the Indian, touching his shoulder as if to stroke an invisible pet.

"So do I. Around here they've got their hands full, though."

He rewarded my weak joke with a smile. Then he slipped through the Crawl and out of my sight.

I sent a quick prayer after him.

Who to?

Who knows?

*   *   *

By the time I got back to the shed, the quad was coughing up smoky phlegm of its own. I didn't like its chances of one more trip, let alone two.

"The stuff is getting harder to cut through."

I glanced up. It was creeping down the wall on the inside.

"The ambient heat from the fire seems to be changing its consistency," Schaum observed.

I couldn't help it. I gave Daac The Look.

"Can you stop it?"

She shook her head. "I don't know what it is exactly. I *lived* in this building. He kept me away from his cultures."

Loyl held out his hand. "I know there's another way through the wall. The way they brought me. Give me the dagger. I'll do this trip and come back for you."

"No." I didn't want the *karadji* out of my sight, especially with Loyl Daac. It also meant Mei, Schaum and me alone in a shed of creeping Crawl. Uh-uh. No way.

"You'll never find the other entrance, and we can't all fit. I heard the motor, Parrish. You're overloading it."

Stubbornness tightened my lips. We glared at each other.

Mei forced her way in between us and thumped me in the ribs. "Quit stalling. You're gonna get us all killed," she said.

She was right for once. I handed the dagger to Daac. Whoever possessed it had the best chance to get out of here and I didn't trust him.

While he settled himself on the seat I turned to

the old, half-blind *karadji* who'd spoken to me
before.

"Your people sent me to bring you home. Wait
for me once you're through the wall. I'll come as
quickly as I can," I whispered.

"I know." He placed a hand on my shoulder. It
was like a boss-shot of tranq.

"What did . . . ?"

"A gift," he said quietly.

Daac hauled the *karadji* on board and set off in
a different direction. The old one twisted backwards, eyes trained unseeingly in my direction as
the quad moved away.

Creation . . . was that what he'd said?

The calm lasted even after I lost sight of them
past the dim shoulder of the building.

"Boy, you rolled over easy for a tough grrl,
Parrish."

I should have wanted to bury her face-first in the
Crawl but I remained blissfully indifferent to her
jibe. I'd been given a fragment of peace, a gift from
a half-blind man. I couldn't remember having felt
like this before.

Ever.

Eventually the Crawl grew across the door, sealing the shed. It left the three of us huddling together like kids on the concrete lip. Schaum hugged
the flat drive like it was her baby. Her shoulders
drooped, the adrenaline and the glucose starting to
wear thin.

I strained for the sound of the quad and began
to wonder if Daac had left us behind. That thought
shifted to anxiety, and then to straight-up paranoia.

My calm started to slip away. I mourned it like a death.

It didn't help that Mei's mouth got looser by the heartbeat. "He'll never be yours, Parrish."

At that remark my indifference deserted me altogether. "Tell someone who's interested," I blazed. "Anyway, I thought you were Stolowski's one true love. Or is that just more of your cheating?"

She wasn't fazed. "Loyl is our dominant. He has first rights. Isn't that right, Doc?"

Schaum had the grace to blush at the crass notion.

I choked on it. "*Dominant?* You've got a tired case of boss infatuation, Mei. Wake up to yourself," I said.

"The problem with you, Parrish, is you're too much of a competitor. You can't get on with anyone. There's no room for people like you in our new place."

Curiosity got me to respond. "New place?"

"We got plans. This'll all be ours again. Clean the migrants out of Torley's, Shado, The Slag. Plastique as well. Ours."

Ours?

Daac's timing was flawless. Just as I decided to toss Mei out onto the poisoned dirt and watch it eat away her skin, the quad lights spilled past the corner of the building.

He looked like he'd been wrestling inside a wild pig; clumps of wet stuff stuck to all sorts of places.

"It's sealing the wall off. Hurry."

He sat Schaum between his thighs and Mei scrambled up on the pillion before I could think.

Sly bitch. That left me the choice of hanging off Daac's leg or Mei's waist. Both equally distasteful, especially in the light of her most recent commentary.

I really might catch something.

I chose his leg and felt the warm tingle of body contact shoot to all parts of me like a shot of whiskey after a week without food.

Maybe not so distasteful . . .

The quad moped along, spitting and coughing like it had emphysema. Daac steered it more east of where I'd come in. As we closed the gap towards the villa perimeter, we could see the shining spread of the Crawl as if someone had pasted a luminous paint across the wall with a giant brush.

"Did all the different factories get their fuels here?" I shouted over the noise.

Daac nodded. "Was gonna cost the developers too much to clean it up and then no one wanted to live here anyway."

Only Ike. I thought of his geek glasses and neural webbing. I'd seen weird before, but there was something about Ike. . . . "Unwholesome" is what my mum, Irene, would have said. But then Irene lived in a world where wholesome and unwholesome had their very own icons and a definition in the help menu.

In The Tert, shades of gray was a code you lived by—you couldn't afford to divide right and wrong into neat boxes. Take Loyl-me-Daac. Gorgeous, 'zine pixel-fold and carer of his own in a care-less world. Flip the coin and you get racial fanatic.

How would he describe me?

Impulsive and irrational on the one hand, and on the other . . . impulsive and irrational!

I quickly dropped that debate and tried to ignore Mei's busy hands wandering all over Daac's body. If I didn't want to throttle her so much, I'd be tempted to admire how well she pushed my buttons.

The quad died a few body lengths from the villa. We sat in silence for seconds, disbelieving.

"Where is it?" I asked finally, scanning the wall in front of me. A layer of Crawl covered it. No openings in sight.

He pointed. "Up there, where the wall dips, a window has been chiseled in."

"How did you get them through?"

He stretched his arms above his head, miming a push. "With difficulty. I s'pose you thought I'd left you behind."

"Never crossed my mind."

He grinned at me for the first time in a while. Genuine and warm.

I fended off a swell of pleasure by poking at the body of the quad. "Let's strip the faring. Use it to walk on."

I broke off enough for him to stand on.

"Parrish, give me your tee."

I had my crop underneath. Better mine than his, I decided, and for once didn't argue.

He dismounted and tore off the mudguards, using the shirt to protect his hands. I ripped the handlebar faring, salvaging only one piece intact, large enough to use as a body board.

Lucky Teece wasn't here. He wouldn't have

trashed it, even if it had four wheels and might save our lives.

Teece! I suddenly ached to be back in Torley's, drinking tequila at Hein's, listening to Teece and Ibis bicker and looking forward to a great whack of noodles from Lu Chow's.

Daac placed two mudguards on the dirt. "Parrish, you pull Anna. I'll pull Mei."

It might have been fun. If it hadn't been poisonous dirt, if Mei, Anna and Daac weren't my playmates *and* if we didn't have a wall of thickening Crawl to hack through.

Last time Daac and I'd done something this foolish, he'd made me swim up an underwater pipe infested with icy, paralyzing bacteria.

I guess this was an improvement.

We set off across the last, short distance like parents taking their kids for an evening sled ride. I reached the wall first, poison-dirt free, feeling as tired as the clothes I'd had on for the last few days. Daac moved slowly, trying not to upend himself or Mei. Mei crouched on the faring on all fours, like she might spring at me again.

My throat constricted at the thought.

They pulled up hard against the wall. "Mei, hop on my shoulders," said Daac. She shimmied up him like it was something she practiced regularly.

"Now what?" she called.

Balancing on his mudguards, he passed her the dagger. "Start carving. Careful. It's sharper than anything you've ever used."

He stood rock steady as she hacked.

"It closes over as soon as I cut it."

I grunted with impatience.

Daac looked at Anna and sighed. The glucose had totally worn off now and she was trembling, weeping quietly into her fingers.

"Parrish?"

"Can you hold me?" I asked doubtfully.

He looked as tired as I felt and was holding his injured side. None of us had had any food. "I can try."

Reluctantly, Mei climbed down. Daac decided her faring was more stable than his mudguards and they jiggled around each other. Then he braced against the wall, hands gripping the layer of Crawl while I tried to emulate Mei.

Two missed attempts before I managed to climb onto his shoulders. He staggered under my weight, and I held my breath while we steadied.

A face full of toxic dirt wouldn't do much for my looks—nor my life expectancy. I knew he wouldn't be able to hold me for long. That thought, coupled with his ears brushing my inner thighs, sent me hacking like a demon. I found that turning the blade flat and dragging it downwards made incisions that lasted longer, as if the Crawl shrank from the touch of it.

When I had a hole big enough to fit my shoulders, I leaned through and felt around. My hands touched something solid. A rough ledge.

"Found it. Give me a push."

I locked on to the ledge and launched through the hole, falling straight onto the floor on the other side of the window.

I bounded up and checked for Twitchers.

No sign. Only a few broken chairs and food foils outlined in the dim, ambient light.

And then . . . *OK, OK, it crossed my mind.*

A fleeting impulse to leave them behind.

Who am I kidding? Mei would probably find a way to haunt me for the rest of my life. And Daac . . .

Well, never let it be said that Parrish Plessis was an opportunist.

I grabbed the frame of a broken chair and plunged it, and my head and shoulders, back into the closing gap.

I couldn't see them but I shouted, "Use this to stand on. I'll pull you the rest of the way. Wait while—"

My mouth filled with Crawl, so I choked and pulled back. Soon as I'd spat it out, I began the hacking procedure again, forcing the stuff aside with the sweep of the Cabal blade. Minutes later I came within a micrometer of chopping off Mei's nose.

Pity.

Her face appeared. She dribbled goo down her chin and held out her hand. "Loyl said to hurry up."

Hurry up! What the fok did he think I was doing?

I yanked her so hard she popped through like a cork.

I repeated the pattern and managed to fish Schaum through. She collapsed into Mei's arms more bedraggled than before.

While Mei scraped goo off her, I started widening the hole once more. But it had grown thicker and the pressure of it closing forced me back out. I tried again, slashing fiercely, and the dagger slipped from my hand.

No! I plunged my hands in after it and found the bladetip with my fingers. The handle was out of reach. Taking a deep breath I grasped it. The dagger cut straight to the bone, and I felt light-headed with pain.

Inside me, the Eskaalim howled at the thought of blood. The world started to dim. Realizing I might pass out and lose Daac, I took a risk. I accepted the bloodlust sensation a little instead of fighting it. It filled me, lent me energy and dulled the pain. In seconds the Eskaalim presence coursed through my veins.

I pulled the dagger clear and used it to scrape a hole. Then I burrowed through it like a fiend, arms burning with the pain of exertion. Somewhere in the suffocating entrails of the tissue I encountered Daac's hand. I hauled him in like I was starving and he was the last fish left in the last ocean, dimly aware that Mei had me around the waist and was pulling too.

All I could think was blood. Warm, metallic and necessary.

The three of us ended stacked stickily on each other like canned sardines.

I slipped out from between them, seized by the blood desire, and raised the dagger. Daac's throat looked so pale coated in shining Crawl. One stab and I could wash myself in it.

The parasite agreed.

Kill him! It will make you stronger!

I heard Schaum's scream.

That was all.

Daac's punch knocked me out for only a few seconds. But it left me with a muzzy Eskaalim hangover and a really nasty snipe on. It was the second time the guy had punched me in a matter of hours.

My nose and my crotch felt like someone had set fire to them. I touched my nose. Swelling already, but surprisingly straighter than normal. If Daac had improved my appearance by punching me, I'd kill him. Surreptitiously as I could, with them peering at me, I felt my crotch. Bruise on bruise. The exact same spot Daac had kicked me.

"I did that," Mei pronounced. "One good kick there slows most people down. Even the grrls."

What about two good kicks?

Daac held up the dagger. "You were going to kill me, Parrish," he said by way of explanation for the nose.

He's right. For one reason or another I am going to kill him!

He ripped material from his T-shirt and held it out to Mei and me, careful not to make contact. Then he began meticulously wiping himself with the rest. "Wrap your fingers before you bleed to death."

I stared at my hand and remembered everything in a rush. Flesh gaped from the bone. My arm was covered in blood. And my clothes. Come to think of it, so were Mei and Loyl. We looked like bad torture on a good day.

I glanced around at the empty room. "Where are the *karadji?*"

"I told the Clever Men to go. The Cabal will find them."

"You what?" My desire to murder him spiked to new heights. "They'll never survive this place. Tulu and Ike aren't playing by our rules, Loyl."

He sent me an odd look. "What rules would they be, Parrish?"

"There are some things you just don't do. Ike might be messing with bodies but Tulu's messing with bodies *and* souls."

Mei shuddered. "That crazy shaman thinks she can suck our spirit into herself and then Marinette will ride her permanently. Marinette's got other ideas. She wants Parrish. And she's one bitchy loa. Something about getting even with Oya."

I gave Daac a steady stare. "I appeal to all the best types."

No smart reply to that. Instead Daac got glassy-eyed. The way I hated. He was already thinking forward, planning. He bent down and helped Schaum to her feet, checking the flat drive was unharmed.

"I'll get you and Mei to a safe place. Then I'll find Ike," he told her.

She leaned against him, her matted hair leaving crawl-wet trails on what remained of his tee. "I don't think I can walk any farther."

"Parrish and I'll carry you," he said, confident of my alliance, the way he expected everyone to be.

"What about the other shamans?" I said. Would he really leave them?

"This is more important." He tapped the flat drive.

Yes. Of course. Suddenly I was sick to death of him. Everything always came back to what he wanted. What he could gain. Nothing else mattered.

Well, I'd made promises and they didn't include nursing his girlfriend Schaum. With relief I finally knew what I would do. Just as well, because thinking time suddenly got to be a luxury.

Twitchers shouting outside. Noise in every damn place.

We were out in the corridor in seconds, automatically heading in different directions.

Daac turned back and grabbed my shoulder. "Where are you going?" he demanded.

"Keeping my promises."

Genuine surprise took the sting from his anger. "But I'm your only hope of beating the parasite."

"Yes, you probably are."

We locked eyes for one long moment of understanding.

Our differences.

Then I remembered something I'd been meaning to ask. "You said Ike went by another name. What was it?"

"Dr. Del Morte." He shifted Schaum's weight to his uninjured side and headed for the stairs.

Del Morte? Shite! "And Loyl . . . gimme the dagger."

He dropped the Gurkha on the top step as he disappeared.

"Not that one, you pri—!"

Damn!

Chapter Fifteen

I found a dark place to hide and reviewed my compass memory. Glida's attic was north of where we had come out. The *karadji* said the battle had begun but there was still a flanking guard of Twitchers left.

The last Tert war had been brutal and quiet. And for the most part, I knew what it was about. This time I was guessing and I didn't want any part of it. The Cabal versus Tulu's rider Marinette, Ike and the crusty-skin brigade. Tek and voodoo versus some homegrown spirit shit.

The very idea sent chills prickling my overtired body. I knew I was closing in on a physical collapse, but I'd promised Glida I'd take her and the ma'-soops with me. Now that included whichever shamans were waiting for me. I was going to do both those things.

When I got tired, I got pigheaded.

It could be a problem but it also got things done. Even if they were the wrong things.

I moved as quickly as I could, but my hand throbbed and my feet seemed to trip me up. Several times I just lay down in the dark, face buried in my pack, as human traffic crept by me. I was in no state to defend myself but whatever was going on down on the sidewalks had sent the rest of Mo-Vay scuttling to the roofs. Each time I stopped to rest, I fought the temptation to stay there and sleep.

Or just die.

The last time was the worst. A warlike chant had started in the distance. It made the air too thick to move in. I didn't even know if it was real but it sucked me away from consciousness.

You decline more than you know. I will have you.

No!

I kicked up into real time like I was saving myself from drowning in a dream and forced myself on. My resolve was somehow keeping the Eskaalim at bay. Whatever had happened in that alleyway in Mo-Vay had left me sure of one thing at least. While I *could* fight, it *would* be a fight. If I gave in, the possession would be quick and painful.

In the end, I crawled, resting every few minutes, drawn towards the power of the distant chanting.

I didn't make it to Glida's attic. I'm not sure I was even going in the right direction.

She and Roo made it to me, forcing a bitter fluid into my mouth until I revived. When my eyes finally focused, I saw Loser licking his paws in satisfaction.

"He found you, Parrish. Kept hissing and spitting until we followed him," said Roo.

"The shamans?" I croaked. "How many got through?"

Roo and Glida looked at each other. Roo held up seven fingers.

That meant ten or more were missing. Mei, of course, was with Daac.

They helped me back to the ma'soops' attic. It was crowded with bodies but I felt the shamans' relief at the sight of my sorry corpus.

"Let me sleep. One hour, no more," I told Roo. "Have a shaman keep watch with you on the cut-thrus. If anyone tries to get in here, shoot 'em."

"Sure, boss."

That was good enough for me. I stretched out on a row of beams and mercifully blacked out.

Ness and a couple of the shamans performed some spirit mumbo on me while I was out of it. "Renewal," the feather-haired kid called it later. They also let me sleep for two hours.

I felt so good the first few moments after I woke up that it quelled my irritation at how long it had been. Even my optimism had revived a little as well. Maybe we'd all get home after all. Sleep was a wonderful thing.

Loser spotted me awake and limped over to flop on my stomach. I got his message—don't leave without me!

The shamans sat in a rough semicircle around

me, with the ma'soops curled up in the spaces between them. Roo and Glida, holding hands,
launched into an account of my lost hours.

"Thought you needed the rest, boss. Not sure
what's happening out there. Those kids—"

"The Twitchers? Don't mistake them for kids,"
I corrected. "They're animals." I looked at the ma'-
soops. "They'll eat you."

"Well, they're running wild, heading out towards
the canal. The other punters are either hiding or
running like somethin' terrible's about to happen."

"It is," I said flatly. "The Cabal have come to
take back the land before Ike makes a move into
theirs. They don't like what's happening here."

I stared through the gloom of the attic at the
pensive shamans—seven frightened, exhausted disciples of spiritualism, each with his or her own
brand of belief. It was a miracle really that they
were all sitting together in such harmony. I guess
having your brain juice sucked out together was a
bonding experience.

"Who's missing?" I ran my eyes around the
group and stopped abruptly when I recognized one
of the *karadji* by his tattered three-piece suit and
curly hair. "Where are the others? Where's the
blind one?" I demanded.

His hands cradled his large belly as if it ached.
"Loyl-me-Daac tells us to go. You say stay. Geroo
says we should listen to you. We argue. The young-
beasts come for us. I run and get free. I am the
strongest. Afterwards, I am lost. This one found me."

His tone brimmed with accusation that I'd made
the wrong call.

I thought of Geroo, the blind *karadji,* and his gift of calm. *Why did the arseholes always survive?*

I spied a ma'soop peeping out from behind the *karadji*'s shoulder—so small I'd scarcely noticed her before.

"I tell all my famlee go look," Glida confirmed. "She bring him here."

"And you?" I asked the other shamans.

"Can you get us home, Parrish Plessis? We've seen within you and trust your honesty." Ness, the Polynesian *kapna,* spoke for them all.

Within me? Now, that couldn't be a good thing. And there was that damn word "trust" again. I hated it nearly as much as fake tits and false friends.

"Tell us what you want us to do," she added.

Do? I scrubbed at my face with my fingers, appreciative, for once, of my Eskaalim-driven healing.

Or was it the Eskaalim? Schaum didn't seem to know what it was. To date I only had the word of some dead shaman and my own hallucinations. I played out the idea that maybe I'd been pumped full of some long-acting PCP that Ike or some other goonie had manufactured.

And yet it was a real presence. Every heartbeat, I knew it was there.

Well, whatever it was, I'd use every reserve I had to get the remaining *karadji* to the Cabal and the others back to Torley's. The rest of my problems could just damn well wait their turn.

"OK," I said, levering onto my haunches. "Here's how it goes. We stay in pairs on the pavement. Except Roo and me. I'm heads, Roo's tails. If we have to go through the roofs, it's single file.

Same order each time. Remember who's before you and after you when we do it that way. Each of you"—I pointed to the shamans—"is responsible for one of the ma'soops. Take care of them or . . ."

I didn't need the threat. Understanding and agreement was in their nods and their serious expressions.

Glida translated my instructions to the ma'soops. They chattered excitedly, but when she barked at them they settled into the laps of their keepers.

"Glida, you're my partner. I need you to navigate through here. When we go single file, you're my number two."

Reluctantly she and Roo unclasped hands.

I hid my smile.

And my envy.

I took Glida's light strip and scouted down on the pavement but things had worsened. Mo-Vay changed as I watched—morphing as if it were alive. Plas, timber and neon growing quicker than the jungle after monsoon. As the moon rose higher, the whole place stirred with unheard purpose. Twitchers ran the alleys, wild with new weapons and the change.

Like us, the rest of Mo-Vay scrabbled into the rooftops for safety. It made our progress slow. So did the task of keeping so many bodies moving together.

Punters barricaded the attics like tiny fortresses. A few times we managed to pass by as other groups fought. But most times I had to do the snarling, blade-waving thing.

I did it well, but I knew eventually someone would call my bluff.

It happened too soon.

As I held a gang at bay, Ness fainted at my feet. Seeing my concentration drift as the shaman collapsed, they came at us en masse. Knives and planks and whatever they could lay their hands on. I waded in with my fists, too scared to use the Gurkha in such a small, dark space and cause a massacre.

I repelled the first wave, but in a matter of seconds they were all over me again.

"Glida, get the others through," I bellowed.

Roo hustled to my aid and we fought with fists, like street kids. Only his were metal and relentless. Trouble was, I had two fights going—one against our attackers, the other against my Eskaalim-driven desire to rend them apart and daub their blood over me.

I tried to contain it. These people were just trying to survive in a crisis. Same as us. I even managed to keep a weapon out of my hands. Then one of them jumped the *karadji* carrying the smallest ma'soop.

I had a knife out before I knew it. It slid through the attacker's skin—effortless and lethal. The smell of blood sent the rest of the gang scuttling into their corner.

Roo hauled the body off the *karadji* and the ma'-soop. The *karadji* was shaken.

The ma'soop was dead. Crushed under the weight.

I carried the child's body into the next cut-thru

where Glida had herded the rest. The light was poor, but they all knew, like they were somehow wired together. Listening to their wails, I felt their loss set hard on me. I had to see them out of this nightmare alive. Which meant not staying here a minute longer than we had to.

"We go down to the pavement," I said. "Our . . . chances are better there."

What I really meant was, Down there at least I can see who I'm fighting. Anything else was a lie.

"Glida." I motioned to the feral to lead us down.

The ma'soops cried in a unison of pain and huddled together.

"They won't leave Cha," she whispered, distraught.

I gently levered myself in amongst them as they grieved over the littlest of lives. "This won't happen again." The words came out strident with emotion but they seemed to understand.

A couple of them clambered on my back, hugging me. One took my hand and stroked Cha with it. I felt her fading warmth and my own impotence.

"Let me carry her," said the *karadji.*

I nodded. "Glida, tell them we'll take Cha with us until we can find a place for her."

Somber and timid they followed me down into the moonlight. In the shelter of a doorway we crowded together as refugees. With Glida's help, I talked to each ma'soop, looking at them properly for the first time. Despite my intentions, Cha's life had been forfeited without me even knowing her name.

I didn't want that to ever, *ever* happen again.

When I'd stumbled on Bras in the Villas Rosa
months before, I'd felt the same way. Humanity
wasn't worth canrat shit if we didn't bother to know
each other's names.

Shyly, the ma'soops spoke.

Walbee, Biiby, Bettong, Fat-tail, Wombebe, Quoll,
Cuscus.

I ran impressions of them in my mind. Quoll
glowers. Black spots on his tail. Wombebe . . . cockroach skin that bulges like smart armor. Fat-tail . . .
he struggles to keep up. Biiby, two sets of ears, one
encased in the other—loud noise causes him pain.
Bettong's toeclaws unbalance him when he walks.
Walbee, she's Glida's favorite. Cuscus? What
about her?

I looked at Glida.

"Cus sees what we all hear," Glida explained.

There was a name for that sort of thing. I'd heard
of it—when the senses got crosswired. Ibis would
know it. If I could just get the ma'soops back to
Torley's alive to ask him.

I told them all to say, "Parrish."

They each uttered a mutation of it.

Around me I felt the approval from some of the
shamans. Without prompting, each offered their
names. As with the ma'soops I memorized something about them.

"I am Ness. You know I can give renewal." *Polynesian* kapna. *Waist-length hair. The oldest.*

"Stix." *Implanted scalp feathers. Chlorine eyes.
Lithe young body.*

"Chandra Sujin." *Tattooed face. Silken voice.*

"Arlli, I tell futures." *Veiled.*

"Tug. I am a healer." *Tug, powerful, big hands.*
"And this is Talk Long," said Tug.

A mute. "What does Talk Long give?" I asked.

The silent shaman raised a set of tranquil, green eyes. A color I'd never seen. The eyes of someone not meant for this world.

"Talk Long gives calm," answered Tug.

I trembled. I needed an awful lot of that.

The surly *karadji* spoke last. "Billy Myora. I don't talk my stuff." I stared at his unblinking eyes and plump, unconditioned body and wondered if he even was a *karadji*.

Whatever he was, I had no wish to know his secrets.

Afterwards, though, a mood change took the group. I felt a sense of connection creep into my own heart—the beginnings of a chosen involvement, not something forced on me by the Cabal. While it dispelled my irritation, it also amplified my anxiety.

Between Glida's local knowledge and my compass implant, we hurried northwest. Around us the pavement bulged with bizarre life. The bulbous wall growths that had first shocked me were now charged with a sickly luminescence like aged neons. The scars on the walls leaked rivulets of a clear plasmalike fluid. It puddled in crevices and dips and began to crystallize and shine.

"Don't touch anything you don't have to. Especially that," I told the shamans.

Their expressions spoke of abomination.

"We must hurry more. King Tide brings it on," Stix whispered.

I looked at Ness for confirmation.

She nodded. "The 'voyants say this tide will be significant. It has long concerned us."

"Why so?"

"Not only the water rises on the tide but the earth's crust lifts. Nature responds and things breed extraordinarily. They die so, as well, when it wanes. It has been said that this tide will bring on a biological singularity."

"Things will grow?"

"And die."

So this is what the Cabal feared. Their invasion was already a given, but they wanted their *karadji* clear before the wild-tek spawned. "How can you know this is related? The sea is so far away."

Ness shrugged sympathetically at my ignorance. Stix began to cry. She twisted in his arms to comfort him. He almost carried her, staggering under the weight. I thought of taking his load but sensed a complex relationship between the two that invited no intrusion.

"This can be healed." She touched his cheek.

I wish I had her faith.

Talk Long came behind Stix and concentrated on the rise and fall of his breathing. Gradually Stix calmed.

Suddenly I saw inside Loyl Daac's world. I saw how belief prevailed over truth every time.

Maybe belief *was* the only way.

We circled around a bristling tower of fiber. It glowed a pulsing siren of red. Ten feet up from the base a body hung. We watched it being slowly tractored up and down and across the glass shards, its blood seeping into the optics. The tower was bleeding the body. I guessed it was one of the shamans who'd gone on alone and glanced at the others. No one spoke. No one confirmed my suspicion, but a grim mantle fell across us all.

I shuddered, remembering how my hand had stuck to a tower in the same way. How the blood had leeched from my fingers.

As I harried them onward, the sheaves of glass started to sing to us. The noise was discordant beyond description, a last bawl of life-agony that pleaded for help.

Cuscus screeched in terror, scratching Billy Myora until he dropped Cha's body, digging her marsupial claws deep into the *karadji*'s leg.

Glida ran to them, forcing the ma'soop to let go. She scooped the distressed child into her arms, uncaring that the claws fixed straight into her arm.

Billy Myora bent over, clutching his leg. "What she doin'? Wha's wrong with her?"

"She sees *blood*. Everywhere. Around us," said Glida.

"Carry her," I ordered.

But as we moved on, Biiby scrabbled free from Chandra Sujin. Crazed with the noise, he ran back towards the tower like he would fling himself at it.

I caught him just short of it. His heart beat wildly against my arm. He clamped his doubled ears in pain.

"Keep moving," I yelled hoarsely to the others. "Whatever you do, don't stop."

We skirted the towers after that, veering east or west, though the singing stayed in our ears. Biiby whimpered and tugged his ears constantly as if they hurt. Glida stripped a piece of her clothing and persuaded Biiby to wrap them. After that the ma'-soop fell silent, as if he'd lost his connection with the world.

I dropped back to walk alongside Myora. The *karadji* clutched Cha's body tightly under his arm.

"We should burn the little one soon."

He nodded, watching ahead intently.

"You said Loyl-me-Daac warned your brothers not to wait. Why did Geroo disagree?"

He waited so long to reply I thought perhaps he wouldn't. Only as I moved to take the lead again did he speak.

"He b'lieve you the wise."

"What do you believe?"

"I b'lieve you got them killed."

Much as I wanted to, I couldn't argue.

The pavement remained passable and mostly level, but webs made of a tough fiber had begun to grow from the gutters and across the alleys and walkways. Everything glowed under the bulging moon.

The first few times we retraced our steps and found other routes, until I realized we were spending more time moving backwards than forward.

The world began to narrow. Claustrophobia crept upon me.

Fat-tail and Bettong whimpered in fear and Arlli wept tears of exhaustion. Her veil stuck wetly to her mouth.

Glida tapped my elbow. "Mo-Vay won't let us go," she whispered. "It makes us stay."

"It *will* let us go," I growled. I pulled out the
Gurkha and stalked to a web blocking the access
of the alley we were in. The big blade worked labo-
riously, slicing the fibers so they fell about and on
me. When the hole was wide enough, I motioned
them to step through.

"Quickly!"

I moved to follow last but the strings caught and
reattached as I brushed past. They pulled taut on
me in a trapping dance. A shadow skittered down
the lengths of web.

My gut said, *Spider!* My mind reasoned, *Not!* I
strained to see but my head was caught fast.

"Roo!"

The Pet spun and ran back to me. He glanced
up, digits unsheathing blades . . . and froze.

"What is it?" I demanded.

"S-p-p-ider!"

"No, it isn't! It just looks like one. Spiders don't
grow that big."

"But it has."

"I don't care what it is, shoot it! Then take the
blade from my hand and cut me out!" I kept the
panic from my voice. Just. "Roo, listen to me. It's
mek. *Spiders don't grow that big!*"

He nodded like he understood.

And did nothing. Terror had him.

And the web had me. It began to vibrate. I felt
the sticky strings tighten as the creature clambered
closer. From somewhere in the depths of my pack
Loser howled. His fear let mine loose.

"Roo, shoot it," I shouted. "Or so help me—"

My threat choked off as the spider straddled me,

its body blocking out the moonlight. It exuded a rancid, freshly killed smell—a bio smell that reminded me of a 'Terro. Meaty bones. It belied my insistence the thing was mek. Compound eyes glistened along the underside of its abdomen. Barbed quills jutted from its legs.

My gut turned liquid.

"Roo!" I heard Glida's plea. She squeezed in under the spider's rancid abdomen, seized the Gurkha from my hand and pulled it away. I felt the sides of the web shaking as she hacked.

"Shoot it," she screamed at him. "Now!"

Her voice penetrated something in his mind that mine hadn't. He fired straight up into the shadow spider's head. I know because the explosion deafened me and rank insides splattered over my face.

Way too close, Roo!

Glida's side of the web sagged and broke. I rolled a second before Roo fired again. This time he took out its right side and legs. They detonated into thousands of single sensor units that crawled erratically over me, piercing my skin, running in and out of my nose and ears—and other places I couldn't bear to think about.

I visited total, abysmal dread.

The Eskaalim gorged on it. I got unbearably hot. Boiling, bubbling, burning-white hot. Like once before, when a woman had tried to rape and murder me.

Screams tore out from my chest, over and over. An image came . . . molten Parrish, thrashing and staggering and falling. Out of the web. Burning alive.

Burning alive, until a boy embraced me and beat out the flames with his mek arms and legs.

The cooling came slowly. So did coherent thought and the sound of the shamans chanting in soothing time. I immersed myself in the sound like it was burn salve.

"She's alive. Barely."

I struggled to know the child's voice.

"What are you doing?" Another. Sharp with distress. Not a child. *Ness.*

"Let her." This one was Glida-Jam. "It might help."

Let her . . . what?

I started to remember. Pain cascaded. An agony of burned skin. My face raw to touch.

"Be still, Parrish." Firm, clear words on a thick, primitive tongue. "Wombebe and Tug help."

Wombebe? Shy. Skin like a cockroach. Wombebe.

I kinked one corner of my mouth to smile. Pain rippled . . . then stopped where they touched. Something hardened on me like a crust everywhere Wombebe's tiny hands rested. It took the pain away. How breathtaking, how exhausting life is without pain.

I felt cooler now, and stiff all over.

I opened my eyes and blinked away grime. "What the freak . . . ?"

Shamans, ma'soops and Glida leaned over me

under the now full-blown moon. Their faces showed relief and something else.

Loser panted loudly at my side, hair singed to stubble.

Roo crouched at a distance in the shadows, head down, limbs twisted abnormally.

"What the freak . . . are you all looking at?"

Ness handed me the overlay of her robe. I stared at my body like it belonged to someone else. My shirt had disintegrated and I was naked from the waist up. My fatigues had blackened like they'd been too close to a fire. Even my boots had heat blisters.

Wombebe took my hand and smiled for the first time I could remember. "Youse bootiful."

Beautiful. Never have been. What's changed?

They told me what had happened while Roo kept watch apart from us, sullen and distant.

Glida's gaze lingered on him. "Roo feel bad. The web-'sect. He got scared."

My thoughts regathered like leaves falling in the same spot. Layers of meaning and memory drifted into place.

"Web-'sect? You seen one before, Glida?"

She thought for a moment. "Not like that. But others . . . at night they goes around changin' things."

I tried to smile some reassurance at her, felt my cheek tug, and frowned instead. "What's on me?"

Ness answered. "Your burns would have killed you. Wombebe healed them somehow. But you've been left with a—a mark."

I didn't much like the sound of that.

Wombebe crawled over to me at the sound of her name. "Bootiful Parrish."

I put a hand to my cheek.

The skin felt like scale.

Chapter Sixteen

It stretched along the ridge of my cheekbone. "What do I look like?"

"Parrish like me," said Wombebe. She sucked her finger and rocked slightly on her small haunches and stubby tail.

Vomit soured the back of my throat. I swallowed rapidly to keep it down. This kid lived with a body covered in cockroach skin and legs that resembled a marsupial. I could handle a cheekbone's worth of scale.

Or could I?

I stood up too quickly and the night spun. "We go in a few minutes."

The shamans and ma'soops got themselves ready to move while I sought out Roo. He heard me but didn't look my way, stiffening in the dark.

"Roo?"

"You can't trust me at your back, boss. Next

time . . . I'll probably do the same thing. I froze. Then I nearly shot you."

"You also covered my body and snuffed the fire. You're the *only* reason I'm alive."

He shook his head. "Wombebe did that."

"Wombebe healed me. You put out the fire."

Finally he looked at me. The childish poise had gone from his face. It left an adult's doubt and insecurity. "Thought I was cool, boss. Y'know, thought I could get the job done. I never seen nothin' like that web-'sect. I was . . ."

I rested my hand lightly on his shoulder, where the mek met flesh. "So was I."

He didn't shrug me off but the stiffness stayed. I could hear the whine of his digits as he tried to loosen the blades. The heat of my flames had melted the mechanism. Roo was damaged and he had no Angel inside him to make it better.

"What's wrong in this place, boss?"

I took a deep breath, searching for a way to explain it. To myself as well as Roo. "I don't know for sure. Wild-tek has taken over. You heard of that?"

He shook his head.

"The land here's been soaked in poisons for years. There's been a . . . reaction between the chemicals and it's gotten out of control. Somehow it's changing the hydrocarbons—the plastics and the wood. Early nano industry began here as well. Could be that's part of it too."

"But the place is . . . like, growing?"

"In a sick kinda way, yeah. The shamans reckon

this King Tide has spiked it. Made everything re-
produce faster."

"What does 're-pro-duce' mean?"

Oh great. The facts of life! "Uh. It . . . uh . . .
means . . . like babies. Only it's stuff."

He cracked a tiny grin at my embarrassment and
I realized he was winding me up.

"What's this Ike scud got to do with it?" he
asked.

I hesitated over detail here. The less Roo knew
about Ike, the better for him. And yet Ike was the
one who *made* Roo. How could I keep that sort of
info from the kid?

"He's been doing a lot of this sorta thing. Now
someone's paying him to spread it."

"That's a problem."

"Yeah. He's responsible for the ma'soops. And
the Twitchers. And probably this as well." I gestured to the fibrous web strung across the entrance
to the nearest alley. "He's been playing God."

"He ain't the only one to do that," he said
bitterly.

My conscience twinged. "Roo, I think this guy
Ike maybe is Del Morte."

Unreadable emotion suffused his wan face.

I instantly regretted telling him. "I can't be sure
about that. I might be wrong," I added quickly.

He nodded like he was listening, but his eyes had
gotten vague with preoccupation.

"Roo!" I said sharply.

He nodded. With effort he turned his attention
back to me. "So why aren't we on their case?"

His straightforward thinking made me smile. "Little matter of getting you guys home first."

He seemed to accept that. The stiffness had left him in favor of a trembling energy. I let my hand slip away, but as I made to get up and walk, he grasped my wrist.

"You sure you got your priorities right, boss?"

Roo's words haunted me as we pushed through the night, racing the spread. It itched at my psyche the way the new scale itched my cheek. I'd never been shy of confrontation. The Cabal were fighting Ike and Tulu for their lost land. Was that a battle I should be choosing as well?

The main conflict I guessed would be near the canal. Perhaps I hadn't missed the party yet.

We stopped for a short rest sometime before dawn.

The moon was on the wane and the world felt like it was tipping over, emptying itself. I stared at the grotesquely budding landscape and knew that those left in Mo-Vay would be taken by it, the same way the body had been leached of blood by the tower. Human fertilizer.

I checked my bearings with Glida. She'd curled into a ball on the pavement, making herself as small as possible. "Never been here. It's too weird now."

She was right.

The night could no longer hide the changes. Behind us the villas had 'creted over with Crawl. The one closest to where we huddled had thrown out a strut like a tree—a load-bearing upright that could support another room. A red gelatinous substance slowly welled from inside the strut. It hardened quickly, building in either direction.

Roo had said the place was growing. He was too damn right. And it was too damn creepy.

"Move on," I said.

But such little rest had the ma'soops moaning with exhaustion and lack of food and water. The shamans were in worse shape. Days of lying prone had taken its toll on their muscle conditioning. Ness could barely walk.

I got edgier. How far would the changes spread across The Tert? What about the Mo-Vay people who had fled? Where would they all go? What about the Twitchers?

I carried Wombebe and Fat-tail. Wombebe stroked the scale on my cheek like it was silk. I batted her hand away but it didn't deter her. Fat-tail hung around my neck, chittering in my ear. Neither of them was heavy but my strength was failing too.

And this time I doubted I'd get up from it.

With relief I noticed the villas around us were less Crawl affected. Then I heard the noise of skirmishes. We had to be close to the canal.

A pressure built in my head. Vivid, unwanted visions bloomed. They sent me stumbling, catapulting the two ma'soops to the pavement.

"What?" Roo and Glida tried to help me up.

I flung them off, pressing hard on my temples. The force of my fingers seemed to squeeze my mind high above the ground. I saw the area clearly despite the graininess of predawn, even my own

fallen body. I felt free from it and yet connected—
an accretion of desires and beliefs barely tethered
to a flesh husk.

We were close to the banks of the canal where
I had crossed days before. To the west, near the
remnants of the monorail, the canal banks teemed
with frightened people fleeing the transformation.

I watched the mad confusion and violence. Some
tried to swim but choked and drowned in the
copper-laden water. Others flung themselves at the
skeleton remainder of the monorail, hoping to
somehow climb across, but finishing impaled on the
jagged uprights.

Up and down the banks, small groups clashed.

Hidden by the chaos, Kadais fought with stealth
and deadly accuracy, picking off isolated Twitchers.
A flash of iron-copper weapons, a shimmer of form,
and they gouged the hearts from their opponents.
I circled the scene, fascinated by their skill.

Then a blur, like a mirage, caught the corner of
my eye—a smear of distortion. I drifted over, curious. *Twitchers guarding it.* I dropped closer but the
air became slippery as a sand dune. Instinctively I
knew Leesa Tulu was there. Ike too.

I backed away and swept on toward the Outer
Tert side. Mei squatted there with others from the
Cabal. The force of their combined chi power
steadied large, roughly made rafts rowed by warriors. They rocked and took water in the middle of
the canal while a spirit battle raged above it.

It should have been invisible—was it really
happening?—like the early puffs of a strong wind.
But I could see it—malicious salvos from Tulu and

a pulsation of earth-heat from the Cabal. Opposed forces—one fighting to overturn the rafts, the other to keep them upright.

Mei stared up at me as if distracted from her task by a physical jolt.

"You!" she accused. *"What are you doing in my head?"*

"How can you know it's me?" I thought back.

She stood, fists clenched. *"We're linked, damn you, Parrish. How the crap did that happen?"*

"You're the shaman," I retorted. *"Explain it!"*

I tracked her thoughts as she remembered our union in Mo-Vay. Some bond had been forged then. Unwanted by both of us. Unwanted but undeniable.

"Get out of here. We're trying to keep the rafts steady."

"We? Who are you betraying this time, Mei?"

"The Cabal want to know if you have their— aggh—"

The Cabal swarmed through her and along our connection, reaching for me, hungry with need to find out the fate of their brothers. I banked sharply and fell, desperate to escape them.

"Loyl!" I screamed as I fell to my death.

Chapter Seventeen

They caught me before I crashed. Stix, Chandra
Sujin, Ness, Arlli, Talk Long and Tug straining
to bear my weight, even though I had no substance,
settling me gently on the ground.

When I became conscious, Roo and Glida helped
me up. My nose bled from falling flat on my face.
I wiped it and shook them loose.

"Boss?" Roo's eyes were dark with strain. "We
ain't got time for this."

The pressure had gone from my skull, replaced
by a peculiar light-headedness. I sensed the satisfaction of the Eskaalim presence, as if it had orches-
trated my escape. "If it happens again, keep
everyone moving."

"What about you?"

"I'll catch up."

He looked unhappy but didn't argue.

I went to the shamans where they squatted together in the creeping daylight on a clear patch of

pavement. I didn't bother to ask them what had happened. "Thank you," I said.

Ness opened her eyes wearily. Sweat glistened lightly on her brow like fever. "You were lucky."

Lucky Parrish? I doubted it.

I thought of the mirage. "What was happening in that blurred spot?"

"The Cabal ask their spirits to fight the bitch loa," said Billy Myora. "They call the fire."

"How do you know that?"

The shamans mirrored my question in their faces. Billy hadn't been linked to them. How could he know anything?

He gave us a sly smile and pointed to a fresh crack in the pavement. "The serpent moves through here."

And then what? I'd had a gut full of religion. For something that was meant to give comfort, it had a long track record of getting people killed.

"What about Mei? How did she know me?"

"You are psychically linked," said Ness.

"Joke, right?"

She placed a hand on my arm. I felt a tingle like a double shot of tequila. She removed it as if proving a point. "We all are—from our shared experience. That is why we were able to help you. The elder *karadji* will use this connection as well, if they can. My guess is that they need you to defeat Tulu."

"What can I do that they can't?"

"Your psychic energy is uncommonly strong— though raw. That's why you have not shape-changed. The parasite battles hard to possess you, but you resist. You have it . . . trapped."

"Y-you can sense it in me? You believe it's real?"

"As real as we are."

I don't know that I liked that answer. Lately, real had become very unreal. "Well, the Cabal can have Billy, but I'm taking the rest of you home."

The shamans exchanged glances. For the first time Arlli pushed her dirty veil back from her face. Her skin had started to blister into ugly lesions from exposure to the Crawl. In fact all of the shamans showed the beginnings of it.

"You can't," she said. "See this?" She brushed the sores. "We have to protect our own people from this sickness, even if that means we fight *with* the Cabal."

I glared at Billy Myora. "The Cabal are colonialists. They just want more territory," I argued.

Myora shrugged as if my thoughts were of no consequence to him, but he listened intently.

"No, Parrish," said Tug. "They seek what was theirs. To heal it."

I folded my arms in disagreement but my head told me it didn't matter if they were right or wrong. Whatever the Cabal's motives, it had to be better than letting this wild-tek infect the entire Tert.

"What do you want me to do?" I asked.

Ness spoke for them all. "Stay and fight. Perhaps gain them ground."

I sighed. Couldn't someone ask me to do something easy?

"I'll stay, but you—*all of you*—go home." I turned back to Glida and Roo. "The *karadji* owe me for him." I nodded at Billy. "I'll use it to get

you across. Roo, you must take the ma'soops back
to Torley's. Tell Teece to find room for them in
the barracks."

"If you use your psychic link again, to bargain
with them, you risk losing yourself," Ness warned.

"Sure." The space around us had begun to creep
with noise and movement. "The canal is only a few
blocks away. Let's get there first."

I stood and urged them forward.

Fat-tail grabbed my hand and pulled me along.
"Tor-lee's, Tor-lee's," he chattered.

His excitement spread among the ma'soops. They
clicked and squealed with renewed energy. Wombebe
snuck under my elbow, her scaly hand stealing into
mine. She clicked and whistled in sadder tones.

"M-iss Parr-ish," she said.

I pushed her ahead of me. "Don't." I didn't need
that sort of extra attachment. Not now.

Her scaled face fell.

As we hurried on, Roo fell into step beside me,
his round, young face gloomy. "I'm useless. My
targeting system is out and my blades are melted."

"Just take them," I said flatly. I had no energy
left for holding anyone's hand. I needed to untan-
gle myself from all of them if I was going to do
what I had to.

"But Teece told me to stay with you, no matter what."

I fixed him with my most dogmatic stare. "Tell
me, Roo, what do you call Teece?"

He scratched his hair, eyes fretful. "Uh? Teece,
I guess."

"What do you call me?"

"Boss, boss."

"So you work it out."

He scratched again and gave me a resigned, tired nod. "Guess I'll take them home then."

Home. I kept thinking about that word as we found a spot to shelter in amongst the last line of villas that ran along the canal.

Ness and Chandra Sujin drilled me on how to relink with Mei and the Cabal and explained how they would try to block them if need be.

Ness clicked her tongue. "Concentrate, Parrish."

I closed my eyes and attempted to focus my thoughts.

"Empty your mind. A meditative state will allow you to leave your body," said Ness.

But my mind had other ideas. It resisted, running away from my control like a scared kid. "Can't do it," I muttered.

"Yes, you can!" hissed Chandra Sujin. He tugged fiercely on my arm.

"What about the parasite? It killed the others. It killed Vayu. You're risking your lives as well," I said.

"Yes, we are."

This time I herded my mind into a corner and invoked the taste of tea with sugar. My mouth watered. Without realizing it, my mind lifted and drifted. A vista unfolded below me like one of Jamon's war-sims—except that these contestants had only one life.

"See the channel of light issuing from the far side? That is the Cabal. Get close enough to begin your link with Mei." Ness spoke in my head.

"How?"

"Is there something you share in common?"

"No! . . . Well . . . perhaps . . ."

Daac's image spontaneously filled my mind. Teeth flashing, dark skinned, intense. His fingers inside me, giving pleasure.

"Stop!" Mei's shrill voice shattered the picture.

It got her attention. *"I need to link with the Cabal, Mei."*

"You aren't strong enough—"

"Save it!"

She gave a mental sigh. *"Always the tough one, Parrish. Remember you asked."*

She diverted a thin stream of her energy towards me. I felt it unite with the Cabal and tug like a fast watercourse.

A storm of power coursed into me. It peeled open my mind and burst my senses with colors and aromas.

Ancient memories unwound before me— dreamtime rituals of ocher-daubed faces. Wimmens business—drinking dugong blood, dilly bags full of cramping berries . . . Then newer ones of stolen lives, urban subsistence and lost stories.

An instant later the torrent of knowledge vanished but the energy raged on like a cyclone, tearing me apart. I felt Ness and the others struggling to bind me, keep me whole.

"I want these people to bare safe passage across the canal," I said.

The Cabal buffeted me in reply. *"Where are our karadji?"*

"Only Billy Myora lives."

"Then he was right."

"Who was right?"

"Bring Myora to us."

"Only if you give these people safe passage across."

"We don't bargain."

The wind roared and shrieked. Ness's grip weakened. Then Stix's. Slipping . . . Tug. Arlli. None of them strong enough. I began to unwind. Soon I would tear and the watercourse would drown me.

A shadow fell. A shadow with broken teeth and dripping saliva. The teeth scraped across my neck, hoisted me up high onto its back.

"Can't stay on. It's too fast." I panted.

I slipped down and the water picked me up and slammed me. Thought blackened. Life squeezed out of my pores. I felt it leave . . . violet and violent.

No!

No!

The Eskaalim's protest doubled mine. It lent me strength and resolve. I grabbed the watercourse with my hands and twisted with all my strength.

It writhed and buckled in pain.

"Give them safe passage or I'll choke you and Billy will perish."

"We cannot. The houngan battles us."

"Find a way."

The channel contracted in one angry, complicit thought.

"We try. Bring Myora and we will send someone."

"Parrish? Parrish?"

Glida was shaking my shoulders. Dry saliva crusted my face. My jaw ached with clenching.

Slowly her face came into focus, flushed with color by the glow of the fires razing Mo-Vay.

"How long?" I asked.

"Too long." Her eyes were wide and scared. "They attack. Roo shoot them. Tug gone."

I looked around. The ma'soops huddled around Roo's legs. Two bodies lay a short distance away. Thankfully they weren't Twitchers or we'd be dead. A sticky brown substance oozing from the pavement had already begun to coat them.

My heart hammered at my throat. The shamans lay spread-eagled behind me. All except Billy Myora and Tug.

Myora squatted in the first patch of sunlight, staring at the tide-swollen canal.

"He no help," Glida said. "Roo try make he. Ness say no—better not."

"Where's Tug?"

She shrugged.

"He came out of the trance before the rest of you and left. I figured I better stay and watch, not follow him. We dragged you away from the others," Roo explained. "They were screaming. When we moved you from the circle they stopped."

I crawled over and felt their pulse in turn.

Relief threatened to black me out. They were alive. "You broke their trance?"

"B-bad thing?" Glida stammered.

"I don't know." And had the Eskaalim and Loser really saved me from the Cabal? A liaison that meant . . . what? I didn't . . . couldn't think what. "Where's the canrat?"

"Gone."

"What do you mean, gone?"

"When we dragged you from the circle he started howling. Then he just bolted."

"Remind me to get him some sugar dough."

Roo and Glida exchanged the-boss-has-really-freaked glances. I didn't let it worry me. Freaked was better than dead.

I think.

"Come on. Get them up. You've got a boat to catch."

An oarsman in fatigues and dull gold piercings battled the dark, swelling water of the canal to collect them. A faint blur dogged his journey and I wondered what the Cabal had sacrificed to get the raft past Tulu.

When he landed none of the shamans argued about leaving. They'd spent their courage surviving.

I singled out Roo. "You got ammo left?"

He patted his leg compartment. "A round for each piece."

"That should do. There's plenty of snakes and lizards on that side. They're starving. Kill some straight away and eat them but leave the diamond pythons alone," I told him.

He only wrinkled his nose slightly. He was as hungry as the rest of us.

The raft took two trips to ferry them across. The Gurkha and I forced Billy Myora to stay until the second trip. It might not work against the Crawl but on human flesh it was dandy. He regarded me with sullen indifference and I wished again that old Geroo had been the one to survive.

Ness gave me a renewal before she went—exhausting herself to fainting. Stix gave me a scowl that could have meant anything—probably condemnation of what Ness risked for me.

Arlli removed her veil and handed it over. "It will help you go unnoticed," she said. "Give it to me later."

I took the filthy piece of gauze, smarting at her faith that I'd return.

Glida and Wombebe were the last to get on the raft with Billy. I squeezed Glida's arm.

She nodded. I could see the gratitude and apprehension in her eyes. Neither made me feel good. I watched the raft to the other side with heavy relief. Roo would see them home.

I *believed* that.

A drizzle had started up. I cupped it in my hands and wet my tongue, sucking greedily. The canal turned brown, as if the fresh raindrops had stained it. To the north, below the clouds, the air crackled with a peculiar, unhappy light. Like two worlds rubbing each other raw.

Mei was right. For a grrl who didn't like spirit shit, I was becoming a real buff.

It struck me then that none of them had said a word about Tug leaving.

I spun in a circle. "I can't protect you. I doubt I can protect myself. You can come but you're on your own," I shouted out.

He materialized from an alleyway and approached. "You will need me to heal."

I wanted to groan aloud to match the agitation in my belly, but a trickle of excitement quickly superseded it. The Eskaalim was back, stronger. I'd let it loose in order to survive against the Cabal's spiritual power. Now I would pay for it.

I glanced around for Loser. The damn unpredictable canrat hadn't reappeared.

Not able to think of another reason to stall, I moved on, keeping to the cover of the last line of villas, following the canal north.

As the clamor of chaos and fighting got louder, I forced my way into the top-floor vantage of a villa. With Tug's help I kicked the boards from an old window. Twitchers roved the banks for several klicks in either direction of the maelstrom. They waded in amongst the mob, hauling them from the sides, trying to drive them back to Mo-Vay.

Tug grabbed my hand and pointed back east.

The skyline of Mo-Vay glowed with an unsavory crimson tinge, as if the roofs were bleeding into the new morning sky. The fiber optic towers glinted: beacons in the sunlight. A heavy scent floated in—cloying, damp, electrical energy and recomposing matter.

On the gutter of the nearest villa, secretions ·burst and dripped from abscesslike growths. Dark mold stained the walls behind us, and below thick webs spread across openings. Tiny tremors heralded small eruptions in the pavement. The whole of the Inner Tert seethed and mutated with eerie purpose.

"What have they done?" I whispered. The bloodlust simmered deep inside me, but fear chilled my skin.

Tug shivered at my side. "Maybe it's too late. Even for the Cabal."

I looked back to the canal. Several rafts bobbed upside down, slowly sinking, their oarsmen drowned. Were these the decoys the Cabal had risked to get their last *karadji* back?

Was he really worth it?

Along the canal a dull noise built. Suddenly the water began to break its banks: a puddling that turned into a stream, and then a flood across the pavement. Twitchers and punters caught in the rising water convulsed and collapsed.

On the other side more Cabal launched their homemade rafts. With the upsurge of water, the Cabal seemed to gain a tiny momentum. Tulu's salvos began to fall short and their earth-heat dissolved them in hot, conquering gusts.

Where had the extra strength come from? Surely not Billy Myora.

As the water flooded the first line of villas, hope revived in me. Where it came into contact with the wild-tek, it sizzled and steamed, dissolving the offensive substances.

"Maybe not. I don't think the wild-tek can cross the water—must be the copper in it."

"But what about the people? What will happen to them if they don't get out? What will happen to us?" asked Tug.

In answer to his question Priers crammed the sky with 'Terras hanging from their bellies, their 'corders extended to full range.

The gust of their props lent Tulu a physical edge,

and the Cabal's rafts began to wallow and tip dangerously, the oarsmen fighting natural forces.

A mob pawed the banks screaming for the rafts to come and save them. Some fled farther north and south, looking for another way.

Guilt assailed me. I'd just bargained to get Roo and the ma'soops rafted across. But what about these people?

Too many of them, I reasoned.

Or was I just the same as Loyl Daac—*selecting* who deserved to be saved?

Tug watched me, sensing my uncertainty. He would follow my lead, and his trust was just another burden.

I shook a fist at the hovering Priers. "I have to get to Tulu. She's stopping the Cabal's rafts from crossing," I said. "Wait here. Watch for them. When the rafts reach this side, get as many people on board them as you can. If something goes wrong and things go to crap . . ."

"I couldn't abandon others, Parrish." Tug flexed his powerful hands as if wanting to touch something.

I shrugged. "Suit yourself."

I slipped out of the building and onto the pavement. Arlli's veil cloaked me in an anonymity that made me uneasy—as if I had no identity. I reached for the comfort of the Cabal dagger and remembered Loyl had it.

Where was he?

I ran east, pushing past punters running the other

way. The majority of them still clustered in villas near the old monorail crossing, watching for the rafts, downwind of the maelstrom. Fear and confusion ravaged their faces. I'd seen it before, in the recent gang war. Yet this was different. These people didn't understand their enemy or know how to fight it.

Nobody recognized me. Nobody stopped me. I shut out their panic and concentrated on controlling the blossoming urge I had to kill anyone who bumped me. The closer I got to the maelstrom, the deeper and more violent my mood became.

I felt like I was being followed. Using the ferals' mask to block the stench, I ran as close as I could to the flood line. My eyes skimmed the surface of the murky water. Haze arose where it intermingled with the Crawl.

Would the copper stop it? Or would it accustom and continue to spread?

A racket behind me drew my attention. I turned, searching the teeming pavement for the source. A moment's glimpse at something dropped the base from my world.

A shout and a splash as a pair of Twitchers tossed something into the flooding canal.

Not something. Someone.

The hat spun away and the body floated for a second before the water gobbled it down.

I recognized the hat, and the sweet face.

Chapter Eighteen

R^{oo!} My throat closed over. *He must have come back for me! He must have . . .*

Shock and anger took over. With all the energy and malice the Eskaalim could lend me, I burst through the crowd to get at the Twitchers, taking them both from behind with a kicking blow that knocked them down and jarred my foot. Senseless to the pain, I fell on the pair, hoisting one of them to the same fate as Roo.

I twisted the other one's neck like a screw top, until my shoulders popped with the strain. He managed to drag my veil and mask away before he sideswiped me with a metal baton.

I heard my ribs crack. Felt my flesh rip. A flare of unnatural light in the Twitcher's eye told me he'd wired the others. In a minute a swarm of them would be here and I'd be dead.

I twisted harder until bones cracked and he flopped unconscious.

I knew it wouldn't last long. His recovery time would be quick.

So what? I'd had enough.

Roo deserves more than that, I quarreled with myself. That single thought got me up.

I hobbled towards a villa. Punters who witnessed the event helped me, running interference as more Twitchers arrived.

I struggled up two flights of stairs, into an attic and across a cut-thru. A rust stain seeped through the walls of the attic. I touched my headband on so I could see, and kept away from the stain. I wasn't sure what contact with it would do and I wasn't willing to find out. The memory of the body fixed to the fiber optics tower having its life sucked away was still fresh.

Like Roo . . .

I took a second to strap my half-melted boots a bit tighter. With a conscious effort I sank deep into myself, giving over more to the Eskaalim. I needed the extra adrenaline to keep the pain at bay.

It flooded through me with a welcome numbness.

I knew if I could live long enough to get near Tulu, I would have a payback need that'd see me through hell.

But the closer I got to the maelstrom, the harder it got to move. My legs felt like they were bogged in Crawl. I saw dead Kadai in alleys.

The idea that they were mortal distracted and frightened me.

I veered away from the canal to where Tulu hid

herself. Her salvos drew me to her, a barrage of twisted spirit juice spewing out to challenge the Cabal. All the worst stuff she'd harvested from the minds of The Tert shamans and me.

You didn't get it all, bitch. I shouted the thought over the cacophony in my head.

My insides felt crowded to bursting. The Eskaalim, the spirit guides, and now a link with Mei and the shamans. I made multiple-personality disorder look lonesome. If I wasn't already crazy, then I was definitely on the low road.

I grabbed at one notion to keep me afloat and wrapped myself around it.

Stop Leesa Tulu!

Single-minded revenge charged with the unholiest of bloodlusts kept me moving past a swell of Mo-Vay punters, freaked and milling like animals, and skirting around a knot of Twitchers.

I located the maelstrom at the top of a villa set, half a klick back from the canal. Tulu wasn't getting too close to the action.

More Twitchers circled her building at a frenzied pace. If Ike was calling their moves, he had a major hard-on.

I ran scenes in my mind. Frontal assault? Subterfuge? Distraction? Decoy? None of them seemed right and I could die waiting to find the correct way. If only I had a decent weapon. A firestormer. A semi. If only I had the damn Cabal knife!

I thought about trying to ambush Tulu using my mental links, but passed on the idea immediately. Whatever small talents I possessed were trivial and untried next to hers.

Besides, she'd harvested spirit sap from a shed full of shamans. Who knows how juiced she'd got on that cocktail? Or how strong it had made Marinette?

I shuddered at the memory of the evil loa. Marinette had an acute case of total vice.

No, I needed to stay with what I did best. Rash and reckless.

Make that rash, reckless and vengeful! Ike would find out just what it felt like to have his flesh liquefied.

As I crouched, watching for an opportunity, the Twitchers guarding the doorway suddenly deserted their post and ran towards the back of the villa.

Unable to believe my fortune, I loped awkwardly across the alley, flinging myself in through the open door. Stairs—straight ahead; living room—to the right.

I took the stairs.

A quick recce at the top revealed rust pus seeping through walls. Otherwise the place was empty aside from some unhappy vermin. Murmurs, though, drew me out towards an enclosed balcony. These villas must have been top of the range in their day. Balconies, en suite sans and auto-dim on the windows. The window dim had failed years ago, leaving the glass door with a kind of smoky smudge.

I tugged at the slider and felt the suck of the pressure change. Crouching down, I peered cautiously around the sliding door. Through the crack I saw Tulu outlined, staring north at the canal. I could practically feel the chi stream launching from her towards the water. She had two Twitchers guarding either end of the balcony to deter climbers.

A noise from below drew me back to the top of the stairs. I stuck my nose around the balustrade, expecting a Twitcher. But it was Ike, fully kitted in exoskel and combat hood and wedged into a mobile command plinth. The skel rippled on him, wheezing and murmuring. The hood had to be running the Twitcher command.

Roo's killer.

He lifted the hood to get a proper look at me.

I wanted to rush down to him and pulverize the puny body under the skel. As if guessing my intention, he murmured something into his pickup.

Pain jarred my mind.

Where the hell . . . I glanced back. The balcony door was open. The two Twitchers had pierced my shoulders with large, spiked clamps.

I gasped for breath as they jerked me off my feet, and a second inferno of pain lit through me.

Parrish on a spit!

More like Parrish spitting!

Following on the heels of the second pain came a second wind of animal hate and fury—a rush of numbing endorphins. It sent my senses into hyperreality.

"Bring her here," ordered Ike coolly, patting the base of the plinth.

They stepped down in unison, with me strung between them. At the bottom they dangled me like a crucified puppet in front of him.

I could see it in his face. Ike wanted to chat.

I tried to think across the top of the pain.

What was his weakness? The skel shielded him from any bodily attack. That left his neural webbings and face, and only while the hood was up.

One chance.

I gave him my best high kick, my foot catching underneath the side of the helmet, knocking it askew. I didn't even wince.

The Twitchers jerked me backwards but I kicked again, just connecting, booting the hood clean off his head.

He screamed and spasmed as the neural sponges tore free of his neck and skull.

I screamed as the Twitchers dumped me.

They both fell to the floor, writhing and frothing with seizures brought on by the withdrawal of Ike's neuro-ghost.

I rolled clumsily away from their feet and squeezed the clamps off. Then I crawled over to the sponges, rending the filaments.

GET UP! the Eskaalim urged.

Ike was already moving, up out of his plinth and running on skel-fed legs.

I chased. Damaged foot, bleeding shoulders, dizzy. *Stay with him. Stay with him.* A mantra.

I did at first. But eventually my injuries slowed me to a weaving hobble. I staggered from one alley to another, not even sure that I was still going in the right direction. Like it always had, only sheer stubbornness kept me upright and moving.

Overhead the thrum of low copter noise filled my senses. I gazed upward. Two Priers playing chicken.

What the fok were the bastards doing?

I wanted to spit at them but my tongue wouldn't coordinate. Couldn't they see what was happening down here? Where were the rescue craft?

I hunched my shoulders against their inhumanity and stepped doggedly on.

In the end, I didn't have to find Ike. He jumped me as I skirted the base of a fiber optic tower and slipped in a large puddle of blood dripping from a body suspended above. We rolled together in it.

He got his arm around my neck and with the added strength of the skel began to crush my windpipe. It should have broken my neck. It should have ripped my head right off. But I caught the glint of the fiber optics thrusting up behind us as he squeezed and I forced us into another roll.

We slammed together into the tower and he screamed as the wet, freshly torn back of his head and neck adhered to the glass. He tried to kick me away but I flung myself straight back, digging my feet into the ground, forcing him against it. The skel began to contort as it made contact with the tower, strangling him alive.

Bonus!

I wedged him fast as he kicked and gasped.

It was quicker than I hoped.

Then the kicking stopped and I collapsed against him, breathing heavily.

When I was recovered enough to right myself, I tore his glasses off, compelled to see into the face of the man who had made the Pets and the ma'-soops, as if it might somehow explain what he had done.

His corpse stared, unblinking. Literally. The guy had no eyelids. Underneath the line of his eyebrow ran a blurred arc of incomplete symbols.

A cold, altogether unhealthy tremor ran the length of my overheated body. I suddenly knew where the two little flaps of flesh sitting in a box in my gun safe belonged. I now also had a pretty good idea who Ike was working for.

The tattoo was a quod mark for a life sentence. You got that only for crimes against the media. You got bailed out from that only when the media decided you'd be more useful working for them.

I'd assumed Ike's backers were privateers. Other gang lords doing their dirty stuff in someone else's backyard, maybe even planning a coup. I knew that the Twitchers were black-market meat. Stolen. Hijacked. Whatever. Even the presence of an operational 'Terro could have meant more stolen goods.

But this . . . there was no doubting the connection. No wonder Ike'd been able to maintain a power stepdown large enough to run the veiling device.

He had media cooperation. Which meant . . . the media and the Militia were propping up an entire operation based on totally immoral genetic experiments, i.e., murder.

Now, there was a headline.

I was no saint but I believed and tried to uphold basic human dignity. I'd left Vivacity and come to The Tert to escape the media's intrusions and controls over people like Irene. I figured that even the bent and broken, the down and dirty, got one small kickback for living their miserable lives in their own stink hole— the media and their Militia buds couldn't touch them.

The worst they could do was voyeur from above.

Well, crush my delusions!

I slumped backwards. From my blood-occluded horizontal view I watched the glass tower tractor Ike's body upwards, stripping pieces off the skel as it went, then flesh. The whole process was like an animal being skinned and deboned.

I stayed there as long as I could stand it.

His death wouldn't bring Roo back. Or change what I'd just learned about my world. It sure did nothing to ease my guilt or my anger or my grief. But at least I knew Ike wouldn't be engineering any more freaks. For himself or anyone else.

Most of me wanted to stop then. I think I could have even died—given a moment's peace.

But a stubborn, determined sliver wouldn't let me off the hook. I hadn't finished what I set out to do, and finishing had somehow become more important than anything else.

Later, my compass implant and sheer bloody-minded endurance got me back to the door of Tulu's villa. I was nauseous with pain and fluid loss but crazy to stop the voodoo witch. She was still up there. I knew because I could feel Marinette's power.

Driven by the thought of the loa, I crawled up the stairs and peered clumsily through the smoky glass of the sliding door. When it opened of its own accord, I sprawled inward like a kid caught eavesdropping.

Tulu's eyes flickered in my direction, but her look was distant, inhuman. Marinette was riding her, and the loa was pissed off.

Blood pooled beneath me. My blood. It wet my face. I wanted to lie down and drown in it but the stubbornness wouldn't let me.

Not yet!

Tulu stalked over, her fingers twitching, her arms flapping again. She made eerie owl sounds and garbled a sermon of utter filth.

When she got close enough I tried to kick her feet from under her. But my legs flailed weakly, as if they belonged to someone else. She seized the baton hanging from her waist and began to beat me across the hands and face—strong, hard whacks that cracked my finger and face bones.

I moaned aloud, unable to do anything to stop her. As consciousness slipped, a blurred object leaped from near the doorway and clawed her face. She flung it away with irritation, anesthetized to the pain of its scratches by the energy of her loa.

The object landed awkwardly on the floor near my face.

Loser!

Tulu jumped on him, crushing his head hard into the floor. Loser went limp.

I felt his presence leave me like someone had stripped off a layer of my skin. Mental and physical pain went beyond. It left me with the insane clarity of near death.

I wasn't going to survive this—I knew—but I could still make it hard for her.

My mind fired off instructions.

Distraction! If her attention stayed on me, not the Cabal, it might help them get more Cabal across and do what they needed to do.

I just need to live a bit longer. There was only one way I could do that.

With every last cell I embraced the Eskaalim.

Keep me alive, I beseeched it. *Keep me alive so she has to use her power to kill me! Keep me alive so they have time . . .*

Things grew grainy like I might faint.

Please . . .

The Angel reared before my eyes, triumphant, blood spilling in rivulets from its gold-red wings.

Finally, human. The change will come immediately.

It wasn't a noble choice—noble didn't have a place in my erratic last thoughts. Just stubborn perversity. Tulu and Ike and their media benefactors weren't taking over my world, even if I had to turn werewolf to stop them. I'd set off down one path a long time ago and I saw no reason to turn back.

"Take me!" I whispered aloud, and waited.

Chapter Nineteen

"How could I resist an invitation like that, Parrish?"

An amused and familiar voice seared a path to my scrambled brain. My eyes flew open.

"You!"

Daac had the Cabal knife pressed to Tulu's throat, and a sardonic smile just for me. Relief didn't even begin to describe how I felt. I opened my mouth again but the words stuck. My throat closed over and my skin itched.

Convulsions started. The change had begun.

Stop. I don't need you now—

Too late!

I fought to keep it at bay, but the Eskaalim swarmed along a bargain struck a heartbeat too soon.

I was drawn down a funnel of darkness blacker than charred remains.

Parrish?

The thought accompanied tiny, rough licks on my face and an awful stench. *Loser!* I knew the smell even on my way to death. Mangy canrat fur.

Parrish, I can't help you anymore. But another one who can is close by.

His thoughts became faint. The tongue licking got weaker. A weight lifted. The smell went with it and sadness enveloped me.

I opened my mind eyes and gazed along the ruby sand of an endless beach. Shadowy dunes hunkered behind me. I got to thinking about life.

Did I want it? Would I still be human? Did it matter?

Blood waves lapped at my feet. Behind me the dunes were fading.

Large, warm hands touched me.

Tug?

Hi, boss!

Don't call me that! Roo called me that.

I'd gotten Roo killed. He should have been with me, not left in charge. That was my job. What sort of a person was I?

I took a step back towards the oblivion of the dunes.

Fingers closed on my wrist. *You can stop them. But you must want to.*

I sniveled a bit and sulked. *Of course I frigging want to.*

A smile. *Come on then. The healing will be the worst.*

Trusting the smile, I stepped forward into the sea of blood.

The battleground that was my body twitched and

trembled as if being kick-started. My system pulsed with an upheaval of electrical messengers telling my cells to transmute and heal. Then the pain took me somewhere else.

"Parrish, wake up!" A voice as hoarse and insistent as my body was sore and resistant.

"Don't nag, Irene," I croaked.

I unstuck my lids and blinked my eyes clear. It wasn't Mum. We were on a balcony in Mo-Vay, and Tulu and the Twitchers were gone.

So was Loser's body.

Daac helped me sit up, leaning me back against the wall, dripping water into my mouth. His skin was warm and mine felt like scale.

"Where's Tulu?"

"Got away in a Prier. But not without a reminder," he said grimly and showed me the bloodied blade of the dagger. He had claw marks down his arm.

I sighed shakily. "Looks like she left you one as well. What about Tug?"

"Who?"

"Shaman with big hands?"

Daac shook his head. "No one here but you and me, Parrish."

"But he healed me."

His eyes narrowed. "You're healed, yes. But not by any shaman."

"What do you mean?" I demanded.

He touched my scaled cheek—gently. I didn't like it when Daac did gentle. I usually forgot all my reasons for not trusting him. His finger dropped to my chest and traced the line of my collarbone.

Nice. But not really the time . . .

He cleared his throat as though something had got caught in it. "Y-you changed. I saw it, a . . . shape-change. When you changed back you were healed."

That got my attention.

"Crap I did!" I sat up straighter, running my hands over my body. I felt like my skin had been removed and pegged on drying racks. Inside, though, was another matter. Inside I felt like I'd been chopped, minced, rolled and tossed many times over.

His hand strayed to my stiff, dirty hair. "No one needs to know," he murmured. "We can keep it between us while we find out if we can reverse it."

My heart hammered a bit.

He slipped his arm under my shoulder and squeezed some water into my mouth from a tube. His breath fanned my face. Before I knew it he had wrapped both his arms around me and leaned his head on my shoulder. "I'm just glad you're alive," he said.

Glad I'm alive.

His words spread salve on my battered body and mind. I leaned into him and a deep, deep weariness rolled over me—the sort that you knew would stay with you for a lifetime. A tear sputtered down my face and onto his chest. "The ch-change . . . What did I look like?" I whispered.

He touched the line of scale on my face. "This.

Your whole body was like this. You were you, but with a covering of . . . armor."

I turned the image over in my mind. My own private skel. Cockroach. I tried to laugh but a violent shaking overtook me. I couldn't stop it.

He held me tightly until the worst of it went away.

"But I feel the same inside," I said at last.

His arms tightened. "I'll get Anna to work on it straightaway. We'll find a way to beat it."

A wave of gratitude flooded me.

He took my chin in his hand. "But you must come and live with us. It's better that way."

I nodded. I could see the sense in it. It just wasn't how I'd dreamed we might make our peace or be together, but he was right. "I have to go home first. Settle some things."

"I'll come with you."

I shook my head. "No. But if I get crazy in the meantime, you have my permission to hunt me down and shoot me."

We shared a grim smile.

I wanted to stay where I was, getting drunk on his kindness, but something drove me to unclasp his arms. Habit. I slowly climbed to my feet, holding out my hand. "The dagger."

He gave it to me this time without argument.

I wiped Tulu's blood off it. There didn't seem to be anything else worth saying, so I left.

Chapter Twenty

Outside the villa Twitcher bodies littered the pavement like bits of scrap. Ike's death had tangled their primitive rewiring and set some against each other. But it didn't account for all of them.

I trod warily back towards the canal, swinging the Cabal knife in a warning arc before me, advertizing its presence. It kept the bestial shapes in my peripheral vision crouched behind corners and ducking down below balcony rails.

The Cabal would need more than one small dagger if they were going to take back this land.

Around me the flood had subsided, leaving a messy tidal sweep of dead bodies. I stopped looking at faces after the first few and climbed to the roof of a villa a row back from the canal. A handful of Cabal warriors camped on the other side by a fire. They sent the raft for me when I signaled them.

The crossing was slow even though the tide had

fallen. On the other side they'd fashioned a pathway across the spillover to avoid the poisonous residue.

I navigated the planking and walked up to them with a curt nod of appreciation. They didn't welcome me into the circle where they sat sharing smoke and talking softly. Doll Feast had been right about them—theirs was a men-only club. And I no longer had any desire to be a part of it. I dropped the dagger in the circle and kept walking.

I found Glida-Jam waiting not far from them. She sat cross-legged in the morning shadows of the vine-strangled villas, cradling Wombebe. Her eyes were swollen from crying.

I couldn't look at her.

Wombebe wriggled free and galloped to meet me. I knelt into the ma'soop's embrace, taking time to gather my thoughts and memories.

She chattered in broken words, trying to tell me about everything at once. Then she broke off. "Tug?"

I shrugged. "Not sure."

She closed her eyes as if seeking his trace in her mind. "Tug gone. Roo gone," she said sadly.

I turned to Glida. "I told Tug to wait and get people onto the rafts. But then I thought he came to me when I . . ." I said, confused. "It felt like he healed me . . . somehow."

Glida listened without comment. Without the forgiveness I craved.

Depression descended hard. My body count climbed still. The *karadji*. Tug. Loser. I didn't un-

derstand why they did it. Why they risked themselves. Plainly put, I wasn't worth it.

"Why did Roo come back?" I had to know that.

Glida's lip quivered. Her utter desolation hurt
me far worse than the physical pain I'd suffered.

"Not follow you. Find doctor," she said.

Of course! Roo wanted to see Del Morte again.

My arrogance and lack of insight amazed me. I
should have known. But then I didn't have titanium
arms and legs and artificial organs. I didn't know
what it was like to be Roo, or the ma'soops. My
deformities had been purely on the inside—until
now.

I touched the scale on my cheek. Soon I might
get a lesson on how people really treated outsiders.
The thought didn't thrill me at all.

Billy Myora detached from the Cabal group and
came over. Gone was the three-piece suit. His body
was adorned in the ochre and white markings of
tribal status. Seems, maybe, I'd saved someone
important after all.

He regarded the three of us with a grave expression and spoke in a formal tone I'd never heard
him use before. "We plan to take our land back
now. You have had a part in this, Parrish Plessis.
Consider this . . . payment." He handed me a plat-
ter roughly fashioned from a palm tree pod.

On it was dry food, a tube of drinking water and
some grisly bio-mesh nesting in a chunk of bloody
flesh. They'd hacked the wetware from Ike's head.

I knew what the mesh held, but my heart didn't
even miss a beat.

"It's too late," I said.

He nodded. "There was that risk."

Risk? I turned away, towards the canal, dismissing him. I'd had enough of the Cabal and their secrets. I hoped they could save Mo-Vay, I truly did. But they could take their *goma* and smoke it.

I noticed Loyl climbing off another returning raft. He joined the others, and they made room for him with hand slaps and approving noises. The politics of the Cabal were beyond my reckoning.

As for Loyl and me, we'd done with circling each other. He had the lead now.

I stayed where I was, sharing the food and water with Glida and Wombebe and staring across at the sickness that had overtaken Mo-Vay. It was an invasion a bit like the one in my body.

The flood had left a crystalline residue over everything it had touched.

The irony of it amused me. The copper wastes that had first poisoned the canal had saved us. Hopefully they'd be barrier enough until the Cabal could figure out a way to clean the place up. And they would. I had faith in that. Maybe it was the only thing I had faith in.

With a sigh, I lay down in the shadows of the villa and went to sleep.

A day later I began my trek back to Torley's, Glida-Jam and Wombebe with me, Glida withdrawn, Wombebe scared and excited. A Cabal warrior shadowed us at a respectable distance. I didn't

know whether to be gratified or annoyed so I ignored him.

Ahead of us Mo-Vay refugees streamed all the
way to Tower Town, a straggling procession of
human need that the locals weren't too welcoming towards.

By the time we reached the fringes of Tower
Town, fights and fear haunted every alley and corner. I should have intervened but my heart was
aching tired like my resolve. I badly wanted to see
Teece before things got worse with me. I had to
say thanks and sorry and whatever else came into
my head. Right now, I had no time for anyone
else's need but my own.

What did that make me?

As selfish as Loyl Daac!

I couldn't quite cop the comparison, so, with the
deliberation of permanent exhaustion, I waded into
the next fight I saw and took issue. A group of Mo-
Vay types and some of Daac's devotees, head to
head over chow. The Mo-Vays were trying to buy
meat with hair and skin samples. The vendors
didn't get it.

"It's not currency," I said, waving their samples back.

The M-Vs looked at me confused. Abscessed
foreheads, skin like grated meat.

"Ahh've seen yu," said one of them.

I sighed. "Yeah. Probably. But it's still not currency here. We use credit. Real money."

I held my own spike out so he could see it. "Our
world is different. You work for yourselves now—
not Ike. You work for real money. Then you buy."

In other words, get a job, scud!

The banality of the idea sent a frisson of hysteria through me that, once started, might never stop. I hugged myself tight to control it.

The vendor spat on the ground and rubbed the stock of a worn sawed-off meaningfully. "Buy or move on. You're bad for business," she said.

My patience slipped. I didn't like her attitude, so I wrenched the shotgun from her grasp and fired it off. "Dis has blown wide open. Cut these people some slack. They're homeless . . . refugees," I said.

My scowl took in the line of food karts and the gathering crowd. I brushed the foam trays and meat ladles from the top of the kart and climbed onto it.

"That goes for all of you," I shouted. "Tell everyone. Dis is contaminated with wild-tek. You go there, you die. It belongs to the Cabal now."

As if to reinforce my point, a Cabal warrior materialized by the kart, slipping the battered hood of his leather jacket down. Only the punters in front could see him. But it was enough. Word backburned. *The Cabal are here. . . .*

I felt a tiny moment of gratefulness to the somber, lean man. I swept my arm wide to include the M-Vs. "These people can't go back. Let them find somewhere to live here."

"We don't want 'em," shouted a reply.

"And who're you?" someone else yelled.

I opened my mouth to reply, and shut it again. It was a question I couldn't answer anymore.

I took Glida and Wombebe to Vayu's old place on Torley's outskirts. The other ma'soops and shamans were there. They greeted us with hot herb tea and a chatter of news. I insisted on the san first and barred myself in there until the water ran clear of blood.

I borrowed some clothes and wished I could stay there and shut the door on the world, but other—greater—needs drove me home.

I took Ness aside before I left.

"Can you keep the ma'soops here until I can set things up for them?"

She nodded. "I'll try, Parrish. But how will I feed them?"

"I'll organize something," I promised. "Just give me some breathing space. I need a little time."

She didn't touch me, but her gaze scorched my mind. What she found there tightened her expression. "Time is one thing you'll never have," she said.

Glida was waiting outside for me. Her dejection was the hardest thing of all. I still couldn't say sorry about Roo. There were no words for it. No words at all.

I wondered if she hated me. I didn't blame her if she did.

I hated me.

Teece was in my den. He didn't hear me enter. The Mueno guards at the door had let me through without a word.

I watched his broad back and shaggy hair as he traded insults with Jamon's tacky bookkeeping icon. I was so comforted to see him I wanted to throw myself into his arms. A sound bubbled up in my throat. Not an attractive one. Somewhere between a moan and a sob.

He swung in his chair. "Parrish?" His voice held relief, surprise, pleasure and something else all rolled into one.

The something else put me off balance. Literally.

I stumbled against the doorframe like I was standing out in a cyclone. I knew I was spent in a way that allowed no quick recovery. I badly needed to lie down.

He crossed the space to me in a blink. Taking my weight he eased me out into the living room and onto the couch. His faded blue eyes brimmed with concern.

I held his hand tightly, refusing to let go of it even when he wanted to get me a drink.

"What have you done to yourself?" His free hand reached automatically to the dark scale on my cheek. "Where the hell is Roo? Why didn't he come and get me? I would have come and carried you back if I had to."

Asking about Roo sent my body into convulsions, as if I'd been poisoned, and tears spurted from my eyes. I couldn't catch my breath to speak. My chest strained to fill with air, but there was none left in my world.

He slid an arm around me as I shook and moaned and shattered into a million pieces. He'd never seen me like this. *I'd* never seen me like this.

We sat together until the worst of it had passed, then he got up, rummaged in a drawer and came back with a pack of derms. "They're strong. They'll help you sleep."

I pushed them away. A measure of calmness had found me now—as it sometimes does, after a storm.

I suddenly wanted to talk, where only a short while before I couldn't.

He sat, his fingers linked in mine, listening intently as I gave him a full account.

"I called it wrong, Teece. I should have kept them all with me. Roo would be alive if I'd kept them all with me. Or if I hadn't told him about Del Morte."

His eyes flashed with anger and compassion. "How the hell do you know that, Parrish?"

I shrugged.

"What will the Cabal do now?"

"They think they can heal the place. I think they can too." I thought of the web-'sect and shuddered. "As long as I never have to go back there."

"What about Tulu?"

"Ike is dead and the shamans are free. But she's escaped back to whoever sent her. Her brain fuel has dried up, though. It'll keep her quiet for a while."

"And the refugees?"

I took a deep breath and blew it out in a sigh. "It'll be a mess for a while. Some of them will die. But others will find their place here. Everyone needs a place. I think the Cabal might even help them."

He frowned at my resignation. "What about the Priers you saw? What does that mean? And the . . . eyelids."

"I think it means we're not free here at all, Teece. I think we're living in a maze—a human maze." I said the words slowly.

He let out a breath, long and low. "It's not such a surprise to me. There've been signs."

"Thanks for sharing them." I tugged his hair to take the sting from my sarcasm.

"I was trying to leave the paranoia to you." He smiled. "Besides, I don't know that it makes a lot of difference in the end, Parrish. There are always the few truly powerful operators and then there are the rest of us. It's the way life is. You just have to survive within that and get what you can. It doesn't matter who they are."

Anger rippled through me at such impotent talk. "Yes, it does. It matters a heap. It's about intent, Teece. I despise their intent, so why should I screw my life to live by it?"

He shrugged. His arm dropped away and he moved back so he could see my face. "There's something else, though, isn't there? Something you haven't told me."

Isn't that enough?

I coughed and leaned into him. I couldn't bear to see his eyes when I told him what had happened to me.

Before I could speak, though, the door opened.

Teece sprang up. What the hell was making him so edgy?

"Teece?" A female voice, high-pitched and un- sure. Familiar.

"Honey," said Teece. "Parrish is back."

Honey? She stepped into the low light of the room. Gone were the fake, multiple breasts and the bikini in favor of normal breasts, jeans and a tee—but the cultured voice and the good manners were still the same.

Tingle Honeybee!

I stared between them, confused, as she ran into Teece's open arms. She sheltered there like a child, half his size and as feminine as lace. She turned her face from his chest to look at me sideways. There was nothing coy in her expression, only apprehension.

I found I couldn't do anything to put her mind at rest. I was too stunned.

More than stunned. Heartbroken. How long had I been away? A week?

And yet I, more than the next, knew that time was irrelevant when it came to desire.

"Get out now," I said harshly. "Both of you. And make sure the place is locked on your way out."

I got up, peeled off three derms and whacked them in my arm like they were spears. Trying not to stagger, I headed towards the bedroom.

"Parrish, that's too much! You'll overd—"

I slammed the door on his aggrieved concern.

I just wanted unconsciousness. Lots and lots and lots of it.

Chapter Twenty-one

S leep is never long enough.
  I woke eighteen hours later with a fiercely dry throat and an argument going on outside my bedroom door.

I levered myself up and sat on the edge of my bed, waiting to see whether it got worse or better. Apart from feeling like it was stuffed with dirty rags, my mind felt normal.

I got up and wobbled my way to the san.

Broiled skin and a new set of duds later, I risked a glance in the reflect. My face was pink from the heat. Apart from that it was the usual. Hair styled à la crown-of-thorns, crooked nose, bent face, sullen expression, brown scale on the bridge of my cheekbone.

Scale! That's how Daac had described my change.

So what happens now? I wondered. How does it

take me? In truth I hadn't really figured on staying alive this long.

I fished through my pack and found the bloody wetware the Cabal had given me. I needed to wash it and get Merry 3# to convert it, which meant I could no longer ignore the sounds of fist-thumping in my lounge.

Besides, I was starving. Several days without much food did that to you.

I threw the door open.

Teece and Ibis glowered at each other across my only table. Tingle Honeybee was nowhere in sight.

The pair took a fleeting moment to show relief that I was still alive before they got back to whatever was eating them.

"Don't be such a fool!" Ibis jibed.

"I told you we're not a frigging charity," argued Teece. "How do you think we're going to pay for it?"

"Cool it!"

They stiffened like a pair of dogs who'd forgotten their alpha was back with the pack.

Strangely I felt no curiosity about their argument. I just wanted to get far away from everything I knew. That's when I realized that something had radically changed in me while I'd slept. Maybe it was the inhuman part taking hold?

I'd woken from nearly a day's sleep into another kind of exhaustion—no heart for anything.

When Jamon shape-changed, the worst of the parasite loosed itself almost immediately. Probably because he was three parts a monster already. With Io Lang it had been different. His inhumanity had been a well-guarded secret until I took his fate into my hands.

I hadn't felt remorse over Lang. And now suddenly I was like him! When word got out that I'd changed, *someone* would come after me.

I wanted to get right away from this place before I hurt someone I cared about. And if Daac and Schaum couldn't find a cure for me, I wanted to be the one who decided when to end it, not some idiot vigilante who wanted to get famous.

It meant I'd be walking away from all the things I should be putting right—the beliefs that had sustained me through Mo-Vay. Including the most important unanswered question—who in the media was backing Ike and Tulu, and treating the Tertsiders like a bunch of inferior lab rats?

But this morning I was heartsick. Deeply.

Perhaps Teece was a piece of that. And Loyl. Mostly, though, it was about me. My life.

"Parrish?"

Ibis seemed distant, as if he were on a comm viewer—not an arm's reach away from me.

Teece too.

"Are you all right?" said Teece gently.

My body gave a tiny spasm. I didn't have a place to put his compassion anymore. Or maybe too big a place. Besides, Teece had someone else to spend it on, someone who'd use it properly. I didn't begrudge him it, but I was gut-wrenched jealous.

"I want a full account of the business, Teece. Ibis, I want to see the barracks. Then we'll meet at Hein's. This is important and I'm in a hurry. Don't frig me around." My voice sounded flat.

They both opened their mouths to argue, then they exchanged glances and closed them again. Maybe they could sense a change too.

"Business first?" asked Teece.

I shook my head. "Barracks."

Ibis swallowed like he had someone's balls stuffed in his mouth.

We barely talked on the way there, just the basics as I stopped to get breakfast from a dough vendor.

Meat dumplings and flat scones with syrup. Heaven!

"What's been happening?" I forced myself to ask between gorging mouthfuls.

"I've done what I can. Just like, I suppose, you did in Dis." Ibis gave me a sideways.

"Teece told you what happened?" I stopped eating and stared at him.

"Some. I'm sorry about Roo, Parrish. He seemed like a reasonable . . . kid."

Meat caught in my throat. "Don't talk about him, Ibis," I said harshly.

He looked wounded and changed the subject. "I'm going home after this," he said. "Pat is toey."

I nodded, understanding. "I didn't expect you to still be here. Don't think it's not appreciated. I've just got some things on my mind and they have to be dealt with quickly, otherwise—"

"Otherwise?"

I was tempted to spill the truth. But it wasn't fair. You couldn't dump my appalling kinda karma on someone like Ibis. "Forget it. I'll make sure you get paid."

"Did you really think it was about the money?" he snorted, and unlocked the main door.

Inside a substantial miracle had occurred. The place had been gutted and scrubbed. The san was community-sized but clean. Cribs crammed most of the smaller rooms. The main room, however, was set up for communal eating. At one end a clutter of flatscreens flickered with games and simulacrums. In a corner sat an antiquated, rubber-cushioned pool table.

Ibis caught my stare.

"That was Teece. He had some tek connections. Called in some favors. It's all old stuff, patched-up systems, but they work. He said he'd train them to fix their own stuff. If you wanted, and they wanted, they could maybe do some rudimentary schooling. The pool table was from the shop. It was never going to sell. We had a lot of help on the other stuff once word got around."

"From who?" I asked, mystified.

"People around here."

Part of me wanted to whoop at what had been achieved in such a short time but I just couldn't share it with Ibis. My emotions were like a ghost limb: I felt they were there, but when I reached out I couldn't touch them.

I settled for, "Great!"

Ibis looked hesitant. "Are you sure?"

I put my hand on his shoulder. "I'm sure. Don't ask me to say it better than that at the moment. Just accept that it's more than I hoped for. Way more."

His face cleared of doubt. Now he just looked

beat. His plump face had thinned and grayed in a few short days. I suspected he'd done more of the cleaning than Larry Hein's bots.

"I want them in here tomorrow—get Larry to send word to Link. I've got some extras as well."

"Extras?"

"More lab rats from Dis. I'll tell you about it when I have time."

"Sure. And I suppose you'll tell me you're going to start wearing skirts as well?" he observed dryly.

I tried to locate some real warmth to put in my smile but there was none.

"I'll find Teece now. See you in Hein's when I've finished."

He nodded and left as if he couldn't get away from me quickly enough.

Teece was waiting for me back in my rooms, his arms folded belligerently. Jamon's lips-and-torso accountant was up on the screen counting pixel cred.

I dropped onto the couch, feet up.

"What's the score, Teece?"

"The score is . . . you're loaded. Most of the income's from Lark and Speed, though some of your kickbacks have dropped away since Jamon—"

"What else?"

"You owe The Cure their increment for the Sen sil trade, and the tek wholesalers are getting toey as well. Apart from that most of the local bars are behind on protection payments."

"Pay up The Cure and the teks and then tell them we're finished with them."

His eyes bulged. "You can't do that."

"I *am* doing that."

"You kill the Sensil trade and someone else will run with it. You ruin yourself and nothing will change."

I sighed. He was right. Just like Roo had been on the same matter. And I needed the income to take care of the ferals.

"OK," I allowed. "For the moment."

He looked relieved. "What's on your mind, Parrish?"

If you knew, Teece, you'd probably be the first to shoot me. "I've got some more ferals waiting over on the edge of Torley's. I need them brought to the barracks and watched over. There'll be trouble, though. They look like . . ."

"They look like what?"

I sighed. "Animals."

He wrinkled his nose. "That's a tough one."

I climbed to my feet and stood closer to him. "I've got two more things to ask of you. Nothing else. I want you to stay on a bit longer minding the business." *Actually it's yours, but you don't need to know that yet.* "And I want you to make it work for these new kids. Get them accepted. Make sure they get fed. Buy some immersion sims too, if you can get them to agree to soak."

"You mean *school?*" He whistled. "You don't ask much, do you, Parrish?"

"Only of my real friends."

He took a breath and I knew what was coming. "About Honey and me—"

I stopped him. "You don't owe me any explanations, Teece. I think it's the right move."

"Do you?"

Was he disappointed? I couldn't tell.

He stood up so we were almost touching. The warmth of his body sent my head spinning. If I could just lean against him for a minute or two, things would feel so much better.

His blue eyes were torn and I knew what I was thinking . . . wanting.

A tiny ripple of satisfaction swept me. He cared still, but Teece believed in monogamy. Unlike Loyl he would never be with two women at once. I respected that and stepped away from him.

"And what are you planning while I'm doing your job?" he demanded, not letting me off the hook that easily.

"Er . . . I'm going down the . . . er, coast a bit, working up some new business contacts."

"You can't leave here safely. You're still a murder suspect."

"I'll just have to be smart about it."

Teece flushed with an instant attack of blood pressure. "Smart? It's the stupidest thing I've ever heard you say. I know you, Parrish. You're not going to do business. You're bailing! What about these media voyeurs? Who's going to stop them?"

I stuck my hands on my hips, flaring at his attack. "I'm not running away! I've just had enough, Teece. So what *if* I managed to stop them? You're the one that said there'll always be others."

"Parrish, some bastard is playing with your life. And mine. All of us. And you're just going to roll over."

I felt like my brain had been shaken. A day ago we'd each been on the other side of this same argument.

I knew why I'd changed, but what about him?

I turned and walked to the door. "Take care of the biz, Teece, and . . . take care. I'll be in touch."

He punched the wall as I left.

I found Ibis in Hein's defending a table full of shot glasses.

"Teece won't be joining us."

He eyed me and swallowed another. "Totally piss him off as well?"

I shrugged and picked my split and chipped fingernails. "Yeah. A rare but beautiful talent."

He laughed, tears gathering in the corner of his eyes.

I waved to Larry to bring some shot glasses for me and downed one immediately.

Ibis slumped in his tactile. It grunted in protest and tipped, trying to even up the weight distribution.

"You've had enough," I said.

He stuck out his bottom lip and skulled one more.

"I'm taking a holiday," I continued conversationally.

He sat bolt upright. "You can't do that!"

I downed another. And another. "Can. Will."

We scowled at each other like a pair of kids about to bloody each other's noses until Link's shadow fell across the table. I hadn't seen him since I left for Mo-Vay. He looked taller than I remembered. The mask slung around his neck seemed tiny.

"Can you speak with me outside?" he asked.

No! Go away! "I guess." I got up slowly, my hand dropping automatically to my pistol. "Why outside?"

"Please."

I glanced back at Ibis. He was resting his forehead in his hands and groaning about needing mockoff.

I followed Link out of the bar and down into the closest alley. I'd been in this one before, when the Prier pilot had contacted me for the first time. It sent a prickle of remembrance across my skin, but there was no 'Terro waiting for me, only Glida.

"Glida?" I stared between them. "You two know each other?"

Link spoke. "Everyone knows you brought more of us back from Dis. I—I figured we should get acquainted."

I blinked in surprise. The boy had intelligence stamped on his face. It impressed me. Maybe Teece's job wouldn't be so hard after all. I would have been pleased if Glida's face wasn't swollen from crying.

"What is it?"

"They've taken Wombebe."

My frozen heart cracked. "Who?"

She held out an audio bung like it was a bomb. "They left this for you."

I stuck it into my ear and with a shaking finger pressed hard. The device was meant for messages only. When the crackle cleared I recognized the thin, now familiar voice of the Prier pilot.

*"What you saw in there, what you know now—
it's called Code Noir. Designer slavery. I can't stop
it by myself. I need you. I've got the kid. Stay in the
game and you'll get her back."*

The recording crackled again in pause.

*". . . you should know. You haven't changed. He
was lying. I know because I was there."*

The bung shriveled and fell from my ear to the
ground.

Loyl Daac had lied?

Why had Loyl lied?

I stared at Link and Glida, absorbing what I had
just learned. If he had, that meant I still had some
control over myself and a chance to change things.

Even better, I discovered I still wanted to.

My life crashed back at me like a reboot. With
it I felt the Eskaalim's stranglehold loosen and my
emotions thaw in a white-hot flash of hope. I could
almost hear its long, anguished howl.

I picked up Glida and whirled her around me.

I wasn't just back in the game.

I could still win.

Marianne de Pierres was born in Western Australia and now lives in Queensland with her husband and three sons. She has a BA in Film and Television and is currently completing a Graduate Certificate of Arts (Writing, Editing and Publishing) at the University of Queensland. Her passions are basketball, books and avocados. She has been actively involved in promoting speculative fiction in Australia and is the cofounder of the Vision Writers Group in Brisbane, and ROR—Writers on the Rise, a critiquing group for professional writers. She was involved in the early planning stages of Clarion South and is a tutor at Envision. You can find out more about her on her Web site, www.mariannedepierres.com.

The first Parrish Plessis novel from
Marianne de Pierres

NYLON ANGEL

Bodyguard Parrish Plessis has just cut a
deal with a gang lord that could land her boss in
jail. She's also sheltering a suspect in the murder of
a news story. In this world run by the media, the
truth isn't relevant, it's bad for ratings. Now
Parrish finds herself tagged for murder—and up to
her tricked-out leather tank top in trouble.

0-451-46037-5

**Available wherever books are sold or at
penguin.com**